LOSING SOMMER

NORA SOMMER CARIBBEAN SUSPENSE - BOOK FIVE

NICHOLAS HARVEY

HarveyBooks llc

Printed in the United States of America

First Printing, 2023

ISBN: 978-1-959627-20-3

Cover design: Covered by Melinda

Editor: Andrew Chapman at Prepare to Publish

Author photograph: Lift Your Eyes Photography

This book is dedicated to all those poor souls whose darkness robbed them of the ability to turn life's next page.

1

A FINE GLASS OF SCOTCH

Tuesday 4:45pm

Perry stirred awake as the plane touched down, the roar of the jet engines reminding him where he was. He could hardly believe he'd fallen asleep on the short flight from Atlanta, but considering how little rest he'd had lately, he supposed it was inevitable. As the pilot announced what he already knew, he picked up a few papers from the floor where they'd fallen. Carefully sorting and stuffing them inside his Italian leather satchel-style briefcase, he was glad he'd declined a stewardess on this trip. The ladies the lease company provided were always polite and professional, but they were only human, and people couldn't help themselves from sneaking a peek.

The pilot turned the plane around and taxied back along the length of Owen Roberts International Airport's only runway. Continuing past the main terminal, they reached the apron outside Island Air, the fixed-based operator - or FBO - at the west end of the facility. Once the Embraer Phenom 300/E came to a stop, Perry unbuckled and stood, hunched over in the cramped cabin of the private jet. The door to the cockpit opened and a uniformed man slipped through, donning his cap.

"Welcome home, Mr Collins," he said, unlatching the exterior cabin door and letting it lower to the tarmac below. "Your car is being brought around, sir."

"Thank you," Perry acknowledged, edging past the co-pilot and feeling his legs slowly wake up as he took his time descending the steps.

The hot, humid air was tempered only slightly by the gentle ocean breeze which swept across the low-lying island. Perry inhaled the familiar warmth and moistness which reminded him he'd returned to his favourite place in the world. The sun had lost much of its intensity for the day as it arced towards the western horizon. Checking his Audemars Piguet Royal Oak Minute Repeater Supersonnerie titanium watch, he knew he only had 63 minutes before it dropped beyond view. He planned to be watching it do so from a comfortable chair in front of his home.

A middle-aged woman with dark flowing hair and the white short-sleeved shirt of the Cayman Islands Customs & Border Control approached.

Perry turned to the co-pilot standing in the open cabin door. "Safe travels on the return, and thank you," he said, offering a brief nod before pivoting to greet the woman and hand her his British passport along with his Cayman Islands residency card. "Good evening, Miss Grainger."

"Welcome home, Mr Collins. Nice to see you again. Bags, sir?" the woman asked in a subtle version of the island's musical accent.

Perry raised his satchel. "Travelling light today."

She smiled in return, and he lowered the bag.

"Alone, sir?"

"I am," he replied, watching her scan his passport on a portable unit connected wirelessly to the secure system.

"When's your lovely daughter going to grace us once more with her pretty smile?" Grainger asked, making small talk while entering his details into the tablet she carried.

The wireless unit always took longer, but it beat going inside the office and through the security scanners she was allowing him to skip. Which he'd been counting on.

"Christmas break she'll be down," Perry responded, internally amused by Miss Grainger's phrasing. His only daughter had inherited many traits from her father, and one of them was her stern and business-like manner. Her smile was indeed pretty, certainly in her father's opinion, but her joyous expression was not often shared in public.

"How long this visit, sir?" Grainger asked, handing back his passport.

Perry thought for a moment. "I believe this will be an extended stay, Miss Grainger."

She nodded, typed something more into her tablet before flipping the cover closed.

"Enjoy your time at home, sir," she said, and walked away as a metallic silver Mercedes G-Wagen 550 pulled up and a young man in pressed trousers, white button-down shirt and a dark blue vest stepped out.

Perry handed him forty dollars and slid into the driver's seat which the delivery driver had already moved to his preferred seating position via the memory selection. He placed his satchel on the passenger seat while the young man closed the door, then selected drive and pulled away, turning alongside the FBO towards Roberts Drive.

The security gate raised as the Mercedes SUV approached and Perry thanked the guard with a brief raise of his hand from the leather-wrapped steering wheel. Turning left, he reached over and used the touchscreen display to select music from his mobile phone, which had automatically connected via Bluetooth. Luciano Pavarotti's powerful voice filled the interior of the vehicle and Perry hummed along although he only understood enough Italian to order gelato.

Taking Shedden Road, he crossed over the main highway skirting George Town and turned right on Mary Road, arriving at

North Church Street by the waterfront. This wasn't the fastest way home, but it was far more pleasant, and he turned right again, blending in with the early evening traffic. For a brief moment he considered stopping at Casanova Ristorante and picking up an order of their ravioli Mamma Rosa, his favourite, but he knew it would throw his timing off. He continued but carried a tinge of regret for not factoring in the stop.

Intermittent peeks of the ocean between buildings soon gave way to condo complexes, hotels, and businesses, but Perry still enjoyed the drive, soaking up the welcoming atmosphere of familiar surroundings. Reaching the Seven Mile shopping centre, an unassuming U-shaped array of single-storey retailers, he pulled into the car park and found an open spot outside the Tortuga Liquor Store. Silencing Pavarotti mid-note as he shut the engine off, he stepped from the SUV and walked to the front entrance.

Nodding to the familiar face behind the counter, although he didn't know the man's name, Perry went directly to the locked cabinet of expensive bottles and pointed to the taupe tube containing The Balvenie Twenty-Five single malt Scotch whisky. The man unlocked the cabinet, removed the container, and carefully carried it to the register.

"Anything else tonight?"

"That'll be all," Perry replied, handing the man his Amex Black Card to cover the $1200 price tag.

Three minutes later, Pavarotti was back in full voice, and Perry drummed his fingers on the wheel in time with the music as he drove another mile and a quarter to The Caribbean View Residences, overlooking the famed Seven Mile Beach. Parking in one of his dedicated spots below the main tower building, he gathered up his satchel and newly purchased Scotch. Standing next to the Mercedes, he looked around the concrete underground parking structure. The lighting was dim, but he could see well enough to know he was alone. Perry checked his watch, took one more look around, then headed to the steps.

Perry never took the lift at Caribbean View. Conscious that his business life was often sedentary, he used every opportunity to add exercise into his day, whenever it made sense. Typical of his analytical nature, he'd once tasked interns with producing reports on the average time to reach each floor of his offices in London and Atlanta, then compared the results to the time it took to use the stairs. Fifth floor or above had been the crossover, much to the chagrin of his managers who found themselves chasing Perry up four flights of steps to where he insisted his office be located.

Perry hesitated for a moment at the base of the stairs then proceeded, quickly rummaging through his satchel as he took the familiar steps which reversed direction before concluding at the ground level.

"Welcome home, Mr Collins, sir," a voice came from behind him as he turned left into the rear foyer. He spun around to see an older dark-skinned man in a security guard uniform, standing before the reception desk.

"Good evening, Charles," Perry replied. "I trust all is well?"

"Yes, sir," the man responded. "Walked through dis mornin', sir."

Perry briskly covered the few steps across the tiled floor until he stood before the old man, who raised an eyebrow in surprise. Perry extended a hand, which Charles shook.

"I'd like to thank you for your diligent service, Charles. You should know your efforts have not gone unnoticed."

The older man studied Perry's face, taken aback by his kind words.

"Thank you, sir," he stumbled, but Perry had already turned once more, crossing the foyer and continuing out of the doors to the grounds surrounding the swimming pool.

Several people looked his way as Perry traversed to the separate building to his left. He didn't recognise any of them, but many residents rented their units to wealthy visitors when they weren't on the island. He didn't. His home was his sanctuary, more so than his flat in London or his condominium in Atlanta. He'd been coming to Grand Cayman since the mid-nineties when his parents brought him on holiday as a university graduation gift. He'd purchased a modest condo in West Bay when his first business had begun making decent money, before he'd even owned a home in the UK. In the wake of the financial crash of the late 2000s, Perry's business had recovered well, and he'd finally purchased his dream unit at the Caribbean View Residences.

Unlocking the front door to his ground floor oceanfront villa, he felt a wave of comforting relief flood over him. Walking past the bedrooms, he placed his satchel and the Scotch on the curved kitchen counter, and kept going until he stood by the sliding glass doors leading to the patio. Before him, the pale sand beach extended to the brilliant turquoise water, which gradually darkened until reaching a deep blue beyond the outer reef, half a mile offshore.

He was home.

Perry turned his attention from the lowering sun to his wristwatch. It was 5:42pm and the sun would set at precisely 5:55pm. He hurried back to the kitchen counter and removed the Scotch from its tubular packaging. He stole a glance to his drinks cabinet and noted a similar bottle on the shelf. Almost exactly where he'd left it. Details, suspicions, and doubt swirled in his mind, but he suppressed them. He was home, and he wouldn't let anything spoil that feeling.

Retrieving a cut Glencairn glass from a cabinet, he removed the corked top from the bottle and gently poured himself two fingers of the honey-golden Scotch. A tradition he'd begun on the day he'd taken possession of the condominium and continued ever since. Sunset and his favourite Scotch.

Next, Perry opened his satchel and pulled a bundle of manila envelopes from inside. Each bore a neatly printed label on the front, and he set them out in an orderly fashion across the counter. He stared at each one, mentally scrolling through the contents and double-checking the culmination of months of long hours and much deliberation. Finally, he nodded, satisfied that his business was all in order so he could finally relax and soak up the glorious sunset.

Slipping the satchel strap over one shoulder, he picked up his glass and walked back to the sliding door, unlocking it and gliding it open. The ocean breeze greeted him along with the humidity, which enveloped him in stark contrast to the air-conditioned home. He slid the glass door closed behind him. The patio leading to the beach had been swept clear of the sand and leaves which often blew around, and he sat down on his favourite cushioned chair, knowing Charles had made sure his place was shipshape for his arrival.

Perry set the satchel on the concrete next to the chair and raised the glass to his nose, inhaling the smooth fragrance of the fine Scotch. He softly swirled the glass before taking a sip, closing his eyes as the liquid eased down his throat, exciting his taste buds. The tannins pulled from the oak casks tickled his tongue, and opening his eyes once more, he placed the glass down on the table and allowed himself a brief smile.

Before him, the sun was severed in two by the horizon and the sky around it danced with rich hues from daffodil to tangerine.

"Perfect," he whispered to himself.

It was a rare moment for the man to feel completely relaxed and at ease, his mind clear of all burdens, worries, and concerns. His thoughts emptied of the baggage his corporate life consumed him with. At peace with himself, and the world as he knew it.

Perry reached into his beloved satchel, and as the burning orb dropped beyond the Caribbean Sea, he placed the muzzle of the gun to the underside of his chin and pulled the trigger.

2

"HE DEAD ALRIGHT"

Tuesday 5:55pm

I was a little over four kilometres into my beach run when dozens of birds all took off at once. On my right, a pelican flapped like crazy to launch its odd physique from the clutches of the ocean, and to my left, doves, sandpipers, and several others I had no idea the name of, flew from the trees surrounding a beachfront mansion. Over the music blasting from my earbuds, I'd heard a strange thump, but the mass exodus of feathered creatures was what made me slow down and pay attention. Every person who'd been enjoying the sunset was now standing and staring at the Caribbean View Residences building.

I picked up my pace again and ran past a line of umbrellas and loungers on the beach, spotting a security guard coming from the pool area. He was an older man, but moving in a hurry, so I sprinted towards him.

"What's going on?" I asked.

"Stay back," he panted with a strong island accent. "I don't know, but you oughta stay back, Miss."

"I'm police," I told him as I arrived by his side. "Constable Sommer."

He looked at me in surprise. Not many people expected a tall, blonde Norwegian to be a constable with the Royal Cayman Islands Police Service. Apparently he believed me as he hustled along the beach to the patio of the far building where a few steps led from the sand to the luxury condominium.

"Mighty loud bang," the old man wheezed before coming to a rapid halt at the base of the steps. "Oh, my Lord," he said, crossing himself.

"Stay here, sir," I told him, catching my own breath and quickly assessing what we faced.

I saw a firearm on the ground next to a man slumped in a cushioned patio chair. A briefcase-like bag lay next to him. Blood spatter streaked the sliding glass door behind him, and a large piece of his scalp was simply missing. It was a grisly sight.

"Oh, my good Lord," I heard the old man mumble once more as I walked carefully up the steps, making sure I wasn't treading on anything we'd consider evidence.

I plucked my mobile from the strap on my bicep and quickly clicked a few pictures.

"Miss, why you makin' photographs of dis?" the guard said in disgust.

I ignored his comment and dialled my mentor and indirect boss, Detective Whittaker. The line rang.

I turned to the guard while I waited. "You know this man?"

"It Mr Collins," he replied. "I just spoke wit him, not twenty minutes ago."

"Good evening, Nora," Whittaker answered. "How can I help you?"

"There's been a shooting at the Caribbean View Residences, sir. Appears to be a suicide. Figured you'd want to see this."

"Really?" Whittaker responded. "I can't say I want to see it, but I dare say I'd better attend. Have you called dispatch?"

"No, sir. You were my first call."

"Is the victim deceased?"

"Extremely, sir."

There was a brief pause, and I wondered what I'd said wrong this time. With English being my second language, I occasionally phrased things incorrectly. I also harboured a distaste for unnecessary words, which made some people uncomfortable.

"I'll get the appropriate branches on their way if you can secure the scene and corral any witnesses," he ordered. "I'll be there in fifteen minutes."

"Yes, sir," I said and ended the call, turning to the security guard.

"Shouldn't we cover da man over with someting?" he asked. "Dat's undignified, you know? He was a good man."

"What's your name?" I asked.

He looked up at me, his eyes pained and shocked. "Charles."

"Got any cones or those pole things for blocking off areas, Charles?"

"Stanchions?"

"I don't know what they're called in English, but if they keep people back, then get them."

Charles took one more look at the dead man in the chair, shook his head, then hurried away. People were starting to gather, edging closer in the way crowds formed and moved like a single entity, gaining confidence as a pack.

"I'm police. Stay back," I shouted, and the feet stopped shuffling in the sand. "Did anyone see this happen?"

"What did happen?" a man in board shorts who should have been wearing a shirt over his fat belly asked.

"If you don't know, then you didn't see anything, so you can leave. I'm looking for anyone who actually saw what happened."

The fat man gave me an angry look, which I ignored.

"I heard what sounded like a gunshot," a woman said, holding up her hand.

"We all heard the gunshot, ma'am, that's why I asked if you *saw* anything."

Sirens wailed in the distance, so I knew it wouldn't be long before I had help with the crowd control, but it was becoming clear no one had actually witnessed what took place. Not that it was hard to reconstruct what had happened. Charles staggered down the steps from the pool with an armful of waist-high poles, struggling to carry them with their heavy circular bases. I ran over and helped him with a few.

"How we know you're a cop?" another man asked from the crowd.

I pretended not to hear him as the question had no bearing on what I was doing.

"Hey, lady," he yelled louder, pushing to the front of the two dozen people now forming a semicircle on the beach. "How do we know you're really a cop?"

Charles and I dropped what I now knew were called stanchions at the base of the condo's patio steps, spread them out, and strung the retractable belts between them to form a barrier. Either side of the steps, the raised patio deck and planters completed the partition.

"Hey lady," the guy persisted.

"You'll know for sure when I arrest you for obstruction, you idiot," I barked, sick of his stupidity.

Honestly it really didn't matter whether I was or wasn't. I was doing what needed to be done to protect the crime scene until our scene of crime officer arrived. The man, on the other hand, was standing on the beach shouting 'hey lady'. It was why they would probably never let me carry a gun. He was tempting target practice.

"Make sure no one comes up the steps, Charles," I said, and carefully skirted around the dead man in the chair.

Mr Collins was his name, according to Charles. The former Mr Collins, I supposed, seeing as he was now considered to be nothing more than the corpse of the victim.

I inspected the sliding glass doors and determined I could open it enough to step inside the condo without the splatter going behind the other pane. I didn't need SOCO arriving to find a blood-smeared mess over the glass. Using my shirt so I didn't leave prints on the handle, the door slid so effortlessly, I almost flung it open, just catching it in time. I went inside. It was dimly lit as the last vestiges of daylight were being chased away by a dark blue sky, soon to turn black. Only the hall light was on, throwing a narrow glow between the living room and open-plan kitchen.

I checked my trainers weren't leaving prints, and apart from a few errant grains of sand, they seemed fine. The place was beautifully decorated, spotless, with not a cushion out of place. To one side of the kitchen, a glass-doored cabinet housed bottles of liquor with many labels I recognised. Next, my eyes fell upon the curved kitchen counter. Spread out were a series of manila envelopes, each with a label marking their intended recipient. I took a step closer and began reading them. The first two were names I didn't know with a business address below them, but the third simply read, Kayleigh. There was something very personal and sad about seeing the name and I wondered who she might be. His wife? Daughter? Mother? Who would be the people missing this man? I moved to the final envelope and raised an eyebrow. It read 'Detective Roy Whittaker'.

"Who's in there?" came a voice from outside and a torch light made me squint as I turned around.

"Constable Sommer," I shouted, holding up a hand. "Stay there, I'm coming out."

I couldn't tell who the policeman was, as to me he was nothing more than a bright white light, but he must have known me as he didn't say anything more or try to come inside. I slid out through the glass door and pulled it closed behind me. Two uniformed constables stood on the patio, one trying not to look at the victim and the other unable to take his eyes off the hole in the man's head.

"Why would someone do that to themselves?" the second policeman muttered. "Look at this place," he continued, finally averting his gaze. "This guy has it all, man."

"Had," I corrected. "And just because he has an expensive condo doesn't tell us anything about his life or how happy he was,"

I responded, watching the ambulance crew trudge through the sand towards us. "I'm Constable Sommer and Detective Whittaker is on his way."

"I know who you are," Smith replied.

I determined his name from the badge on his chest while he looked me over. I hadn't met him before as he worked from the George Town station - I was West Bay - but by the tone of his voice it appeared he wasn't a fan of my work.

"What's Whittaker coming for? Pretty straightforward what happened here. Sure isn't a crime scene."

"Actually, it is," I contested, squatting down near the body and looking at Mr Collins' right hand.

Blood dripped from the holes in his chin and scalp, pooling directly below the wounds on the concrete.

"Suicide isn't a crime in the Cayman Islands," Smith informed me. "You'd know that if you'd lived here more than five minutes."

I didn't waste my time looking up at him, but continued examining the body while I replied, "Carrying a firearm is, so for that alone it's technically a crime scene."

He scoffed. "What are you gonna do? Charge him for it?" He looked around for his partner to make sure he was getting credit for showing me who was smarter, but the other constable was losing his lunch in the planter.

I stood. "No, I'm going to follow the evidence and find out how the firearm came to be on the island. Then, maybe we'll be charging someone." I elbowed past him to greet the medical team. "I'm Constable Sommer. The crime scene is secure, but there's nothing for you guys until SOCO are done."

"Are you certain the victim is deceased?" the female EMT asked, a large lady with shiny dark skin and big, bright eyes who peered around me. "Oh shit. Yeah, he's deceased alright."

"Guess we should pronounce him," her partner said, not appearing to be in any hurry to approach the body.

"Sure, just try not to disturb anything," I warned them,

knowing they had to verify a lack of pulse, despite the obvious fatal injury.

The female EMT pulled latex gloves on her hands and slowly walked over to the victim. She reached over and touched two fingers to the corpse's neck. The body slipped in the chair, then the weight of Mr Collins' head and upper body dragged him over the arm, and slammed his corpse onto the concrete patio.

The crowd gasped, and the EMT leapt backwards, shrieking. So much for my secured crime scene.

"What did I just say?" I blurted and ushered the EMT back to her partner.

"He dead alright," she babbled. "I callin' it right here. He dead."

I looked down the steps to where Charles' pained eyes were looking back at me.

"Dat's why you take dem pictures, huh?"

3

BOOT

Tuesday 6:20pm

"Tell me what you know so far," Detective Whittaker said when he took me to one side shortly after arriving.

I walked him through the gunshot and finding the body, explained how I'd gone inside and how the body came to be spreadeagled on the patio.

"Here," I said, showing him the pictures on my mobile. "This is how I found him."

"And his name is Collins?" Whittaker asked.

"Yes," I replied, waving Charles over, who'd been joined by another member of staff.

The vomiting constable had recovered enough to begin taking statements, and he frowned at me as his witnesses walked away. Whittaker extended a hand to them both in turn, introducing himself. Charles still looked to be in shock and the lady with him, who told us she was Valerie and worked at the front desk, appeared bewildered.

"Charles, please explain when and where you saw Mr Collins this evening," I instructed.

Charles nodded, then described his interaction with the victim. "He seemed completely normal, I'd say. Although he took da time to thank me for what I done for him."

"Was that unusual?" I asked.

Charles's brow furrowed, producing twice as many wrinkles across his forehead. "It weren't... how I know him to be, I must say. He a very nice man, don't get me wrong, he always polite and all, but he don't usually take time for much more than da hello and check on tings about da place."

"He didn't appear distracted or unhappy?" Whittaker asked.

"Not at all," Charles quickly replied. "More like da opposite, I'd say. You sure he did dis himself?"

I hadn't seen a shred of evidence to suggest this was anything but a suicide, although I couldn't say that to a witness.

"We'll thoroughly investigate the circumstances, I assure you," Whittaker said, saving me from coming up with an appropriate response. Which wasn't my forte.

"How long has Mr Collins owned here?" I asked.

"Longer dan I work here," Valerie said, turning to Charles.

"More dan ten years I'd say," Charles responded. "I know he bin comin' to da island for a lot longer dan dat, too. He tell me so."

"Married?" I asked. "Was he alone when you saw him?"

Charles nodded. "He married, but I ain't seen Mrs Collins in a while. His daughter come down some."

"Mrs Collins here not too long ago," Valerie offered. "Just for a couple of days."

I nodded and turned back to Charles. "And to your knowledge Mr Collins arrived today?"

"Dat's right. Service come collect his car earlier. I gave dem da keys myself. He landed dis afternoon."

"Okay, thank you. We'll check with the airlines," Whittaker commented.

Charles shook his head. "He don't fly on dose planes, sir. He has one of dem fancy jets dat bring him here."

"A private plane?" Whittaker asked.

Charles shrugged his shoulders. "I 'spect it is, sir. I tink he da only one on dere."

I managed to stifle a laugh.

"Can you let us in the front door please, Charles?" I asked instead.

He nodded and pulled a key card from his pocket. We walked around the building, pausing briefly to greet Rasha Howard, our lead scene of crime officer, before continuing to the condo. On the way, Whittaker called his contact at the Cayman Islands Immigration Department and enquired about Collins' entry that day. From what I heard on my end it sounded like the man would call back. Arriving at the door, Charles swiped his key and stepped back.

"Make sure no one else comes in for a few minutes, please Charles," Whittaker said, resting a hand on the old man's shoulder.

Charles nodded, and I realised the detective had given him a task more for the security guard's sake than that of the inquiry. Whittaker had a way with people. I felt calmer now he was here, the other constables stood a little straighter, and the casual chatter had lessened as everyone became more focused. Not from fear of the boss, but a desire to make their best efforts in his eyes. It was a talent I firmly believed I would never possess.

We stepped inside to the well-lit hallway and could see the activity on the other side of the sliding glass doors now lights had been erected outside. Whittaker slowly continued into the living room and looked around with his hands on his hips.

"Anyone else been inside except you?" he asked.

"No, sir," I replied, waiting a step behind him. "Did you know this man, sir?" I asked.

He turned and looked at me. "Not that I recall. What's his full name?"

"Perry Collins," I replied, having overheard Valerie mention the victim's first name to the puking copper.

Whittaker thought for a moment. "Doesn't ring a bell. Why? Should I have heard of him?"

I shrugged my shoulders. "I don't know. But he seems to know you," I said, pointing to the kitchen counter.

We both slipped nitrile gloves on and moved closer to study the envelopes. Whittaker quickly moved to the last one and stared at his own name.

"I'm not hard to find with the right internet search," he said, more to himself than to me.

He turned and looked out through the blood-splattered glass. Rasha was organising the two officers she'd brought with her, who had all donned Tyvek suits.

"Turn a light on, please," he said, and I found a row of wall switches, trying them until the living room and kitchen lights came on.

Everyone outside looked our way, and Whittaker beckoned Rasha inside. She did the same as I had earlier, carefully sliding the glass door open and slipping through.

"What have we got in here, Roy?" she asked, looking around the room.

"These envelopes appear to be the most comprehensive suicide note I've ever seen," he said, pointing to them. "One is addressed to me, so if you wouldn't mind photographing them, I'd like to open it."

Rasha inspected the envelopes, standing on tiptoes in an effort to see them better. She's a good 15 centimetres shorter than me, but shapely unlike my tall, lean, uneventful figure. She turned to me.

"Nora, take a series of pictures with your mobile, please, and just open the one, okay?" she instructed, not waiting for a response before turning back to Whittaker.

"I'm not to be trusted taking pictures?" Whittaker asked in an amused tone.

Rasha flicked an unruly curl of hair from her face with a gloved hand and smiled. "I don't have to explain to Nora how to name them and where to send them."

"Hmmm," Whittaker grunted.

"Move," I said, lining up to start taking the shots. "Please, sir," I added when I realised I was being that abrupt thing people whined about.

I heard Rasha chuckling under her hood as she made her way outside.

After I'd taken photos from every angle I could think of, I called to Whittaker, who was moving around the room, studying the details. He came over and carefully picked up the envelope, allowing me to photograph the underside before he opened it.

"Notice the choice of pictures in this place?" he asked, his eyes sweeping the room.

"Expensive-looking art on the walls," I replied. "Only family picture is a younger woman. I'm guessing daughter."

Whittaker nodded as he examined the metal clasp of the envelope, carefully squeezing the tangs together and opening the flap. From inside he retrieved a single sheet of paper which I took more photos of. It was on the personal letterhead of Perry Collins. The message had been produced on a printer, but signed with an ink pen.

Attn: Detective Whittaker with the Royal Cayman Islands Police Service:

I, Perry Collins, have taken my own life of my own free will and desire. Please keep this in mind when investigating the details, as I'm sure you will.

The firearm used in my suicide was smuggled by me onto the island today. No one was at fault in not finding it – I used their goodwill in my favour. Please do not judge them harshly for their oversight.

Regards, Perry Collins.

Whittaker shook his head and rubbed his chin until he noticed the nitrile glove against his neatly groomed goatee and stopped.

"How strange," he said quietly.

"Strange how, sir?"

He read the note again before turning my way. "Taking one's own life is usually the desperate act of someone at their wits' end. I can't imagine the despair an individual must feel to see this as their only solution. Yet this man appears to have planned his own demise in great detail."

"Maybe he was terminally ill," I suggested, measuring my response to the detective's thoughts.

"That's certainly my first presumption," he agreed, placing the paper down on top of the envelope and turning his attention to the bottle of Scotch.

"Is that expensive?" I asked.

"So much so I have no idea how much it costs," he replied.

We both looked outside once more and saw a perimeter of vinyl sheets supported by tall, metal stakes had been erected to shield the scene from the beach, and Perry Collins' body was being carried away in a body bag on a stretcher.

"Between the security guard's description of his usual demeanour, his decorating preferences, and the way he's organised his departure," Whittaker summarised, "I'd say Mr Collins was an analytical man."

"Mostly," I replied, not intending to share more thoughts at this stage.

That was another talent the detective possessed. I found myself talking more openly to him than anyone else I knew. Except perhaps my friend AJ. But that was different.

"How so?" he asked.

I groaned to myself. Now I had to explain my comment, and I didn't feel like I'd fully formed my opinion yet. His mobile buzzed, and I hoped for a reprieve.

"Private jet, landed just before five this evening. Entered through the FBO. Plane left already back to Atlanta where it originated," Whittaker read aloud, then looked at me. "Continue," he urged.

So much for a reprieve. "The painting," I said, pointing to the windowless north wall where a large original painting of a worn boot hung in a modern black frame.

Detective Whittaker peered over his glasses. "What about it?" he asked.

His tone was inquisitive rather than judgemental.

"It's a classic still life, using only three colours," I pointed out.

"There's more than three colours in that painting," he responded, walking closer.

"Correct. But they were produced with three base colours. Black, white, and red."

"Hmmm," he murmured. "And what is that telling us?"

"The painting is pure artistry," I said, walking over to stand before the piece. "Creating this image using only three paints in a style that could be four hundred years old, and placing it as the centrepiece in a strikingly modern condominium, is brilliant. And creative."

Whittaker nodded. "I didn't know you were an art aficionado."

"I'm not," I replied. "But my mother loved art and she would take me to lots of galleries in Oslo and get excited about paintings."

He smiled at me, which made me uncomfortable. I hated talking about me.

"Sarah Freeman," he said, reading the signature from the painting. "You think this is four hundred years old?"

"No. I think the style is timeless. I'm guessing this was painted in the last twenty years."

"Oh," he replied. "Okay. But maybe his wife picked this out."

"He hates his wife," I said, once again wondering how the detective had me bumbling out so many words.

He laughed softly. "I'm not sure the lack of pictures of his wife tells us he hates her, Nora."

I sighed. Sod it, I figured, I might as well keep going now. "If he still loved his wife there'd be pictures. If he still respected his wife, there'd be pictures for his daughter's sake who still visits. There's none. So he hates his wife, and if she placed that painting on the wall, he would have taken it down. It's his, which means he has a creative side to his personality."

"Or he's a collector, and it's a great investment," Whittaker said.

"Wouldn't be on the wall."

"Why?" he asked, and again his tone was curious.

"Did you see his wristwatch?" I asked.

He nodded. "I didn't study it, but it looked nice."

"It's Audemars Piguet, which I don't know shit about, except they're crazy expensive. But the model he chose is understated. Look at the drinks cabinet," I continued, moving to the kitchen. "I know most of these brands, and they're high end, like Maker's Mark, but nowhere near the price tag of the bottle he chose for his last drink, right?"

"I'd say that's true," Whittaker agreed.

"Apart from another bottle of the same Scotch," I noted aloud, wondering if that dispelled my initial theory. "Anyway, what I'm saying is Collins wasn't flashy. He didn't try and impress people, but he personally enjoyed and admired nice things. And the main reason I'm saying he had a creative, or at least not completely analytical side, is his timing."

Whittaker looked outside again where white-suited techs were swabbing samples from the windows and collecting brain matter from the patio.

"His timing? Seems like he came here from the airport, poured himself a drink, and killed himself."

"At sunset."

"A coincidence?" Whittaker offered.

"The sun dipped below the horizon, and bang."

"Really? Just as the sun set?"

"Yup. Pure logic would have been to do this wherever he came from and save himself all the travel and hassle."

"I think suicide is illegal in America, at least in some states, so maybe there were legal reasons to come here," Whittaker said.

I shrugged my shoulders. He'd dragged my opinion out of me, I'd be damned if I'd bother defending it. He stared at the painting for a moment, then looked over at me.

"I'd like you to work this case with me."

"Is there a case to work?" I asked. "No reason to think he didn't kill himself. I don't see any sign of foul play."

"Agreed. But the gun situation needs to be followed up on, regardless of Mr Collins' wishes. That's not his call to make."

I couldn't argue with that as I'd already made the same point.

"I'd like us to put a little time into following up and seeing if we can understand why this man took his own life," he said, looking me in the eyes. "I think you can help provide me with insight in this case."

I felt frozen in place. Detective Roy Whittaker had known me for three years. He knew some of what I'd endured in the past, and he'd turned a blind eye to certain transgressions I'd made. He'd mentored me, supported me, and reprimanded me fewer times than I deserved, but never had I spoken a word to him about my own battle with depression and thoughts of taking my own life. And yet he seemed to know.

"I'll call Sergeant Redburn at West Bay station in the morning and let him know you'll be assisting me for a day or two," he said, and walked down the hallway to the front door.

I persuaded my reluctant feet to follow.

4

HAIR, NAILS, AND DREAMS
COME TRUE

Tuesday 8:15pm

I stood on the pavement in front of the Caribbean View Residences, and wondered if I should have taken Whittaker up on his offer of a ride. My Jeep was in my friend's car park next to West Bay dock, four kilometres away, but after his intuitive comment about my help, I needed to be alone. But I also had somewhere to be and would now be late. With little other choice, I headed north to complete my run, returning under the streetlamps instead of the now darkened beach.

My legs took a while to warm up again, and I was just feeling loosened up enough to push harder when my mobile buzzed with a text. Some people are social butterflies. I'm the opposite. A social moth? The thought amused me. Although the analogy didn't seem quite as good when I looked up and saw moths and assorted bugs banging their heads against the lens of the streetlamp above me.

I slowed and slipped my mobile from its strap and tried reading the text without busting my arse. It was from Jazzy. The teenage kid I was temporarily fostering. Permanently, it seemed, but I wasn't ready to admit that. She knew I planned on being home late, so now I was worried something was up. I stopped and opened the text.

'How late? Need help with homework.'

'Google,' I texted back, and set off once more, keeping the phone in my hand.

'Not allowed. Cheating,' she wrote back, and I almost tripped reading it.

She was a fourteen-year-old who'd been abandoned and lived on the streets by pilfering anything she needed. Now she was worried about looking up the answer to her homework on the internet. Despite my less than stellar influence, I decided the kid had a chance of growing up to be a decent human being.

I checked the time. Eight twenty-two, and I wasn't even halfway yet.

"*Dritt*," I mumbled, and called her.

Thirty minutes later, after being of very little help with Jazzy's maths problem, I climbed into my faded blue CJ-7 and started the engine. Letting the old Jeep warm up, I tried to cool myself down from sprinting the final kilometre. By the time I drove away, my heart rate was close to normal, but the sweat continued to trickle down my face in the humid night air.

Heading south, backtracking along where I'd just run, it only took a few minutes to reach the Discovery Beach Club condominiums. I passed by slowly, but it was hard to see much beyond the neatly landscaped entrance with tennis courts on both sides. I parked on the inland side of West Bay Road, a hundred metres farther on, nestling the Jeep under a sea grape tree, away from the streetlamps. I walked back in the shadows of the woods lining the road and slipped along the edge of the entrance towards the parking between the tennis courts and the three-storey condominiums.

On my right, the management building was dark, but I noted a security camera covering the complex's entrance. It was unlikely it was monitored live, but regardless, I preferred not to be recorded. With lights concentrated on the short driveway, I was hopeful the camera would pick me up as little more than unidentifiable movement in the shadows, staying low behind the shrubs.

At the corner I paused, scanning the cars, and spotting the silver BMW X5 SUV in front of the downstairs unit the driver owned. I carefully looked around for other vehicles worth noting. At two to three million dollars per unit in the current market, owners at Discovery Beach Club tended not to drive fifteen-year-old Renault Clios. Like the red model in the far corner by the tennis court with the driver's door plastic trim missing. A car I recognised.

My intention had been to watch the Clio arrive, but Perry Collins and his messy exit from this world had ruined that plan. Now, I had no clue when 'Baby-G', as Roxanne Brookstone liked to be called, would leave the condo. At four hundred dollars an hour, she'd be happy to stay all night, but I doubted her client would be. He had a wife who'd wonder where he was at some point. Although I couldn't imagine how she could care anymore.

Staying tight to a small maintenance building, I quickly moved to the fence surrounding the tennis court, hoping the building hid me from any cameras facing that way. Continuing along the edge of the courts, I found a dark corner under a line of trees at the edge of the property. I was ready to get off my feet, but the thought of sitting in an unseen fire ant nest kept me standing.

A door closed and I heard two people speaking French. A couple made their way down the exterior stairs from the third floor and walked to a blue Audi. They embraced, holding each other close, and passionately kissed. She even raised one stilettoed foot behind her. It was probably all quite romantic if I wasn't standing in the shadows in sweaty running clothes, worried about fire ants and waiting for a prostitute to be done servicing a disgusting old man.

The woman slipped into her car with one more kiss from her

lover, then backed out of her parking spot and drove away. The man watched her leave before taking his mobile from his pocket and typing a text as he walked back to the steps. I wondered if he was sending an amorously charming note for Miss Audi to read when she got home, or letting another girlfriend know he was now free.

"Ouch," I yelped as something bit me, and the man paused on the second floor, looking out across the car park.

I crouched down and swiped at my ankle, picturing a swarm of ravenous insects smothering my skin. The man moved on and I leapt from under the tree, squatting down on the pavement in front of the little Renault. I couldn't feel anything else biting me, but my legs tingled as though a million little feet were running all over the place. I furiously rubbed with both hands.

I heard a door close, so at least the man was gone, but I dare not stand up in case anyone else happened to be looking. My ankles itched like crazy, but that could be the scratches I'd just inflicted on myself too. Then I heard the footsteps.

A light flashed across the front of the Clio. "I got mace," came an island-accented female voice.

I stood up. "That's illegal," I said, looking at Baby-G holding her mobile up, shining the torch at me.

I held up a hand to block the bright light from blinding me.

"Who da hell dat?" she asked.

"Turn the damn light off and lower your voice," I whispered sharply.

"Dat da foreign police lady?"

"Nora. Yes. Now turn the light off," I repeated, finally lowering my hand once she'd turned off the torch function.

Baby-G swung around, checking the car park for anyone else. "What dis all about, girl? You bustin' me? I ain't done nuttin'! You undercover or some shit?"

Nothing about this evening had gone to plan, especially the part about being seen. Now I had to find a way out of this mess without throwing away months of work.

"Get in," I told her, and moved to the passenger side door. "Drive us out to the road so no one sees us."

She frowned at me, not moving at first. Baby-G was shorter than me, but that's where any reasonable comparisons ended. Saying she was full-figured only painted a part of the picture. She certainly carried a few extra kilos, and probably outweighed me by fifty percent or more, but the largest portion of her mass was housed in her voluminous breasts. How she remained upright was a testament to her leg strength and ab muscles, which were carefully concealed under her belly paunch. She'd once told me the 'G' part of her moniker was a nod to her cup size. I didn't even know they made bras that far up the alphabet. Of course, they'd be at the opposite end of the shelf to where I shopped, so maybe I'd missed them. Where the 'Baby' part came in, I had no clue. When a woman has boobs each bigger than her head, it's hard to picture her as an infant.

Roxanne was actually quite pretty, with beautiful almond-toned skin, and long, colourful braided weave extensions which wrapped around her head before cascading down to the middle of her back. In my opinion she'd make an amazing magazine model, if she hadn't chosen a different career path… which was probably a lot easier to get into than the fashion business.

"Whatever," she mumbled, and unlocked her car.

I quickly scrambled into the passenger seat and examined my legs while the interior light was on. I saw a bunch of little white stripes from my fingernails, but no bugs, so I closed the door.

"Why ain't you in uniform?" she asked as she drove out of the complex. "You look damn fine in dat uniform too. I'm just sayin'."

"I'm off duty," I replied. "Pull over by that Jeep."

She did so, putting the Renault in park and killing the headlights, but leaving it running. "I'm ready for a hot bath, glass of wine, and my own bed, girl, so best you get on wit what you doin' here."

I still hadn't formulated a new plan yet, or at least one which stood a chance of working, so I laid a few cards on the table instead.

"How bad would your business suffer if that particular client went away?" I asked.

Baby-G looked at me and frowned again. "Honey, dere bin people trying to take dat man down for years; ain't nobody managed yet."

I wanted to tell her that I was going to do it, one way or another, but I'd already compromised myself enough for one night. She didn't need to know that he was the last one on my list, and I'd rather see him dead than behind bars, but I'd settle for either.

"That's not what I asked," I said instead.

She sighed and shook her head. "You tink I like spankin' that fat old man's hairy ass while he wait on his blue pills to kick in? Girl-friend, only way I take his calls 'cos he have me arrested if I don't."

"I'm not sure that's the case these days," I replied. "He's running out of friends in his corner."

"Dat son-of-a-bitch like a cat wit nine lives," she said, her braids swinging from side to side as she shook her head and waggled a finger in the air. "I just hopin' dat wicked heart of his give out one time, 'cos girl I'm tellin' you, when dat happens I'll keep spankin' till he done dying." Her eyes got wider and she drew in a sharp breath. "Shit. I didn't mean none of dat, now. Don't be sayin' I threaten him or nuttin' like it."

I couldn't stop myself from laughing, and Baby-G looked at me as though I'd gone mad.

"You ain't wearin' one of dem wire things now, are you?"

"No, I promise you," I said, managing to stop laughing. "We're on the same side."

Baby-G's furrowed brow slowly morphed into a smile. "I tink I like you," she said. "You let me go on home one time before when I sure I busted. You ain't like most coppers."

She wouldn't say that if she knew my original plan which had involved her being exposed along with her client, but it had been a crappy idea anyway. She was right; McKinley Woods had been accused of rape, sexual assault, harassment in the workplace, and yet his trials kept getting postponed, and he was still serving on the government, albeit in a lesser role.

"Give me a number I can reach you on," I said. "Then go home and scrub that *drittsekk* off your body. I'll get in touch when I have a plan in place."

From a small, glittery purse, she pulled a business card and handed it to me.

"Don't be givin' a girl hope den leavin' me hangin', now," she said, lifting her chin and looking at me suspiciously.

I read the card. 'Baby-G. Hair, nails, and dreams come true.' Below that was her phone number.

"We could make magic wit dat lovely blonde hair of yours," she said, running her hand through my sweaty, knotted hair. "But you need a shower worse than me, girl."

I quickly opened the door. "I'll call you," I said, and hurried over to the Jeep, giving my shirt a sniff on the way. She wasn't wrong.

5

GRILLED CHEESE AND A CONFESSION

Tuesday 10:30pm

Parking the Jeep on Conch Point Road, I ducked through the hole in the tall wire fence surrounding the former Spanish Bay Reef Resort property and traipsed through the woods to my little shack by the water. I turned off the torch function on my mobile when I saw the lights were still on inside. Sometimes Jazzy left them on for me, so I quietly entered through the front door, but she was sitting on the sofa reading a book.

"Hey," I greeted her.

"Hey," she returned, sparing me a brief glance from the pages.

"What are you reading?" I asked, kicking off my trainers.

"*Dolphin Island*. AJ gave it to me," she replied, and I noticed her thick island accent had softened more than I'd realised. She was enunciating her words more clearly. I'm sure it had been a gradual change, and I couldn't decide if it was a good thing, a bad thing, or just a thing that didn't matter.

When it came to books, I preferred non-fiction, so my friend, AJ

Bailey, was a better resource for reading material. And movies. And games. AJ was sort of normal. Probably because she'd experienced a regular childhood. I had, mostly. Until I was fifteen. Things went a little sideways after that.

I walked to the kitchen, which is to say, I took about four steps. The shack, which I'd been given by a wonderful old man named Archie Winters, was a simple, open-plan room with all the living area towards the front and the bedroom in the rear. The one interior door led to the bathroom. Technically, there was a second door, but it was just a wardrobe.

I was trying to decide between showering or eating something first when I heard Jazzy's book drop to the coffee table.

"Where have you been?" she asked.

"Working," I replied, peeling off my stinky tank top as I walked towards the bathroom. I didn't think I could eat anything while I smelled this awful.

"I don't think so," Jazzy said, which stopped me at the doorway.

I turned. She was kneeling on the sofa looking over the back towards me, her wild, frizzy hair out of proportion with her petite frame. Her brow was furrowed in an intense stare.

"Where do you think I've been?"

"I think you're seeing someone," she said, not appearing happy about the idea.

"I am?" I replied. "I hope he's someone nice who doesn't talk too much."

She rolled her eyes. "I'm not a little kid. Why are you hiding things from me?"

"Maybe it's none of your business," I said, and immediately knew I shouldn't have.

I was too used to being on my own and not having to explain myself to anyone. At least since my boyfriend had been murdered a few years ago. But it had been different with Ridley. We'd operated as one. Both existing within a private world we'd wrapped ourselves in. An oasis and escape from the _dritt_ I'd been through before then.

After Ridley's death, all I'd wanted was to be alone. But things were different now. I was responsible for this kid, and we shared our home and our lives. She was also right. I'd been hiding a lot from her and lying about it for several months.

"I'm not seeing anyone."

She shrugged her shoulders. "You can bring him here, you know. I can make myself scarce if you want to, you know… do the thing."

"*Do the thing?*" I echoed, trying not to laugh.

She just stared at me with her big brown eyes.

"I could get you earplugs," I said. "Or maybe you'd prefer to swing a chair around and check it out with a bag of popcorn?"

"Aargh," she gasped, her face contorting in disgust. "Forget it. You carry on sneakin' 'round and tellin' me stories 'bout it all!" she said, shaking her head and slumping back down on the sofa.

Her island accent had come back in a hurry. So had my total lack of parenting skills.

"*Faen,*" I cursed under my breath. "I'm not seeing anybody, but I do need to shower. Then I'll explain. Okay?"

She sat up and looked at me again, nodding. Her frizzy mop wobbling in sync.

"Make me a grilled cheese," I said, and she rolled her eyes again.

But I heard her opening kitchen cupboard doors as I stepped into the shower to wash away the sweat, filth, and horror of the day.

I took a bite of the grilled cheese sandwich Jazzy had made me while she looked at me expectantly. I had no idea where to start so I chewed slowly. Finally, there came a point when I had to either take another bite or start talking, and taking another bite would be like giving her the middle finger.

"Do you remember I told you about The International Fellowship of Lions private resort?"

Jazzy nodded. "Yeah. The place you said you were kinda conned into working for. You said the people who ran it are in prison."

"Which is true," I replied, trying carefully to choose my words. A process which didn't come naturally to me. "But the members were criminals too, and many of them got away. Some were from abroad and couldn't be touched, and a few had hidden their memberships well enough that they weren't personally tied to the crimes."

Jazzy looked thoughtful so I took another bite.

"What crimes?" she asked.

I'd hoped to avoid this question for at least… forever, or until she was older, if it *had* to be discussed. Now I sat next to a fourteen-year-old who'd already lived a life no kid should have to suffer, and I had to decide how much depravity to expose her to. It was like choosing the cooking time for dinner. Too little and it's useless, too much and it's ruined… except we were talking about a young woman's innocence and ability to handle the evil inherent in human beings. Nobody's life is destroyed by missing one meal.

"I'm not a child," she said, as though reading my mind.

"You're not," I agreed. "But you still have the opportunity to enjoy a *childhood*. There are some things it's best not to know about for a while."

The other side of the argument is that evil doesn't wait for its victims to be ready. Jazzy was the prime age for trafficking. *What if I didn't give the tools to recognise a bad situation before it was too late?* As with almost everything in life, there were no perfect answers. All I could do was turn the oven up to eleven and keep peeking through the glass.

"We were all carefully recruited," I began. "Brainwashed into thinking what we were doing was okay, and after one year working for the resort, we'd be given money and a new identity."

"Why did you need a new identity?"

"Turns out I didn't, but at the time I thought it was important."

She bit her lower lip before asking, "What was the work they made you do?"

I sucked in a deep breath. This was the part where it became hard to see through the grubby, steamy, oven window.

"We provided company for members of the resort."

"Company?" she repeated, her eyes searching mine. "You mean sex, don't you?"

I nodded, holding her stare, and searching in return for the girl's reaction. *Disgusted? Disappointed? Unbelieving?* Would I now be less of a person in her estimation. A broken version of the woman she thought she'd known. I felt broken inside, so she wouldn't be wrong.

"You were young," she whispered.

I nodded again. "That was what the members paid a lot of money for. Girls between your age and seventeen."

Jazzy flinched a little. The mention of her age seemed to drive the point home. "They convinced you this was all okay and normal?"

"They found us throughout the Caribbean, but we all had several things in common," I explained. "We were running from something, our situations were desperate, and we were looking for a way out. That's how they lured us in. Not with handcuffs or threats, but with promises and a place we could call home."

This was the most I'd talked about my experience in a long time, and it didn't feel good. Some people liked getting difficult things off their chest, but I wasn't one of them. I preferred these memories stay shoved away in a dark recess where they could bleed out over time. It was too much to face at any one time.

But out they'd been drawn, and I was pretty sure they'd caused the oven to catch fire and destroy all hope of dinner.

Jazzy looked down at the sofa without saying a word, for what felt like forever. I'm the queen of awkward silence, but this had me scrambling for something to say. Except I didn't know what to say. *Just kidding, it wasn't that bad?* It was that bad, and there are plenty of people out there today who'd run a scheme just like that again. *Why?* Because there's *drittsekk* lining up with cash in hand looking for the chance to participate.

As I sat there in a soft cotton tracksuit, with wet hair and a half-eaten toasted cheese sandwich in my hand, I was sure the 'truth' had driven a wedge between us that no words or actions could remove. I felt a lump in my throat.

And then the kid looked up, shuffled closer, and wrapped her arms around me.

I'm not a hugger, but I accepted this one. I even dropped my grilled cheese on the sofa.

She hung on for a while, finally releasing me and moving back to her side of the sofa. She inadvertently sat on the rest of my dinner, but that was okay. I was ready to move on to wine anyway.

"What does all this have to do with where you've been in the evenings lately?" she asked, while I poured myself a drink and a second much smaller glass for the kid.

I'd almost forgotten where and why the conversation had started, so her question put me back on track.

"The members," I said. "There were three who had managed to slip through the police's net at the time, but still lived in Cayman. A case I worked a while back revealed them to me. One, Rowland Chesterton-Clark, had died."

"That's good," Jazzy commented.

"The second, Randall Cosgrove, we arrested as part of that case," I said, leaving out the part about his complicit wife Estelle's unfortunate drowning while trying to escape. "And the last one is a man who's managed to evade the law for a long time. If I tell you who it is, you have to promise you'll never repeat this to anyone."

Jazzy tipped her head to one side. "I think this whole conversation falls under that umbrella."

"That's true, but this part is especially so."

"Okay, okay. Who is it?"

"McKinley Woods."

"Dat politician guy?" she squealed, her accent showing back up again. "Dat man a creep."

"More than you should ever know. But that's where I've been most nights I'm out late. Following him and trying to find something to pin on him that will actually stick."

"Got something?"

"I did have, but now I can't use it because it'll hurt someone else who doesn't deserve it."

Jazzy nodded slowly and I pushed myself up from the sofa. "Now you know, so can I go to bed?"

"Sure, but don't be hiding shit from me in the future," she said, grinning. "We gotta be straight with each other."

"Okay," I agreed, wondering how our roles had suddenly reversed. "Go clean your teeth. And wipe that sandwich off your arse."

I left Jazzy jumping up, muttering the word 'gross' as she brushed the crumbs from her bum.

***

Ten minutes later, in the dark shack, I lay my head on the pillow and closed my eyes. With so much talk of the resort, I prepared myself for the all too familiar onslaught of haunting memories. The unfamiliar hands, loveless one-sided lust, and ultimately, the beating and rape which brought an end to the nightmare.

But to my relief, the image of Perry Collins crept into my mind, his scalp opened up by the bullet exiting the top of his skull. I wondered what he was experiencing now. Against historically indoctrinated beliefs, absolutely nothing was my guess.

Whittaker's intuition was correct; I'd once craved that relief. For a time, I'd considered turning off the switch to make it all stop. No more hurt, pain, and despair. Nothing at all, just a world moving on without me.

But seeing the man, and walking my mind through his beautiful home, something didn't add up. Maybe we'd find he had a terminal illness or a tragedy he couldn't move past, but I had an inkling that wasn't the case with Perry Collins. His escape was from something else.

6

LOGISTICS

Wednesday 6:30am

I was up early and out of the house without waking Jazzy, whose alarm wouldn't go off until well after I'd left. When she'd first lived with me, the slightest noise or disturbance would jolt her awake, but she'd finally settled down and now crashed out like a normal teenager.

Arriving at the George Town central station, I wasn't surprised to see Detective Whittaker's Range Rover SUV already in the car park. I went inside and ran upstairs to his office.

"Good morning, Nora," he said, being informal as no one else was within earshot.

"Sir," I greeted him.

"I spoke with Perry Collins' wife last night," he said, sitting back in his chair. "She's flying here today, along with their daughter."

"How did she sound?" I asked and he looked at me like I'd said something wrong. Again.

"It was a death notice, Nora. She was understandably upset."

"Of course," I responded, unsure why he'd missed my point. "Upset, as in shocked and sad, or upset as in annoyed?"

He thought for a moment, considering the wife's reaction or trying to understand my thinking; I wasn't sure which.

"That's a hard question to answer without personally knowing Mrs Bradford-Collins. At first she was shocked and could hardly speak, and then her main concern appeared to be their daughter."

"Only one kid?" I asked.

"From what I saw in the immigration file I was able to access, yes, and his wife only mentioned Kayleigh," Whittaker explained. "Although I think she's his from an earlier marriage."

"Was he sick?"

"She said he was healthy."

"Were they having problems?"

"She said they were separated but working on it. According to her it was all very amicable."

I nodded, sensing Whittaker was ready to move on with whatever he had on his desk.

"Starting at the airport?" he asked.

"I'll try to trace his steps from arriving last night. Odd he mentioned the immigration people, don't you think?"

The detective shrugged his shoulders. "Seems like he didn't want them to be in trouble."

"Sure, but why would they be?" I countered. "We wouldn't have any idea when that gun came into the island, or whether he'd brought it himself. He could have purchased it here on the black market. If he'd said nothing, we'd have spoken with the officers simply to understand the victim's movements, but nothing more."

Whittaker looked up at me and tapped his pen on the table. "Then perhaps there is something more."

I nodded and turned to leave.

"I spoke with Sergeant Redburn last night. I didn't want you out there alone, so he's loaned me Tibbetts as well."

"Thank you, sir," I said over my shoulder.

I would have been happy to conduct the investigation on my

own, but I knew why the detective preferred to keep me with my regular partner. Jacob was a good man, and while he wasn't ambitious, he was far more cautious than me, so we tended to complement each other and find an acceptable balance. At least that's what I'd been told by my superiors. I'd still prefer to get the shit done my way and save some time.

Jacob was waiting in the lobby with the keys to a patrol car he'd requisitioned.

"What you got me into now?" he asked with a grin as we walked outside into the morning heat.

"I got you out of another boring lap around West Bay handing out speeding tickets," I said as we got in the car.

It was his day to drive. We alternated.

"I heard some fella shot himself," he said, phrasing it as a question.

He looked at me when he reached the road.

"Coffee, then FBO at the airport," I directed him before replying to his question. We had a little time to kill before I figured the manager would be at the FBO. "Lucky you weren't there last night. It was pretty gory."

Jacob wrinkled his nose. He didn't have a strong stomach. "I heard one of the George Town fellas lost his lunch."

"Right in the flower bed," I confirmed.

He wrinkled his nose again.

While Jacob drove us to a coffee shop, I gave him a quick overview of what we knew, which didn't take long. Man flies into airport. Goes home. Shoots himself. Back in the car, the rest of the journey was filled with endless questions to which I had few answers.

He parked outside the Cayman Islands Customs & Border Control building near the FBO, and we went inside.

"Sommer and Tibbetts," I said, introducing ourselves to the receptionist. "We'd like to speak with the officers on duty at the FBO late afternoon yesterday."

The woman turned and looked towards an office behind her.

"That would be Officer Grainger. She's in with our supervisor now."

"Only one person was on duty?" I asked.

"That's usual for the FBO. Not enough traffic to require more than one."

"When do you tink she'll be available?" Jacob asked.

From her expression, the receptionist seemed unsure, so before she replied, I walked over and knocked on the office door.

"Oh! You shouldn't..." the receptionist began, but an annoyed voice from inside the office asked who was at the door.

"Constables Sommer and Tibbetts; we're here to speak with Miss Grainger," I called out.

A moment later, the door opened, and a man in a white customs and border control shirt stared at me. He was an older gentleman with grey hair and a neatly trimmed moustache. The epaulettes of his shirt had several gold stripes, which probably meant he was important.

"What about?" he snapped.

"A gentleman arrived last night on a private plane. I'm told Miss Grainger was the immigration official who would have met him," I replied, peering around the man.

Behind him a dark-skinned lady in a similar uniform sat in a chair. Her look of concern led me to believe our visit was not the day's first problem she'd faced.

"Miss Grainger came to me a few minutes ago about the very same subject," the supervisor said, opening the door wider. "I'm sure it'll save us all a lot of time if we discuss it together."

"Thank you, sir," I said, slipping into the office.

Jacob followed and the supervisor closed the door, returning to his seat. There was only one other chair, next to Grainger, but I was happy to stand. Jacob wasn't sure what to do, so he stood too.

"I'm Chief Officer McLaughlin," the man said, "and I'd like it noted that Officer Grainger voluntarily came to me this morning."

"Why did you do that, miss?" I asked.

I could see she looked terrified, now that I was standing closer, her lower lip quivering slightly.

"I screwed up last night," she said, her voice strained. "We see Mr Collins quite often, and there's never been a problem before."

"Was there a problem last night?" I asked.

"Well, no," she replied. "But I heard he'd died from a gunshot wound. Suspected suicide. It was on the news this morning."

"Okay. Why does that concern you?" I asked, hoping my presumption of innocence would put her more at ease.

Generally, my manner doesn't put anyone at ease, but I do try sometimes.

"He only had a satchel with him," she continued. "And his car gets delivered onto the tarmac. So, to run him and his bag through a scanner, we have to walk back inside. We've never had an issue with him, so I skipped the scan," she finished, her chin dropping.

"Obviously, this is a failure to follow our strict procedures," McLaughlin began, but I held up my hand.

He looked surprised, but he stopped talking. Those fancy stripes probably meant most people didn't tell him to shut up too often. I felt Jacob nudge me but ignored him.

"Miss Grainger's screw-up is your problem to sort out," I said, turning my attention back to the woman. "Our concern is tracing the deceased's movements last night, and finding out how a firearm came into his possession."

Grainger fidgeted in her chair, then looked up at me. I felt bad for her. From what I'd seen and heard, she was doing everything right after doing something wrong. I hoped she'd get a slap on the wrist and put back to work. I figured after this incident she'd be an exemplary employee. It also started to make sense why Collins had mentioned the immigration staff in his note. He must have sensed she'd come forward and admit to her error. Pretty broad and generous thinking for a man who was about to kill himself.

"How did he seem?" Jacob asked. "You know, was he agitated or upset?"

Grainger slowly shook her head. "Just like any other time I met the man. He's always polite. Never says much, but always polite. I asked after his daughter, and he told me she'd be down at Christmas. Poor girl."

"What time did Mr Collins leave here?" I asked.

"Around five," Grainger replied. "The passport scan was at 4:58, so a few minutes after that by the time I was finished, and his car arrived."

"His car was delivered to the airport?" Jacob asked.

"Yes. There's a service which picks it up from his home and brings it here," McLaughlin answered. He turned to me. "Do you have reason to suspect he had the firearm with him? It could already have been here, correct?"

"Correct," I replied. "But he left a note. In it he asked for leniency for your staff, sir."

McLaughlin couldn't hide his surprise.

"Leads us to believe he brought the gun into the island at some point, past your staff. We'll contact law enforcement in the US to see if the gun was registered to Mr Collins."

"I feel terrible," Grainger whispered. "The idea I helped that man take his own life is just awful."

I shook my head and placed a hand on her shoulder. "Don't lose sleep over it. You may have helped him do it in the way he wanted, but you didn't affect the final result."

I thanked them for their time, and we walked to the car.

"I know you were trying to make her feel better, Nora," Jacob said as we got in. "But I don't tink dat came across da way you intended."

"It didn't?"

"No," he continued, pulling to the road. "You still made her feel like she had a hand in da tragedy."

"But she probably did," I pointed out.

Jacob sighed. "Maybe. But she feel bad enough already, don't you tink?"

"Drive the fastest way to West Bay Road," I said, ready to move on.

I'd told the woman not to lose sleep over it. Collins was going to kill himself whether he had a gun available or not. In my estimation, people who have mentally crossed that line are going to find a way. But I wasn't about to debate that, or my words, with Jacob.

I started a timer on my phone to log the travel time, and we drove in silence until we neared the first liquor store on the road behind Seven Mile Beach.

"Pull into Tortuga's," I told him, and he frowned at me.

"We can't have drink in da car," he said, slowing but unsure whether he should stop or not.

"Pull into Tortuga's," I instructed again. "We're not here to buy anything."

"Oh," he grunted and found a spot to park.

"I noticed the box the Scotch he'd drunk came in had a Tortuga's price label on it," I explained as we walked to the door. "Didn't see an obvious spot for it in his drinks cabinet, so he may have bought it on his way home."

Jacob tried the door, but it was locked. A sign on the door informed us they didn't open until ten. I cupped my hands around my eyes and peered inside. A man was restocking shelves in the far corner of the shop. I looked at my watch. It was 8:50. I knocked on the glass and held my badge up. The man squinted, looked at his own watch, then shook his head and walked over. I could hear him shouting "We're closed", but he stopped when he finally saw the uniforms and badge.

"Sorry to bother you," Jacob said the moment the door cracked open.

Apparently, he'd decided I wouldn't open with that line. Not sure why he thought that.

"Were you working last night between five and five-thirty?" I asked.

"I was," the man replied, standing in the doorway and not inviting us in. I detected an English accent, most likely London area.

"Do you recall a man coming by around that time who bought a very expensive bottle of Scotch?"

"I don't," he said. "But I doubt I would."

"Why's that?" I asked, thinking maybe he was working in the back while someone else handled the register.

"I wasn't working *here*," he said, and grinned.

I frowned, then realised that was actually quite funny, and grinned back.

"You can let all your air conditioning out, or you could invite us in," I said.

He stepped back and let us walk inside, locking the door behind us.

"I'm Jack," he said. "Assistant manager of a few of the branches. I was at another store yesterday, but I can call the guy we had in here if you like?"

"Or we could look at the CCTV," I suggested, nodding at the camera over the check-out area.

"Easy enough," he said and waved for us to follow him into a back room.

It took a few minutes to log in, access the right camera, and find the time in question, but it didn't take long to see that Perry Collins had known the bottle he was after. There appeared to be no rush, yet no wasted time in his actions. He was calm, and from the employee's reactions, polite.

"I don't get it," Jacob said as we left.

My lack of response was his cue to continue.

"Da man look like he out for a pleasant evening, you know? Da immigration lady say he appeared perfectly normal, dis tape look like he buyin' a bottle of booze like it just anudder day. How dat be when he already plannin' on blowin' his own brains out in a few minutes?"

I paused at the car and looked over the roof at my partner. "Because the hard part was already done."

Jacob scoffed. "Da hard part pullin' dat trigger, I reckon."

"That's because you can't imagine doing it. The hardest part for Perry Collins was deciding his only course of action was to kill himself. After that, it was simply logistics."

7

MISSING

Wednesday 10:30am

"What now?" Jacob asked as he drove us to West Bay Road in front of the shopping centre.

I thought for a moment. I'd turned twenty-one and hit my two-year active-duty anniversary a month ago, and was now eligible to officially enter detective training. But I still had to wait for the next wave of classes to start. Meanwhile, Whittaker had been unofficially grooming me with projects like this. One of the things he'd been banging on about was prioritising the lines of inquiry and following them through to their conclusion. It was easy to start jumping around as one lead looked more promising than another, but it was important to complete all of them, until you were satisfied there was no more relevant information available.

In all the cases I'd assisted on so far, he'd been in charge, and I'd mostly taken care of tasks he'd sent me to do. I sensed this was different. He was taking a back seat role and letting me set my priorities.

I started the timer on my phone again. "Turn left. We'll go to the condo. When you get there pull into the underground parking."

While Jacob drove north, I dialled a number at the station with my mobile connected to the patrol car's Bluetooth.

"The ME's not even started yet, Nora," Rasha greeted me with a mixture of impatience and amusement.

She was a bit like my friend AJ in that their soft English accents made even insults sound more pleasant.

"I need to check on the gun," I replied.

"Oh, I have that, dear," she responded. "It was registered to Perry Collins in Georgia. He purchased it just under three months ago and took a firearms class at the same time."

"So, he had a permit?" I asked.

"Georgia doesn't require one," Rasha replied.

"Seriously?"

"Unbelievable, but true," Rasha replied.

"Did he own any other firearms?" I asked.

"This was his first on record. I also checked the UK, where as you know, it's almost impossible to own a handgun, but farmers and landowners often have shotguns or hunting rifles. Nothing on record there."

"You tink da man bin plannin' dis for three months?" Jacob asked, shaking his head.

"Fortunately, that's not for me to figure out," Rasha replied. "Gotta go."

"Thanks," I said, and ended the call.

"Dis fella, wit all da money and jets and what-have-you," Jacob continued. "Perfectly healthy, and got himself a daughter to worry about, who he gotta know gonna be mighty upset about dis, yet he take three months or more to plan out killin' himself. Don't seem right to me."

"We don't know he bought the gun to kill himself," I pointed out.

"True, I spose. But timin' is close enough."

Jacob slowed and turned into the Caribbean View Residences

condominiums, stopping briefly at the guard shack before being waved on. Keeping left, he then drove under the main building. I stopped my timer when we reached Perry Collins' boxy-looking Mercedes SUV, and noted the drive time.

I couldn't argue Jacob's point. Buying a gun that close to his suicide suggested it had been on his mind for a while, but wasn't proof of anything. He could have been concerned for his personal safety, or planned on shooting someone else, for that matter.

We got out and I walked to the Mercedes, standing by the driver's door. Looking around, I spotted the walkway to the lifts, and put my camera on video.

"Jacob, start from here and walk to the lifts. We'll retrace his steps."

"You filming me?" he asked, meeting me by the driver's door.

"Yup. So, shake it like a Polaroid picture."

"What?" he said, spinning around.

"Just walk to the lifts, *fjols.*"

Jacob laughed and started casually walking around the SUV to the hallway leading to the lifts. We passed a stairwell on the left, and I stopped recording once Jacob stood in front of the farthest of the two lifts. I pressed the button and the doors opened. Jacob held a hand against the door to stop it closing on us, and he peered inside.

"Looks like it need a security card to get farder up dan da first floor."

I looked around the hallway which dead ended after the lifts. It was spacious, with bare grey concrete walls and a single light overhead with a protective cage. A security camera was also mounted to the ceiling, closer to the back wall. It was one of the modern dome types. I turned and faced the way we'd come in.

"This way," I told Jacob, and he followed me up the steps.

The stairwell was wide, and the same grey walls surrounded us until the landing halfway up. As we turned 180 degrees, the walls became painted white, and the steps covered with hardy commercial carpet. A more decorative light hung from the midpoint of the landing, and the brightness increased enormously once we walked up onto the ground floor of the tower. A reception desk sat on the opposite side to our right beyond the lifts, and an open-plan restaurant filled most of the street side of the expansive area. A bar seemed to be part of the restaurant on our immediate right, and tall glass doors led to the pool on our left.

"He either came out of the lifts or walked up the stairs, then left the main building through these doors," I thought aloud. "The entry to his condo is outside to the left."

We both stood still and looked around. It appeared as though every detail in the building had been meticulously designed and crafted with no expense spared. Dark woods were offset by the tall doors and windows filling the building with sunlight. It was easy to see how the restaurant and bar would transform into an intimate setting once the sun went down.

Another domed security camera was mounted on the high ceiling, facing the rear entrance, and stepping towards the lobby I could see it was actually a double unit, with a second camera covering the front.

"Can I help you?" came a pleasant voice from the reception desk.

"Good morning," Jacob greeted the lady. "Who should we see about da footage from dese cameras, ma'am?"

"That would be our security team," she replied, smiling at Jacob then looking at me in surprise.

Being the only Scandinavian female constable with the Royal Cayman Islands Police Service garnered the reaction a lot. I'd even had a few people think I was some kind of prank, like those people you pay to show up at a friend's birthday and sing, or take their clothes off. I hoped the lady didn't think I was about to strip in her lobby, but from the look on her face, it could have been crossing her mind.

"Is Charles here?" I asked.

"No, he's off for a few days," she replied, her expression moving to a different kind of concern. "Is this about last night?"

"Who can we talk to about the CCTV?" I asked, ignoring her question.

"I'll radio Darcy; he's on duty today."

She picked up a handheld radio and Jacob moved a little closer to the counter.

"Yes, we're following up on da incident last night," Jacob told her quietly, which earned him another smile.

After she called for the guard, I told her we needed to access Mr Collins' condo, so she called the man again and asked him to meet us over there. I timed the walk out of the back doors and across the pool area to the south building, noting the duration along with the other times I'd recorded.

"You need inside?" the security guard asked, and we turned to see a rotund young man in a uniform similar to the one I'd seen Charles wearing.

Except this guy was sized for his a few cheeseburgers ago. The buttons were gamely hanging on by a handful of threads, but they were one all-you-can-eat Sunday brunch away from giving up. We stepped aside so he could swipe his card and open the door.

"We also need the CCTV from yesterday afternoon, three until seven. Every camera," I said.

"Yes ma'am," he replied in a surprisingly soft voice. "I'll call our monitoring company and ask for the footage."

I followed Jacob inside the entrance hall and we both donned nitrile gloves, although I was sure Rasha had already processed the home.

"Who's the security company you use?" I asked, turning back to the guard, who'd stayed outside.

Which was good, because he was sweating profusely, and he'd turn the tiled floor into a slick-track if he came inside.

"Caribbean Security Systems, ma'am."

I grinned. "Patti Weaver's a very nice lady," I commented.

"She is," the guard beamed back. "She makes the best chocolate chip cookies. She usually brings some if she stops by. I'll tell her you said hi, Miss…"

He squinted to read my name badge, so I turned away.

"Tell her Constable Tibbetts sends his best wishes and thanks," I said.

Patti was indeed a lovely lady, but I'd used up all my favours with her in the past. It was probably better to keep my name out of it.

"Okay," the guard replied hesitantly. "Please close the door when you're done."

Once he'd left, we walked down the hall to the living room where I explained the events from the night before. Jacob listened carefully as I described finding Collins and then the envelopes. Afterwards, he stood by the sliding glass door and stared at the patio outside. The blood and splatter had been scrubbed away, leaving a spotless patch on the concrete contrasting with the time-stained area surrounding it.

I left him to contemplate, and walked into the master bedroom, opening drawers, and looking in the spacious closet. I was certain a man as organised and well planned as Collins wouldn't leave anything lying around that he didn't want people to see, but his possessions might give me a better idea of his personality.

Everything was arranged and sorted by clothing type. His colour palette ranged from greys through soft blues and tans. No black, no bright hues. He had two pairs of shoes for every occasion. Dress shoes, trainers, flip-flops, and boat shoes.

The bathroom felt like it was half the size of my whole shack. I found the usual shaving kit, soaps, shampoos, nail clippers, and hairbrushes. No prescription meds. No razor blades or nooses tucked away. I returned to the living room, where Jacob was looking in the refrigerator.

"Anything of interest?" I asked.

He grinned at me. "I tink da man eat out a lot. Not much in here."

"He probably emptied perishables before he left last time," I suggested.

"True," Jacob agreed, closing the door. "Not much point stockin' up dis trip."

I looked at the painting on the wall again. So simple, yet so much care and effort had gone into the work.

"Dat's a fine paintin'" Jacob said, surprising me.

"Do you paint?" I asked.

"Not for years. Did some when I was younger. Not dis good though."

"Ready?" I asked. "Let's see if the CCTV has been organised."

"I'm ready. Gives me the creeps tinkin' da man shoot himself right dere not but a day back."

We both looked at the patio one more time, then Jacob turned and hurried towards the hall. I went to follow him.

"Wait," I said, looking at the drinks cabinet at the edge of the kitchen. "Something's not right."

Jacob came back and joined me in front of the cabinet.

"What's wrong?"

I pointed to a space on one of the shelves. "There's a bottle missing."

8

SHADOWS

Wednesday 1:00pm

Sitting in front of a computer at central station, I found the pictures Rasha's team had taken of the condo the night before. They had been thorough, so I scrolled past hundreds of shots as they'd moved from the patio into the home. Finally, I came across some of the kitchen. The drinks cabinet hadn't been of particular interest, so no pictures were focused on it, but several had it in the background. I found the clearest view and zoomed in.

The camera they used took really high-resolution photos, but it had been dark outside and the interior lights were more for mood than brightness, so the picture turned pretty grainy. Still, it was good enough for me to see a beige box in the spot I'd noticed empty that morning. A box I know I'd seen there the night before. I thumped the table with my fist.

"What you all het up about?" Jacob asked, walking in the room.

He'd dropped me at the station while he went to speak with the car service driver. He came back just in time to find me annoyed at myself.

"I missed this last night," I grumbled.

"Missed what, now?" he said, leaning over my shoulder. "You said da was a bottle in dere last night, and so dere is."

I copied the photograph and dropped it into the investigation file, then scrolled back through the SOCO pictures until I found a clear one of the box on the counter. I copied that one too, then opened them both so Jacob could see.

"Last night, I noticed that they were the same. I should have had Rasha bag it then."

"Why? Because he forgot he had some already," Jacob responded, straightening up. "Had a few tings on his mind, I expect."

"Would you forget about having a thousand-dollar bottle at home?" I asked.

Jacob whistled. "Can't says I would, but dat man make in a week what I make in a year, so it like a bottle of fizzy pop to him."

"It was important enough to him that he chose it as his last drink," I pointed out. "But maybe he wanted to be sure he had a bottle."

Even as I said the words, I didn't believe them, which annoyed me all over again. Jacob loved to chatter, and occasionally, I found myself drawn into conversing far more than I'd like. If I'd thought this through more, I wouldn't have conceded that Perry Collins didn't know what he had in his drinks cabinet. From everything I'd seen about the man so far, I'd bet he could tell us every bottle in there… if he hadn't blown his own head off, that is.

He couldn't tell anyone shit now, and I was starting to feel like the clues he'd left were so meticulous that I was being manipulated. But this was different. Collins certainly didn't call someone early this morning and tell them he forgot to remove the old bottle of Scotch. Yet it was gone.

I picked up the phone on the desk and dialled Rasha's extension.

"Still not started, Nora," she said.

This time her voice was clearly impatient without a hint of amusement.

"Will the ME do a drug test?" I asked.

"Always," she replied.

I thought for a moment.

"Was that it?" Rasha asked.

"Between last night and mid-morning today, a bottle went missing from the drinks cabinet in the condo," I explained. "It happened to be the same Scotch Collins stopped and bought on his way home."

"Are you sure?" Rasha asked.

It was my turn to be impatient now. "Look in the investigation file. I put two pictures in there, and I'm about to add a third. The one I took earlier. I'm sure."

The line was quiet for a few moments. "Okay…" she finally said, letting the word hang like a question.

"We need to test all the bottles in the cabinet," I replied.

I heard a groan. "No, you need to find the missing bottle and we can test that one."

Fy faen. She was right. *Why would someone remove one bottle if others contained the same evidence? Which could be what? Poison? Why would Perry Collins be worried about drinking the Scotch he already owned if he was planning on killing himself a few minutes after taking a sip?*

"Maybe da cleanin' staff helped demselves," Jacob said, and I turned to look at him.

We couldn't rule that out, either.

"We'll get a tox report from the ME, Nora, but we don't have the bandwidth to start testing a cabinet full of bottles, dear," Rasha said over the phone. "I'll let you know when we have the ME's report."

The line went dead, so I hung up the receiver. My first case I'd been given the lead on, and I was already trying to turn a simple suicide into something more. Jacob was right, and Rasha was right. I was ready to overburden an already swamped department with a wild swan chase. *Or was it geese chase?* But that was plural, I thought.

"What are the big birds you chase when you're wasting time?" I asked Jacob.

He looked at me as though I was mad as a hatter. I knew that phrase.

"You know. Wild big bird chase," I added.

"Goose?" he replied, clearly confused how we'd gone from bottles of Scotch to big, noisy birds.

"That's it," I mumbled. "Wild goose chase."

He was still looking at me, puzzled.

"What did the car service say?" I asked, moving on again.

"Nothing new," Jacob replied. "Times matched. The driver said he never exchanged a word wit him. Usual tip. Collins seemed like he always did. Nothing out of da ordinary."

I nodded as I transferred the photo I'd taken earlier from my phone into the investigation file. It made me wonder again, why would someone take that particular bottle? It was probably the most expensive one there, and the bottle was inside its box, so we have no idea whether it was full or almost empty. If a member of staff with a key card took it, that negated my earlier thought about Perry being concerned if the bottles were spiked in some way.

A text pinged on my mobile. I checked and saw it was from the station's front desk.

"The CCTV footage is here," I read aloud. "There's a hard drive at the front desk."

"I can get it," Jacob said, but I logged out of the computer and stood.

"I'll come too. I need a break."

"Lunch?" Jacob asked, hopefully.

"Sure," I replied, although food wasn't on my mind.

What was on my mind, as we walked through the halls to the reception area, was getting my mind back on track with this case and following up on the priorities.

"Would you call the manager at the Caribbean View Residences and point out the missing bottle?" I asked Jacob. "After lunch, I'll start on the CCTV."

"Sure ting," he replied, "I can run by dere. Show dem what we mean."

Jacob always preferred talking to people in person rather than over the phone or via email. That's because he was a nice guy and he liked people. He enjoyed interacting with other humans. Every once in a while, I found myself feeling jealous of his easy-going manner and the way he instantly made people feel comfortable around him. But those moments were fleeting. I wasn't wired that way.

On my way back inside the building, I stopped by the front desk and collected the package. It was a padded envelope with my name on the front, not Jacob's. Inside was an external hard drive and a note on Caribbean Security Systems letterhead.

Attn: Constable Sommer.
Security footage as requested.
Release authorised by Caribbean View Residences for police use only.
Say hi to Jacob,
Patti Weaver.

I managed a smile. Patti Weaver never missed a trick. I liked her despite the fact she undoubtedly didn't return the sentiment.

Back at the computer, I began the laborious process of looking through the footage. My first task was checking the various cameras and seeing how they'd been labelled, and what they viewed. Most covered areas I wasn't concerned with, but the labelling was logical, so in less than thirty minutes I'd narrowed it down to eight cameras.

Having established a pretty good timeline between the airplane landing and the time I heard the gunshot, I fast-forwarded the recording from an outdoor camera at the front entrance. I found Perry Collins arriving and noted the time from the camera's timestamp.

Next, was the underground parking garage where two views from either end captured the G-Wagen pulling in and parking. I watched him step from his SUV with his satchel in hand, briefly look around, then walk towards the lifts. The camera beyond the lifts showed him turning left and using the stairs. I continued noting the times as I tracked his movements.

Once on the ground floor, he appeared to be heading toward the rear doors, but turned and walked over to Charles, who was standing near the reception desk. They spoke briefly, before Collins turned and left the tower via the back doors. The rear-facing exterior camera on the left side of the main building picked him up walking by the pool area to his condo building. His head was up, his shoulders back, and he strode with unhurried intent. He could have been going to his next meeting, or home to relax. If there was a look for a man about to take his own life, this wasn't what most people would imagine.

Once he'd disappeared into his building, I switched to the camera near his front door and watched him swipe his key and go inside. I noted the camera as the perfect one to see who may have entered the condo this morning before us.

The last view was an exterior camera on a light pole between the pool and the steps to the beach. Angled towards the ocean-facing end of the left building, it caught the sand in front, but didn't cover the patio or decks of the units above. Whether for privacy, or simply the logistics of where the cameras could be mounted, we had no view of Perry Collins' last moments. I watched Charles and myself arrive at the scene. Switching to a straight-ahead view from the same pole, which I'd considered irrelevant earlier, I watched myself running on the beach and recorded the timestamp from the moment I stopped and slipped the earbuds out. Birds flew across the picture. We had a pretty exact time of death.

I stretched my arms and sat back for a moment. Running through a mental list of what we had so far, it was difficult to imagine extending the investigation too much further. Unless the autopsy returned something unexpected, or the other envelopes contained anything other than the organised directives of a man wrapping up his affairs, we could confirm that Perry Collins took his own life.

I couldn't see a way or a reason to pursue the gun issue any further, as he'd obviously brought it on the island himself, so all that would be left was the bottle theft. That would be considered more of an issue for the Caribbean View to sort out internally, unless they chose to press charges. We could add evidence-tampering charges, but that would be more paperwork than it was worth.

My mobile buzzed again. It was a text from Detective Whittaker. Collins' wife and daughter had landed and were on their way to the station. I quickly texted back that I'd meet him in ten minutes, and turned my attention back to the CCTV. I began typing all the timestamp references into the investigation file so anyone would be able to quickly find the key moments with Collins on camera, but then I became curious. I wondered how my re-enactment timing compared.

Flicking open my notebook, I found the video of me following Jacob and watched the timing. We'd gone to the lifts, so I stopped my video as we reached the base of the stairs. I found the same sequence from the CCTV, except I had to use the garage tape for part of the movement, then switch to the camera by the lifts for the last part. I stopped that playback when Perry stood at the base of the steps.

I was about to add the two together when something caught my eye. I could see the victim's shadow cast by the dome light by the lifts, extending behind him towards the underground parking. To his right, which was the left from the camera view, a second shadow was cast from what must have been the light in the stairwell landing.

Next to Perry Collins' shadow was a second one. It was larger, meaning it was closer to the light on the landing. I hit play, and watched Perry briefly pause before starting up the steps. The second shadow moved.

Someone else was in the stairwell.

9

———

EVALUATE. CHOOSE. ACT

Wednesday 4:00pm

I had hoped to reach Whittaker's office before the wife and daughter arrived, but I was too late. Rushing, I almost knocked another detective over in the hallway as I burst from the stairwell.

"*Dritt!* Sorry," I babbled.

Detective Weatherford just smiled and shook his head. He was a big guy, so bumping into him was about the same as smacking the wall.

"Slow your roll dere, Sommer," he said, chuckling as he carried on his way.

I looked down the end of the hall. Two women and Whittaker all stared at me from his office. I walked towards them as though nothing had happened, but I knew the first impression I'd presented was really shit.

"Constable Sommer, this is Mrs Raylene Bradford-Collins and Miss Kayleigh Collins," Whittaker said as I entered his office and shook their hands.

I closed the door behind me, and everyone took a seat. I pulled my chair to one side of the desk so I could face the two women. The wife was slender, medium height, and wore dark-framed glasses. She was dressed in a black skirt and business jacket with a white blouse. Her expression was stern, and her sharp, pointed facial features and piercing gaze gave the impression she was used to being in charge.

The daughter was almost as tall as me. Fair skinned and much prettier than her stepmother. Her sandy blonde hair barely touched her shoulders, and she wore jeans and a pale-coloured shirt. By her side was a rucksack. The older woman had a soft-sided briefcase. Kayleigh's eyes were red and tired looking, Raylene's were intense.

"Let me start by saying we're terribly sorry for your loss," Whittaker began with the standard line he was obliged to use. "Constable Sommer has joined us as she was first on scene, and she's assisting me as we follow up on the details."

"You're certain it was suicide?" the wife asked. Her American accent had a slight southern edge.

I was anxious to discuss the shadow in the stairwell with the detective, but I couldn't see how it would change the answer to that question. Still, I stayed quiet and let Whittaker answer.

"All evidence points that way, ma'am."

"Was he alone?" she asked, her manner direct but not aggressive.

"As best we can tell, yes," Whittaker replied.

I looked at the daughter. She was sitting up straight, her eyes alert despite her obvious fatigue. I noticed Raylene's hand softly covered the stepdaughter's on the arm of the chair.

"Are you both up to answering a few questions?" Whittaker asked. "If you'd prefer to get some rest after travelling, we understand completely and can chat tomorrow."

"No, let's get this over with," Raylene quickly answered, before turning to the younger woman. "Is that okay with you?"

Kayleigh's eyes remained on the detective. "That's fine," she said, with more command than I'd expected. Her accent was English, and I wondered where she'd spent most of her time growing up. From our brief searches, we knew she was going to university in America.

"I'll start with the obvious question in situations such as this," Whittaker began. "Did Mr Collins seem out of sorts, or depressed in any way?"

Raylene sort of shrugged her shoulders and waved her hands. "I'm not sure; we've been spending time apart for the past few months, so I haven't seen him every day." She looked at Kayleigh, who I noticed had moved her own hand from the arm of the chair, folding her arms instead.

"I live on campus, so I hadn't seen Dad in a while, but we spoke three or four times a week. I didn't notice anything strange at all."

It was a good reminder for me that first impressions in times like these can be deceiving. I'd pegged the daughter as being quiet and slightly unsure of herself, but her voice now suggested the opposite.

"Is it fair to say this was unexpected and out of character?" Whittaker asked, and at first, I wondered about his phrasing.

It seemed like he was asking a question which had pretty much been answered, but we both watched for the women's responses more than their words.

Raylene shook her head and let out a huff. Kayleigh's brow furrowed as though she were assessing the question.

"Certainly out of character," she responded.

"Did Mr Collins have enemies?" I asked. "Threats? Anyone who might wish him harm?"

Both women turned and frowned at me.

"What do you mean?" Raylene snapped. "He just said it's suicide. Do you think there may have been foul play?"

From the corner of my eye, I could see Whittaker was also looking my way, no doubt wondering why I was asking the question, but he didn't say anything, so I continued.

"I don't think there's any doubt that your husband took his own life," I said, proud that I'd chosen the words carefully as the image of Perry Collins' shattered scalp flashed through my mind. "But to complete the investigation we have to consider any influences that may have contributed."

"Influences?" Raylene repeated through gritted teeth. She was about to continue, but took a breath and settled herself, staying quiet instead.

"You'd be better served speaking with his business partner about that," Kayleigh said. "But he never spoke to me about any problems with other people."

"We've left a message for Mr Braithwaite in the UK, but haven't heard back as yet," Whittaker said. "As I mentioned over the phone, Miss Collins, your father left several envelopes, addressed to particular individuals. One of them is for you. Our scene of crime officer should be done with them, so I'll get that for you before you leave."

"Why are private documents being examined before they're delivered?" Raylene asked. "If you're convinced Perry killed himself, there should be no need for interfering with personal documents. Is that even legal?"

"I assure you, Mrs Bradford-Collins…"

"For heaven's sake, call me Raylene, Detective," she interrupted.

"Raylene," he began again. "I assure you it's legal and standard procedure until we're wholly satisfied no foul play was involved."

"Which you say you are, correct?" she countered.

"Everything points to it being suicide, ma'am," I quickly interjected, hoping Whittaker would pick up on my reluctance to rule out other factors. "But our inquiry is incomplete. We don't even have the medical examiner's report yet."

The wife eyed me disapprovingly before turning back to Whittaker. Again, she restrained herself and didn't say anything more, but I could tell she was holding far more inside like a coiled spring.

"I could take Miss Collins downstairs and see if we can collect the envelope," I suggested to the detective.

He stood. "Good idea," he replied with a smile. "Raylene, may I get you a water or coffee while you wait?"

She ignored him and stood, along with Kayleigh, who she took by the arm.

"I should probably come with you."

Kayleigh managed a smile. "That's okay. I'm sure we'll be right back."

I led Kayleigh from the office before Raylene could talk her way into joining us, and as I closed the door, I heard her asking Whittaker for more details of Perry Collins' suicide. I wasn't sure she'd want to hear my unedited version. Or perhaps she'd enjoy it more than I thought.

As we walked down the stairs, I dialled Rasha from my mobile. It rang about five times, and I was thinking she'd had enough of me today and wasn't answering when I heard her voice.

"I was getting ready to call you," she said. "The ME's done with the autopsy. No surprises. Cause of death was the obvious. Powder residue on the victim's hand consistent with the gunshot. Appeared healthy. Tox screen is being fast-tracked but won't have it back until late tomorrow at the earliest."

"Okay, thank you," I responded. "Can I collect the envelopes from you? I'm with his daughter."

"Whittaker's and the daughter's are done," Rasha said. "Pick them up anytime."

I ended the call and caught Kayleigh looking at me.

"Your envelope is ready. Follow me," I said and started towards the forensics department at the back of the building.

"Were you the first to find my father?" Kayleigh asked as we walked.

"Yes. I happened to be running on the beach when I heard the gunshot."

I heard what sounded like a gulp behind me, but she kept walking, so I kept walking.

"He hated guns," she said quietly, and I looked over my shoulder.

"He bought one about three months ago. Did he say why?"

"A gun?" Kayleigh questioned. "He's never owned a gun. I presumed he found one down here."

I paused in front of the door bearing a new sign with the words 'Crime Scene Investigation Unit'. I'd heard they were renaming the department to fall in line with current convention. Or TV shows.

Kayleigh was deep in thought, or puzzled, perhaps.

"Your dad purchased a gun and took a firearms training course in Georgia about three months ago," I reiterated. "He must have had a reason."

Kayleigh swallowed, and I heard the same gulping sound. "My father liked to plan ahead."

I nodded and knocked on the door. Another lady who worked with Rasha opened it, and recognising me, handed me the envelopes which were set on a counter close by.

"Thanks," I said, taking them and leading Kayleigh back down the corridor. "I can find you somewhere private to open this."

The young woman took a few moments to reply. "Thank you," she finally said, her voice breaking.

I turned down another hallway to where the interview rooms were located. I slid the occupied sign in place and opened the door, handing her the envelope with her name on it.

"I'll be right outside when you're done. There's no one in the observation room," I added, pointing to the one-way glass.

Kayleigh hesitated, looking at the glass, then back to me. "Would you mind staying in here?"

I shrugged my shoulders. "Okay."

Closing the door, I moved to the desk and took the seat facing the back wall and the observation room. This chair was the uncomfortable one. Kayleigh took one of the chairs normally occupied by an officer. I really didn't want to be in there. This was a private moment, and I wouldn't know what to do if the girl broke down, which would be understandable under the circumstances. The breakdown being the understandable part, not my lack of ability in dealing with emotions. That was a different issue.

She took a deep breath, sat up straight, and slipped a single sheet of paper from the envelope. It was on Perry Collins' personal letterhead, as the note addressed to Whittaker had been. Kayleigh held it in her hands and read the message, her expression stoic. When she was done, I could tell she was fighting to remain composed. After a few moments, her eyes lowered, and she read the letter one more time.

Biting her lip, Kayleigh turned the page around and placed it in front of me. I kept my eyes on her.

"This is a private note to you, miss."

She shrugged her shoulders. "Your people have already examined it. I'm sure a copy will be in the file or report. You might as well read it."

I looked down and followed the words her father had chosen for his final communication with his daughter.

My dearest Kayleigh,

I apologise for putting you through this nasty business, but try to place your emotions aside, and recognise why this was the best, and therefore my only course of action.

I have always lived by the rule I've drummed into you since childhood, and it has served me well.

Evaluate. Choose. Act.

We must always take responsibility for the circumstances we create. In this instance, it would be hypocritical for me to have chosen another path simply because this one was difficult.

Your only responsibility in all of this is to live your best life, and continue to be the exceptional woman you have already become.

With all my love,

Your father.

I looked up, where Kayleigh's bluish green eyes stared right back at me. I guessed she was working on the 'putting her emotions aside' part. I wasn't sure what to say. The letter was in keeping with all I'd learnt of the man in the less than twenty-four hours since I'd narrowly missed passing him by while he was still alive.

The letter was efficiently brief. It contained an undertone of deep emotion, carefully restrained under a facade of succinct explanation. No fluff, no wasted words, no ambiguity… at least to someone who knew him as I presumed his daughter did.

"Does this make sense to you?" I asked, wondering if my presumption was misguided.

Kayleigh slowly nodded. "Raylene and my father had a prenuptial agreement," she said. "It would have expired on their tenth anniversary in two weeks."

10

TRUST ISSUES

Wednesday 6:00pm

I stood behind Detective Whittaker while he looked at the video on his computer screen. He rewound and played it back four times, finally pausing on the clearest image of the additional shadow. Which wasn't very clear at all. But the shadow was there, and it moved.

"Could it be from someone on the floor above?" he asked. "Isn't it the reception and restaurant?"

"The stairs switch directions," I pointed out. "Shadows from that level would be projected onto the back wall of the landing. You can't reflect a shadow."

Whittaker drummed his fingers softly on his desk and thought for a while. "And you've searched the footage before and after? Can't find anyone from another camera angle?"

"I can't find how this person got there at all," I replied. "Before Collins, it was nearly an hour earlier that the last person went down the steps to the parking. Most people are coming from higher floors on the main building and take the lift all the way down. The security guard walks down the steps and does a sweep of the underground level about twenty minutes before Collins walks up. If it is a person, they magically appear in the stairwell."

Whittaker rolled the footage back until the shadow appeared just as Collins arrived at the base of the stairs. We both watched carefully once more as the video played in slow motion. Collins looked, hesitated, continued up the stairs, and the shadow was gone once he went out of sight.

"It has to be a trick of light in some way, Nora," Whittaker said, sitting back. "You could try recreating the scenario yourself, but I wouldn't spend too much time on it. If there's no evidence on camera of anyone positioning themselves in the stairwell, and it doesn't seem to affect Collins in any way, then I'm not sure how it's relevant."

I was about to argue, but I realised he was right. So what if someone was standing in the stairwell? The timelines of the cameras on both floors synced with the time it took to walk up the stairs without a delay, so even if he passed by someone, they didn't appear to influence the course of events.

"What about the missing bottle, sir?"

"I suspect that will be an in-house issue for Caribbean View," he replied. "I would lean on them to do the legwork looking through their CCTV to find who went in the unit after the police left."

He turned and looked up at me. "But if they don't find anything, we may have to look at our own ranks. I hate to think a member of the force would be so stupid, but make sure security follows up with you. We'll do what we must do."

The detective sighed. "Which leaves this business about the prenup agreement."

I moved from behind him and dropped into one of the visitors' chairs. "A piece of paper didn't kill Perry Collins," I said. "So, not sure how it plays into any of this, beyond motive for suicide."

Whittaker nodded. "Agreed. But we haven't seen the document. I have a hard time understanding why a prenup coming to an end would drive a man to take his own life, but I suppose it's possible."

"Kayleigh told me she'd never seen the paperwork either, but her father had mentioned Raylene was stalling on any formal separation. He told her it was because of the timing of the prenup ending after ten years."

Whittaker shook his head. "You'd think if he filed for divorce before the end of the term, the prenup would stand, but I'm not a lawyer."

I shrugged my shoulders. "Do we try and obtain a copy?"

The detective put his computer to sleep and stood. "The other two envelopes are still with Rasha, aren't they?"

I stood too and nodded.

"Why don't you wait and see what they contain?" he said, grabbing his sport coat from the back of his chair. "Revisit the Caribbean View Residences in the morning and have them figure out the bottle business. That'll give you another chance to examine this shadow mystery. Once the other envelopes are released, we need to deliver them, but you'll have copies of the contents to work with."

"Yes, sir," I said, following him from his office, not mentioning that Jacob had already set the first task in motion.

The shadow still bothered me, so I was happy to have a chance to figure it out.

I found Jacob in the lobby chatting with the constable who'd thrown up in the landscaping the night before. The man looked a little sheepish as I approached, but he nodded a greeting.

"We're going to Caribbean View," I announced. "We can go home from there."

Jacob's shoulders sagged. "I was just dere! What's so important we gotta go back again tonight?"

"It's dark," I replied, walking towards the doors.

"Dat's because it's da end of da day, Nora, and we supposed to be goin' home," he complained, following me.

I grabbed the handle and looked back at Jacob before opening the door. "On the CCTV I saw…" I began, but immediately lost my train of thought.

On the other side of the lobby were two men, engrossed in conversation. One was a local solicitor who I recognised but had no idea of his name. He'd represented a client I'd interviewed once. The other was McKinley Woods.

The politician was no stranger to Central Station. I'd lost count of the sexual harassment and assault charges which had continued popping up after the first woman had come forward a few years back. Somehow, Woods had either had the cases thrown out or delayed them coming before a judge. They hung over him like a black cloud and he'd been shuffled out of any key position in government, but like the slime that he was, nothing seemed to stick.

Their conversation was animated, although I couldn't hear what they were saying. My teeth were clenched, and my hands balled into tight fists. I had a strong desire to walk over and stick my Taser against the bare skin of his wrinkled neck.

At the resort, I'd never met the man. Word was he preferred the youngest dark-skinned girls available. Those poor kids. It was genius how they'd programmed us to accept our sessions with the members as something that was healthy and normal. They'd manipulated our young, desperate minds into believing we were simply providing harmless pleasure in exchange for a better life ahead. My hand moved down to my Taser.

"Nora!" Jacob said loudly, his voice echoing around the lobby.

The two men halted their conversation and turned to see what the fuss was about. My eyes met the cold stare of McKinley Woods, and his brow furrowed slightly in recognition. It could have been from the undesired press I'd received from my first police case. *Or could it have been from the menu of girls the members chose from at the International Fellowship of Lions?*

A hand took hold of my arm and I flinched.

"Nora," Jacob repeated.

I shoved the door open and quickly moved outside with Jacob following. The humidity wrapped itself around me like a blanket and the bright lights of the car park pierced the darkness, snapping me back to the present.

"Are you okay?" he asked, trying to keep pace with me as I headed for the Jeep.

"I'm fine. We need to go to the condos to check something I saw on the CCTV," I replied, trying to keep the frustration and anger from my voice.

"Okay, I'll follow you dere," he said, still chasing me. "But what on earth happened just now? You look like you seen a ghost."

I reached the Jeep and finally paused, more interested in being alone than explaining myself. But Jacob's expression was filled with concern, and I knew I owed him some kind of explanation.

This was why I hated getting close to people. Life was so much simpler without these obligations.

"I thought I'd figured out the shadow thing we're going to Caribbean View to recreate, but I had it wrong," I lied.

I couldn't involve Jacob in anything to do with McKinley Woods. I'd convinced myself that I would find a way to take him down through the legal system, but that was until months of surveillance went down the drain thanks to an anthill. More accurately, thanks to me deciding not to involve Baby-G in the slam-dunk case of hiring a prostitute I'd been about to bust him for. But the ants were responsible for throwing me into her path.

Seeing the man up close, moving freely about the world as though the women's lives he'd help ruin meant nothing, pushed me back into a dark hole I'd managed to climb out of. At least I thought I had. Now, I wasn't sure anymore if I could trust myself not to make the man disappear one night.

"Let's get over there, so we can go home," I added, and climbed in the Jeep.

Jacob stood there for a moment, no doubt deciding whether to call me out on what he was sure to have seen as bullshit. But he didn't. Instead, he left without a word, leaving me feeling guilty for lying to him.

———

Twenty minutes later, I stood on the ground floor and looked down the stairs to where the landing made its 180-degree turn, continuing out of my view to the hallway by the lifts. Charles stood next to me.

"It was worse sittin' around at da house," he said, finishing his explanation for why he was back at work.

"I wish our brains were more like computers," I responded. "We could open the files and programs we wanted to access any time. Keep the other stuff closed."

"I ain't too good wit computers," the old man replied. "But I get da gist of your meanin'."

Jacob came into view on the landing, walking up from downstairs.

"Stay there," I told him, and scampered down the steps past him.

Once I was standing under the security camera by the lifts, I looked for the shadow in the hallway. I couldn't see one.

"Move to your right," I shouted, and as Jacob followed the command, I spotted a faint movement on the wall opposite the stairwell.

"Move to the first step," I ordered.

The shadow moved on the wall, and as though I'd focused a lens, became clearer.

"Charles, you still up there?"

"Yes ma'am," the old man replied.

"Could you come down here please?"

"Yes ma'am," he replied, and I waited while he made his way down the steps.

"Stand facing the stairs, please," I asked.

He did so, and his shadow extended towards the parking area, cast by the hallway light in front of the lifts. A fainter shadow also appeared on the wall to my left, opposite the stairs, cast from the landing light. Jacob's shadow had been lost.

"Move to your left," I said, and Charles stepped that way.

"I can't move left," Jacob called down. "I'm against da handrail on dat side."

"That's good, because I wasn't talking to you."

"Oh," I heard him grunt.

I took out my mobile and started taking pictures. With Charles moved just off centre of the stairwell, Jacob's shadow had reappeared, similar to the one I'd seen in the CCTV. I photographed the positions both men stood in, and the shadows on the wall.

"Well?" Jacob asked. "Figure it out?"

Standing next to Charles, I looked up at my partner. "The shadow, yes. It appears someone was definitely standing on the landing."

Jacob spun around, looking up at the reception level, then back down at us. "Okay. Then how dis phantom get demselves here, den leave again wit out being caught on camera?"

I walked slowly up the stairs, squinting at the back wall of the landing with its pristine wood panels and neat trim. Charles followed, and when I stopped beside Jacob, he squeezed past.

"Musta taken da udder way," he said, pressing firmly on the middle panel, which released from its hidden latch and swung open.

Inside, a storage area for cleaning supplies opened to a handful of steps which led to a darkened hallway.

11

GOATFISH, IGUANAS, AND HYPOCRITES

Thursday 6:00am

It was the blue hour over the island; the magical time before sunrise when the black of night has been traded for a deep blue sky. Facing west, it was hard to tell where the ocean ended and the sky began. A tickle of breeze caressed my face as I lay on my back in the glassy water and began my breathe-up exercises.

Freediving was my escape. Alone underwater on a breath hold. Just me and the thousands of wonderful creatures whose natural habitat I borrowed for a few minutes at a time. Spanish Bay Reef was right out front of my shack, and after a short surface swim, I drew in long, easy breaths, and even longer exhalations, dispelling as much carbon dioxide from my lungs as possible and refilling them with fresh, oxygen-rich air.

Holding my final inhalation, I slipped below the surface, and aided by the single kilo of weight around my waist, and the long fins on my feet, I glided down to the sea floor. At 30 feet, sand met the coral fingers extending from the shallows to the deeper water. The reef, a living, growing mass of tiny stony coral polyps, building upon the skeletons of their predecessors, and softer waving fans and sponges reaching into the water column.

A school of blue tangs passed by me, going in the opposite direction in search of their next spot to graze on algae. A sand diver rested on the sea floor looking more like a legless lizard than a fish. I finned over the reef, rising to 20 feet, and spotted a hawksbill turtle crunching on a helpless dome-shaped sponge. A pair of yellowtail snappers eagerly stole the crumbs floating adrift as the turtle's beak crushed its breakfast.

My lungs were beginning to yearn, ready to expel the carbon dioxide accumulating as my body drew all the oxygen from the air. My brain was telling me to leave the ocean where humans weren't meant to exist, and on this occasion, I listened, rising to the surface.

Freediving is a mental battle with the alarms in your own mind. Checking my Shearwater dive watch, I saw I'd been down for nearly two minutes. Well under the time I could spend underwater if I fought the urge to breathe. Next dive, I would accept the challenge of the psychological arm wrestling with myself, but for the next few minutes, I would float and replenish my lungs.

The pre-dawn calm helped flush the noise from my mind, but it couldn't keep the things foremost in my brain from making their voices heard. Usually, it was these serene moments in which I could pare down the problem and see a path forward more clearly, but this morning was proving more difficult. I held my last inhalation and ducked under the surface once more. It was tempting to tell myself I wouldn't surface until I'd figured out what the briefest of meetings in a stairwell could have to do with Perry Collins' suicide, but ultimatums went against the Zen-like mental state I was trying to achieve underwater.

Doing my best to push the pressure of resolution aside, I finned down and began running through the unresolved elements of the case. A tiger grouper hung under a coral overhang and watched me with his mouth wide open, allowing a team of little shrimp and gobies to clean his teeth and gills.

I think it was safe to assume Perry Collins brought with him the gun and the files, and we know for sure he stopped to buy his Scotch. *What was left?* I couldn't think of anything of any importance, or recall the man walking to his condo with something additional to what he'd left his SUV with. At least that I could see. There could have been a flash drive in his pocket or another small item, but nothing was found in his case or on his person. His satchel had been remarkably free of anything other than what he'd needed to enter the Cayman Islands, or wanted to leave for us to find. And a gun, of course.

A small school of goatfish foraged in the sand, stirring up a cloud of debris with their probe-like chin barbels. I swam by, using gentle, long, sweeping motions with my fins, expending the least amount of energy to move around.

It was entirely possible that someone completely unrelated to Collins happened to use the cleaner's hidden door to retrieve something they'd forgotten. Or to do something else, although I couldn't imagine what that would be. A plan to revisit the CCTV and check the footage from one of the other cameras in the parking garage which covered the employees' hallway exit was all I could think of to do.

A porcupinefish appeared over the coral, its chubby torpedo-shaped body moving forward, propelled by its undersized pectoral fins. Its large eyes and seemingly permanently surprised expression made me giggle inside. I gave it a wide berth so as not to threaten the fish and cause it to balloon up to over twice its regular size in defence.

My muscles tensed as my mind moved on to McKinley Woods. Tension was the arch enemy of freedivers, so I quickly pushed my thoughts towards the problem instead of the individual. Catching the man with a prostitute would certainly have added to the woes of the *drittsekk*, but he probably would have found a way to wriggle out from underneath the charge. It was frustrating to lose months' worth of part-time after-hours work, but I needed a better plan anyway.

If only I could tie him to the resort. He'd obviously hidden his membership well enough that he'd escaped the original investigation, which Whittaker had headed up. I trusted the detective would have done everything in his power to find all the culprits, so I had to assume it was a pointless avenue.

My lungs began to ache, and I swallowed, which chased away the urge to breathe. Glancing at my dive watch showed me I'd been down two minutes and 36 seconds, so I knew I could stay down there more than another minute if I managed my exertion and convinced my brain to stay calm.

Which I only managed for a few more moments.

An idea hit me, and the excitement sent me finning to the surface. I burst through the smooth surface and gasped in a deep breath. The answer was to go back to the beginning! Woods had been a member of the resort because he had a sick desire to sleep with young girls. All I had to do was convince him one was available to him. I began swimming for shore.

I'd been following McKinley Woods on my own time, as my information on the *drittsekk* had come from the brother of Carlina Arias, my best friend at the resort who'd been murdered. Her brother had fled the island, and his girlfriend who'd been involved in the illegal scheme to capture number two on the list, Randall Cosgrove, had since joined him. The only one left who knew was a computer genius by the name of Rabbit, but involving her would risk incriminating the woman. I had zero hard proof to show Whittaker. Besides, he'd never have approved of the entrapment I'd planned. Switching to using a minor as bait had even less chance of him biting on the idea, so I was still on my own.

Climbing the ladder at the side of the small boat dock which had belonged to the old Spanish Bay Reef Resort, I grabbed the towel I'd left there and slipped my feet into my sandals. My mind was running a million miles an hour as I stepped along the rough ironshore path to the shack. I could tell the sun had breached the eastern horizon as the lightening blue sky now tinged yellow in that direction.

I neared the steps to the deck and caught movement out of the corner of my eye. Edvard. An endangered blue iguana who had decided to adopt me as his landlord. Well, mostly he hung out in the woods or on the hot limestone in the heat of the day, but the deck had become his evening haunt. Probably because we gave him vegetable and fruit snacks, which we shouldn't do, but he hadn't turned us in to the authorities yet.

"You're up early," I whispered, as Jazzy would still be asleep in the house.

I moved slowly up the steps and Edvard watched me with his head tilted to one side. He used to insist we threw snacks his way, but he'd recently graduated to taking food from my outstretched hand, as long as I was hanging half out of my chair and almost dislocating my shoulder. Apparently, coming ten centimetres closer was simply too dangerous.

"Let me get coffee, and I'll bring you something," I promised, and quietly slipped inside the house, wrapped in the towel so I didn't drip water everywhere.

"Morning," Jazzy grunted, switching on the kitchen light.

Her frizzy mop of hair had staged an overnight rebellion, sticking up in all directions with a few curly strands dangling in front of her face. She did not look happy about being awake this early.

"Why are you up?" I asked, wondering what special event or appointment I'd forgotten about.

My first thought was always a concern over what I'd done or not done that should have been done or not done. I kept thinking I'd get better at this fostering shit, but it didn't seem to be happening.

"It's a friend's birthday so a few of us are buying cupcakes to celebrate," she explained, although her voice indicated she was currently regretting the plan. "Gotta catch the earlier bus."

"Edvard's on the deck," I said, pouring myself a coffee from the pot I'd set on a timer.

I opened the refrigerator door and stared at the lack of human food, not to mention iguana-friendly snacks. Things like laundry and grocery shopping had been a pain in the arse when I'd been alone, but at least then I could triage the least badly smelling shirts and reuse them. Grab dinner on the way home. Now I had to pay attention to that shit and keep the fridge stocked. Or not, apparently. Although laundry still came down to self-preservation. I didn't consider it child abuse to make the kid do her own laundry. Sometimes she threw my stuff in there too, which was an added bonus, although I think that might cross over into child labour laws.

I found a few errant lettuce leaves in the drawer reserved for vegetables and closed the fridge. Jazzy had discovered the last few slices of bread and was making herself a sandwich.

"You need this lettuce?" I asked.

"On a peanut butter sandwich?" she responded, looking at me like I was an idiot despite the fact she was yet to take the jar from the cupboard.

I scooped up my coffee and went back outside to where Edvard hadn't moved a muscle. I sat in one of the chairs and waved the rather sorry-looking lettuce leaf in the air.

"Come and get it."

A few minutes later, with the stupid iguana only halfway to me from where he'd started, Jazzy came outside and sat in the other chair. She sat down and munched on a bowl of cereal while we both watched Edvard inch his way across the deck.

"He's an idiot," I complained.

"If you were at risk of becoming someone's belt, you'd be cautious," Jazzy replied.

"We're short on food. Maybe he could be dinner."

"I've eaten iguana. It's not so bad," Jazzy said, and I guessed she wasn't lying. At least about the eating part.

He finally made it close enough for me to reach out, which of course made him stop. I groaned, hanging half out of the chair.

"Figure anything out this morning?" Jazzy asked.

"I think I did," I admitted.

"If it's busting that arsehole, Woods, I want to help," she said, setting her empty bowl on the table between us.

Edvard finally took the last step and pulled the lettuce from my fingertips. I sat back and looked at the kid with her wild hair and pretty face staring back at me with a resolute expression.

I shivered. I would do everything in my power to keep Jazzy as far away from the likes of McKinley Woods as humanly possible. But I realised I would need at least a picture of a young girl for my plan to work. If it went the way I hoped, he would never need to meet that girl as he'd incriminate himself long before that. *So, whose picture could I use? Someone else's child?*

It struck me as inexcusably hypocritical to do that… yet unforgivable to use the kid I'd rescued from the streets and promised to keep safe.

12

SENSITIVITY

Thursday 7:30am

I was less than excited to be behind the computer looking at CCTV footage again, but Whittaker had talked about only spending a day or two on the Collins case, so I needed to wrap up all the loose ends. Jacob sat at the workstation next to me searching through one camera's recording from the underground parking while I took the other. With the timeline to help us, it actually didn't take long to find a figure entering the door from the parking area. Charles had told us the hallway leading to the stairwell came from a storage room off the parking, and I could see the door from the camera I was viewing.

Ten minutes before Collins arrived, a figure used a swipe card to unlock the storage room door and enter. Thirteen minutes later they left again, keeping close to the shadowed wall in the dimly lit garage, and never looking up. They seemed to know exactly where the cameras were. Jacob's footage revealed even less of the person.

"I can't even say if dey a man or a woman," Jacob said. "Baggy clothes and dat cap on deir head."

I paused the grainy black and white footage as the figure opened the door and began to step inside the room. I opened an internet browser on the computer and searched for standard commercial door heights. I was greeted with 39 million results, but fortunately at the top was a block of text claiming residential and commercial doors have a standard height of 80 inches. In America at least, but it was safe to assume the island followed the same rules, or close to them.

Rummaging through the desk drawers, I found a ruler, switched back to the CCTV footage, made it full screen, zoomed in a little, and measured the door height. Jacob rolled his chair over to see what I was doing.

"Thirteen centimetres," I mumbled to myself, then measured the figure. "Ten… maybe ten and half centimetres."

"Now you gotta convert to inches," Jacob said, pointing to the opposite edge of the ruler. "Just measure in inches."

On the computer's calculator I divided 10.5 by 13 to get the percentage, which I rounded to 80 percent, then calculated 80 percent of 80 inches. Sixty-four inches.

"Or just do dat," Jacob muttered from beside me.

"The person is five foot four inches tall," I confirmed, and rewound the video.

We both watched the figure move along the wall on their way to the door. I fast-forwarded, then played regular speed so we could watch them leave, following the same careful path to minimise their time on camera.

"I can't tell," Jacob said, leaning back. "Dat shirt or whatever dey wearing hide da… you know… bumps da female have, if it is a woman."

"Bumps?" I responded, stifling a laugh. "They're called breasts, Jacob. You make them sound like alien growths."

"I assure you, I don't tink of dem dat way," he laughed.

I brought up the other camera angle that Jacob had been watching. The quality of the recording in the poor light and low resolution made it hard to discern any details.

"Stop dere," Jacob yelped, and I hit pause.

"Back a few frames," he said, and I clicked frame by frame until he said stop again.

The figure was leaving, so walking away from the camera, and was quite distant, but I realised what he'd noticed. With several empty parking spots, there was a short section where the garage lighting illuminated the figure a little more. Protruding from their back pocket was what appeared to be an envelope folded double.

"*Faen*," I muttered. "They didn't give Collins anything. He gave *them* an envelope."

"Why like dat?" Jacob asked, which was exactly the thought going through my head.

Of all the opportunities between the airport and the condos to stop and hand over whatever it was that was so important, Perry Collins chose to do it in the stairwell. He could have avoided the camera dodging and covert hand-off by simply pulling over at any one of a thousand places along West Bay Road.

"Maybe da person thought they'd missed him, and snuck in to see?" Jacob offered.

That seemed like a possibility. Perhaps it was poorly coordinated, or the person got confused. Collins did pause a moment as though he was surprised before walking up the stairs. I squinted at the screen.

"Look at the other pocket," I pointed out, and Jacob leaned in closer.

"Dat a phone, maybe?"

"I think so," I replied, switching back to the first camera angle and bringing up the footage of the figure arriving.

Finding the same spot where the light was slightly better, I saw a highlight picking up the edge of something in their one back pocket, but clearly no envelope.

"It's a woman," I said. "Maybe..." I thought a moment and did the conversion in my head. "Between 130 and maybe 150 pounds."

"Because day have a phone in da pocket?" Jacob questioned,

and by the time I turned to look at him, I saw the lightbulb had gone off in his head.

"Because she put da mobile in da back pocket," he declared. "Dat what more women do dan men."

I nodded. "Not conclusive, but given their size, I think it's likely.

"Why don't I take a picture of da woman to Caribbean View Residences and ask da staff?" Jacob said. "Dey had an access card, so maybe dey work dere?"

I glanced at my watch; it was already 8:30am and I could see how the day could escape us if we didn't divide and conquer.

"Good idea. I'll see if Rasha can release the other envelopes."

Jacob rolled back to the other computer and began printing screenshots of the mystery woman, while I texted Rasha and began walking through the building towards her department. I received her reply a few moments before I arrived at the door and knocked. It opened right away.

"Blimey, were you messaging me from right there?" she asked in surprise. "I just replied and put them here on the counter," she added, handing me the two manila envelopes.

"Just good timing," I replied, leaving out the part that I'd planned on taking at least copies of the contents regardless of whether she was done or not.

I couldn't imagine there'd be any forensic evidence in the envelopes which would change the narrative of the investigation. The contents of the paperwork, however, could be a different story.

"I'll have the scans and details uploaded by the end of the day," Rasha said.

"Thanks," I replied, already moving down the hallway and slipping the first set of documents out of the envelope.

This one was addressed to Jackson, Robins, and Smith, located in George Town, attention Josephine Smith. It contained a short cover letter and what appeared to be a partnership contract between Perry Collins and Nigel Braithwaite for a company called StarLife Semiconductor. Another bundle of papers below that was a mass of accounting numbers and valuations. I returned to the empty office and sat in front of the computer. Jacob had already left.

In the computer browser I searched for StarLife Semiconductor and found a very fancy-looking website describing how the company was on the cutting edge of solar panel technology. According to their blurb, they supplied silicon-based p-type and n-type semiconductors with a ground-breaking technology coming online in the near future. I quickly lost interest and clicked on the company bio page. A picture of Perry Collins was on the upper left, looking in far better condition than when I'd met him.

Nigel Braithwaite's picture graced the upper right, and the text described the two men knowing each other since university and working for other entities in the same field before starting their own company. It spewed a bunch more boring bullshit concocted by a public relations expert, so I put those papers away and grabbed the second envelope.

It was addressed to the same lawyer firm, but attention Horatio Jackson. I wondered who in the world thought it would be a good idea to name their kid Horatio. English might be my second language, but even I knew that boy went through hell at school.

I pulled a spiral-bound wad of papers from the envelope, which according to the cover contained the signed contract between Star-Life Semiconductor and Global Clean Power Technologies. I flicked through a few pages of corporate blabbering until I came across the first signature sheet. Perry Collins had signed on behalf of StarLife. There was no spot for a co-signer, so apparently he had the power to sign on behalf of both partners. The date by his signature was yesterday. The day he killed himself.

Shoving the papers back inside the envelope, I sat back and asked myself once again: *why did Perry Collins blow his own brains out?* Kayleigh had suggested the prenuptial agreement with Raylene had something to do with it, but there was one important element missing if this was all about his marriage. Collins had left envelopes with details for his daughter, his lawyers, and even the detective he'd presumed would investigate his death, but not one word directed at his wife. It didn't feel right that he'd skipped even mentioning her if he was so heartbroken that he was ending it all.

The man was organised and efficient enough to make sure his attorneys had the latest deal he'd put together, and a copy of his partnership agreement so they could shepherd that through the legal process. Yet he resisted the urge to say anything to the woman who had driven him to this moment. Something didn't fit.

My mobile buzzed and I checked the text. It was from Whittaker. Raylene Bradford-Collins was in the building, asking when she could enter the condo. I quickly texted back, 'Can we ask her a few more questions?'

'Probably,' came his reply. 'Let's speak first. I'm in my office.'

Picking up the two envelopes, I dashed from the room and ran up the stairs, remembering to slow before I reached the top, so I didn't knock anyone over. Whittaker was alone in his office.

"Where is she?" I asked.

"Waiting in reception," he replied. "What have you found?"

"More questions, really," I replied honestly. "Jacob is back at the Caribbean View Residences showing people a lousy picture from CCTV of the person Collins met in the stairwell. We think it's a woman. She leaves with an envelope like these," I added, holding up the two in my hand. "She had an access key, so could be an employee."

"Why all the cloak and dagger exchange just to hand someone an envelope?" the detective asked.

"That's one of the 'more questions' we have," I replied.

"I'm sure," he agreed. "So, what is it you'd like to ask Mrs Bradford-Collins? She did just lose her husband. We need to be sensitive to that fact."

He said it like I wasn't sensitive to people's feelings, which made me want to laugh a little, but I resisted.

"As I told you last night, the daughter thinks the prenuptial agreement might have something to do with her father's suicide, but from the paperwork here," I said, holding up the envelopes again, "he arranged all these different business things and said goodbye to his daughter, yet says nothing to the woman who drove him to shoot himself. Doesn't seem right to me."

Whittaker thought for a moment, looking up at me standing in his doorway. "Okay. So, what is it exactly you'd like to ask her?"

"I'd start with why she thinks her husband killed himself," I replied.

The detective frowned. "We've already asked her that, so I feel that falls under the being sensitive with the widow who just lost her husband, Nora."

"*Dritt,*" I muttered. "Then is asking background questions about her husband's business and his partner okay?"

"The questions would probably be okay, but why are we asking them? Do we have reason to believe something illegal is in play, or are you just curious?"

I hated when he brought logic into it and didn't let me do what I wanted to do.

"I can't say I've found anything illegal yet, but there is definitely something strange going on with this case," I replied, trying to tiptoe my way around without making shit up. "Perry Collins just doesn't seem like the suicide type, and maybe behind the scenes his business was in trouble, but from the paperwork I glanced over, it doesn't look that way. Just a couple of questions about his business might help clear things up. I promise I'll be nice."

Whittaker sighed, then stood. "Walk downstairs with me," he said, moving around his desk. "A couple of casual questions, and then we'll tell her she's free to enter the condo." He stopped by the door. "I assume you have no objections to her having access to the home?"

I shrugged my shoulders. "Probably okay."

"Well, thank you," he responded, raising an eyebrow.

I wasn't sure why, so I stayed quiet and followed him down the hall to the stairs.

Raylene Bradford-Collins reminded me of a bird. Her nose was narrow and pointed, and while her eyes didn't dart about, her gaze moved swiftly between subjects as though she were deciding whether to peck them or not. She wore a similar business outfit as she had the day before. I noticed Kayleigh was with her but remained sitting in the waiting area while her stepmother strode over as we approached. She glanced at her sparkly, expensive watch to let us know we'd kept her waiting.

"Detective," she greeted Whittaker, ignoring me.

"Mrs Bradford-Collins, thanks for your patience," he responded. "You're welcome to enter the condo at your leisure. We're all done over there."

The woman hesitated a moment. "I presume, it's all been… cleaned up?"

"They scrubbed the patio really well. All the mess was outside because the sliding doors were closed," I explained. "I think they got it all."

She looked at me strangely, her mouth half open.

"Thanks for coming by and checking with us," Whittaker blurted, just as I was about to begin asking my questions. Then he steered Raylene towards the front door.

I started to tag along and see if he'd decided to speak with her outside, but he threw me a look over his shoulder, clearly urging me to stay there, so I didn't move. *All I did was answer her question. How was I the bad guy again?*

Kayleigh stood as Whittaker and Raylene reached the doors. She looked at me and appeared to want to say something, but didn't.

"Wait," I said, hoping her stepmother didn't hear me.

I pulled my notebook from my pocket and quickly scribbled down my mobile number, handing it to her without a word. Kayleigh nodded, then followed Raylene out the door.

13

HURRY UP

Thursday 9:30am

Jacob had the patrol car he'd requisitioned for the day, so I drove my Jeep to the offices of Jackson, Robins, and Smith. I didn't know exactly what I'd expected, but the building certainly wasn't what I had in mind. I guess I thought the firm would be in one of the fancy office blocks overlooking the water, but it was actually located in an older building on Edward Street, right in the centre of George Town. They were upstairs above a duty-free shop in what was a nice set of offices, but hardly the swanky, ultra-modern vibe.

"I have packages for Josephine Smith and Horatio Jackson," I told the receptionist, a skinny older lady who peered over her horn-rimmed glasses at me.

"You can leave da papers wit me," she said, and held out a hand.

"They've been released from evidence, so I need the individuals to personally sign for them," I lied, deciding on the fly that it couldn't hurt to talk to the solicitors themselves.

After a short staring competition to let me know that she knew I was full of shit, the lady pushed her chair back and stood.

"Wait here," she said, and disappeared into a hallway.

I looked around the reception area. Four Queen Anne-style tapestry wingback chairs surrounded an antique wooden coffee table, and an oak bookcase lined the back wall. The windows faced the waterfront, but the view was blocked by the tall Butterfield Bank building and the backs of several more office blocks with stores on the ground level.

"How may I help you, Miss..?" a lady's voice came from behind me and I turned from the windows.

Josephine Smith was a younger, full-sized version of the receptionist, leaving no doubt they were related. She had a lighter Caymanian accent than the older woman.

"Constable Sommer," I replied. "I have a package for you. Is there somewhere we can talk?"

There was no one else in the reception, but I didn't feel like dealing with the suspicious stares from the woman I now assumed to be Josephine's mother, or maybe aunt.

The solicitor looked around the empty reception area, probably wondering why it wasn't private enough for me, but relented. She led me down the hall to the second office on the left. Her window overlooked a narrow side street with a view of the neighbouring building's wall. She offered me a seat and I handed her the envelope before sitting down. Josephine slipped the contents onto her desk, and her expression tightened.

"I heard the news," she said sullenly. "Who would have thought..."

"How well did you know Mr Collins?" I asked.

The woman looked up from the paperwork. "Not well, but we'd met a few times since he retained our firm about six months ago. Most everything is by email these days."

A thought struck me. "Why was an Englishman with a business based in the UK and America hiring a Caymanian law firm to handle business paperwork?" I asked, pointing to the contract on her desk.

"You've looked at this confidential document?" she asked pointedly.

"It was evidence left at the crime scene," I replied. "It's been examined and released which is why I'm now giving it to you."

Josephine relaxed a little. "I see. Well, Mr Collins hired us to handle any personal business matters which would fall under Cayman Islands jurisdiction once his residency was completed."

I sat quietly for a moment, realising I'd missed a key detail in Collins' background. Now I wondered if any of this had to do with Cayman Islands law versus English or American law. Then I reminded myself the man blew his own head off, so what did it matter. Whittaker was right as usual. I was curious about his reasons, as nothing added up, but at the end of the day the verdict would be the same. Perry Collins committed suicide. Case closed.

"Why were these particular papers so important?" I asked, unable to stop myself while I had the solicitor sitting in front of me. "That partnership agreement is years old, according to the date I saw."

Josephine put the partnership agreement aside and picked up the other documents, thumbing through them. She returned her attention to the cover letter which had little more than a few section numbers referenced. Finally, she looked back up at me.

"Without a warrant, there's not much I'm able to discuss with you, Constable, and I need an opportunity to go over what you've brought," she said, pausing a moment to find a referenced section in the partnership agreement. "But I think it's safe to say Mr Collins is directing me to the pertinent articles which are relevant after his passing."

"Who does get his part of the company?" I asked.

Josephine smiled. "That's a good question, with what will likely be a complicated answer."

I held up the second envelope. "Is Mr Jackson here? This one is for him."

"Horace is offsite with a client this morning, but I can give that to him."

I thought for a moment, pushing aside my deliberation as to whether being called Horace was any better than Horatio, then slipped the bound contract from the envelope. "How come you get one contract and your partner gets another one? Do they fall under different specialties?"

"What do you have there?" Josephine asked.

"Looks like a new deal with an energy company," I said, sliding the bundle across the desk.

She studied the introduction page, her brow creasing more and more as she read. After a few moments, Josephine sat back and sighed, staring at the wall behind me, lost in thought. I waited.

"I think Horace and I have a late night or two ahead of us," she finally said, leaning forward once more. "And yes, he handles corporate contracts and I specialise more in personal agreements."

"Is it possible any of this might affect our investigation into Mr Collins' passing?" I asked, avoiding the use of the word suicide in this context.

Josephine drummed her fingers on the desk and took a moment.

"Is there any doubt as to how Mr Collins passed?"

"It's an ongoing investigation, so I'm not in a position to say," I said, allowing my mouth to curl into a slight smile.

Josephine grinned in return. "Touché," she responded.

I leaned closer. "Here's my problem," I began. "I'm almost certain Mr Collins took his own life. It's why that's bothering me. So far, we've found nothing to suggest he was unhappy or depressed in any way. Perhaps the opposite."

Josephine slowly shook her head. "Hard to know what a person is going through inside, I suppose. He was separated from his wife, I believe."

"Have you met his wife?" I asked.

"I have not," she replied.

"More likely he'd be throwing a party than mourning the loss."

Josephine's eyes widened, and I guessed this was one of those moments when Whittaker would butt in and stop me talking. Maybe his lectures were starting to work. At least I recognised my directness this time.

"His daughter appears very upset," I added, hoping to appear more sympathetic.

"I expect the poor girl is at that," Josephine replied. "Some birthday she'll have in a few weeks."

"*Dritt*," I mumbled, then wondered why Perry's solicitor would know the birthdate of her client's daughter. "You've met Kayleigh?" I asked.

"I have not," she said, suddenly fussing with the papers on her desk and sliding the new contract back into its envelope for her partner. "I should be getting back to work, if that's everything?"

I stood, knowing I'd want more answers, but either something I'd said, or the clock on the wall, had pressured Josephine into ending our meeting. My eyes scanned the sideboard to my right, where a series of wire mesh trays housed piles of papers and files. One caught my eye. It was a manila envelope like the ones I'd delivered, but also similar to twenty more I could see in the stacks... except this one had a distinct crease down the centre. It had been folded double at some point.

"I need to sign for these?" Josephine asked, picking up a pen.

For a second, I wondered what she was talking about, then remembered my excuse for seeing her in the first place. "That's okay," I scrambled. "I just had to place them in your hand."

She raised an eyebrow. "Have a good day, Constable."

I started the Jeep and let the engine idle for a minute while I texted Jacob. I was hoping there'd be an excuse for me to join him at the Caribbean View Residences so I could accidentally run into Raylene or Kayleigh. He didn't reply right away, so I cut across Edward and drove slowly up Dr Roys Drive, figuring I could turn either way when it met Shedden. South to the station, or north towards the beachfront condos. My mobile rang, so I pulled to the side.

"Are you at da station?" Jacob asked.

"No. Got something?" I asked in return.

"Maybe," he began, so I put the Jeep in gear and pulled away from the kerb. *Maybe* was all the reason I needed.

"Charles thinks he knows who da woman might be," Jacob continued. "But she's not workin' today."

"Anyone else corroborate his ID?" I shouted over the building wind noise as I accelerated after turning left on Shedden and immediately left again on Mary Street.

"I haven't asked yet," I thought he said, but it was hard to hear.

I slowed and indicated right, waited for a car to pass, then turned right on McField Lane. The neighbourhood instantly changed from clean and tidy businesses to run down and shabby.

"I'm on my way," I said. "Be there in ten minutes."

I put the phone to my ear to hear Jacob's response, then noticed something out of place in an empty lot on my left. Rubbish and left-over building supplies littered the ground, and a beat-up car was parked at an odd angle with the driver's door open. Beyond the car, a large figure stood over what I thought was another man on the ground. I slowed and pulled over, turning off the Jeep.

"Might be a few minutes longer," I said into the phone, then hung up.

I walked over to the parked car, releasing the safety strap on my Taser as I went. The man on his feet had his back to me. He was enormous. I could fit into each leg of his cargo shorts and his tatty shirt could double as a circus tent. Sweat glistened from his shaved head and although I couldn't hear what he was saying, I recognised his heavily island-accented voice, which rolled like soft thunder. We'd first met a while back when I'd hit him with Whittaker's Range Rover, then tased the big fella, just to put him on the ground.

"Jumbo?" I asked, and the hulk of a human turned around.

His boulder-sized face glared at me, before softening into a grin.

"Miss Sommer," he said, sounding pleased to see me. "What you doin' here?"

His smile quickly vanished as he looked all around for more officers.

The man in the dirt started to get up. "Tank you…" the victim began saying.

Jumbo swung around. "Shut up and stay down," he barked before turning back to me, his eyes still checking behind me. "You alone?"

I nodded.

"What you doin' here, Miss?" he asked again, the smile returning to his young face.

"I was in the neighbourhood," I replied, which was the truth. "What'd he do?" I asked, pointing to the terrified man, who'd obediently lain back down.

"He owes a friend of mine money," Jumbo explained.

"This the warning or the penalty?" I asked.

"Warnin'," Jumbo replied.

I nodded again. "Alright. Hurry up then, I got something to talk to you about."

The big man looked at me a moment, unsure, then chuckled and turned back to the fellow who now wriggled and began spouting off about the injustices of the police. He quietened right down when Jumbo pulled him off the ground and held him up with his feet barely touching the dirt. I leaned against the car and waited.

"You got…" Jumbo started, then paused. "Hey, what day is it today, Miss Sommer?"

"Thursday," I replied.

"You got till… Thursday… Friday…" he said, mumbling the days as he counted them. "Saturday at midday. Hear me?"

The man frantically nodded, dangling from Jumbo's grip like laundry.

"I gotta come lookin' for you again, and I'll be breakin' shit you don't want broken."

I assumed Jumbo took the grunts and moans as agreeing to his terms, as he released the guy, then watched him take off like a cruise shipper spotting a snow globe sale.

"What are you doing in George Town?" I asked, as he leaned beside me against the car, which promptly creaked and rolled away from me under the strain.

Jumbo's usual haunts were all in West Bay.

"Gotta go where da work takes me, Miss," he replied. "You wanna grab some food?"

I looked at my watch. "It's ten-thirty. I don't get to break for lunch for a while yet."

"I was tinkin' breakfast," he replied. "I got a late start."

I was scared to imagine the amount of food that it must take to keep the man running. If I remembered correctly, he was only twenty-three, so his chances of old age were far slimmer than he was.

"What you need help wit?" he asked. "You movin' or someting?"

It was a nice offer. If I ever needed to up and move my shack, he'd be the guy to carry a small house around.

"Nothing like that," I replied. "How would you feel about helping me take down a piece of shit?"

"You know I ain't no rat, Miss Sommer."

"What if I told you it's a politician?"

"Den I'm more inclined to help," he replied. "Who we talkin' about?"

"McKinley Woods," I told him.

Jumbo thumped the roof of his own car, adding a dent to the collection already there. "You just tell me what you need, Miss. Dat man certainly is a piece of shit."

14

VERBAL WARFARE

Thursday 11:15am

"As I told your partner, dis could be any one of a million people, but she does appear to be about da same size and build of Serena," Valerie, the receptionist I'd met before, said, leaning over the counter with the printed picture in her hand. "Someting about her posture too. But like I say, could be anyone really."

She handed me the picture, and I walked over to where Jacob stood with Charles. The old man looked tired.

"So how do we find this Serena woman?" I asked him.

"I gave Jacob her number," Charles replied, and I looked at my partner.

"Voicemail," he said. "I got an address if we want to drop by."

"Okay," I agreed. "Have you seen the wife or daughter here?"

Jacob shook his head.

"Saw dem earlier when dey arrive," Charles relayed. "Tink dey bin in da condo since den."

I chewed over the options in my mind and decided Whittaker wouldn't like many of the ones I preferred. I wanted to find this woman and see if she was involved in the secret hand-off, but I had a list of probing questions for Raylene and Kayleigh.

"Stay here," I told Jacob, "I won't be long."

"Where you going now?" he asked, walking with me.

"To the condo, but you shouldn't come along."

"Why not?" he asked, stepping ahead and opening the door outside for me.

The bright sunshine and humidity hit me after the cool air-conditioned building. I stopped and turned to Jacob.

"Whittaker wouldn't approve of me questioning the family," I admitted. "And I don't want you to get in trouble if he finds out."

"You tink they had someting to do wit him killin' himself?"

"I doubt it was anything unlawful, but sure, I'd say a man's wife and daughter would play into his suicide in some manner."

"Sure," Jacob replied, "But you know what I meant."

I sighed. "*Ja.* I'm not sure. Raylene seems like a *drittsekk*, but that's not illegal or half the world would be in jail. I think there's something more going on which caused Collins to shoot himself, and Raylene is involved, but I've no idea how."

"Or if it's illegal," Jacob added.

"Right," I confirmed. "I don't see how he died any other way than by blowing his own brains out, so unless he was pressured or coerced into doing that, there's no crime beyond a smuggled gun."

"Which we've already determined how he got dat here," Jacob added.

"Pretty much," I said. "So, you stay and chat with Charles, and I'll do the bit we'd be in trouble for."

"I'm coming too," he said, and walked away, heading to the condo building.

"*Dritt*," I muttered, and strode to catch up.

I should have been appreciating his willingness to support me and take the risk too, but it just made me feel guilty. This was another example of the shit that comes with the responsibility for others and obligations. I was starting to feel chained down by the need to concern myself with how other people acted and felt. I much preferred worrying about me and what I was doing without the burden of anyone else.

Jacob knocked on the door to the condo and stepped back. I figured he'd only thought this revised plan through to this point, as he had no idea what I intended to ask the women.

The door opened and Raylene gave me her best annoyed expression. "What now?"

"This will only take a minute," I said. "May we come inside? I wanted to show you something."

"Show me what?" she responded without moving or inviting us in.

"The drinks cabinet," I continued.

"What about it?"

"There's a discrepancy," I said. "Can I show you?"

I was using the most pleasant voice I could muster but she was stretching my ability to be cordial to the absolute limit.

Raylene shook her head and let out a long exhale, but turned and walked away down the hallway, leaving the door open. I went to follow, but Jacob grabbed my arm.

"I didn't have a chance to tell you," he whispered. "Dey found a maid comin' in here on da CCTV. It were shortly before we came by yesterday. Dey reckon she took da bottle."

"Okay," I replied, then carried on down the hallway to the living room.

Kayleigh was standing by the sliding glass doors, looking out to the ocean, but turned when we came in. Raylene waited by the drink's cabinet.

"Your husband stopped to buy an expensive bottle of Scotch on his way from the airport," I began, winging it as best as I could. "But there was already a bottle here on the shelf. Can you think of a reason why he didn't want to drink the bottle he had?"

Raylene stared at me like I was crazy. "What are you talking about?"

I thought over what I'd just said and wondered if my English had failed me, but I was sure I was clear.

"Your husband bought a bottle of very expensive Scotch to drink before he killed himself," I reiterated. "But here," I pointed to the cabinet, "was a bottle of the same Scotch already."

Raylene took a step closer. "Where?"

"Well, someone took it," I clarified. "But it was there on Tuesday night."

"Who the hell took it?" Raylene countered.

"That's not important," I said, trying to stay civil. "I want to know why he'd forget he had a thousand-dollar bottle of Scotch at home."

Raylene glared at me, and we stood a metre apart, our eyes locked.

"Perhaps he had more pressing matters on his mind," Kayleigh said from across the room.

Her interjection diffused the moment, which gave me a chance to compose myself. My Scotch question had been the ruse to get us in the door but had somehow escalated into a verbal war. I had a feeling Raylene was experienced and well equipped to do battle.

"Were you involved with StarLife?" I asked, returning my attention to Perry's wife.

She shook her head and walked to the refrigerator, retrieving a bottle of white wine.

"Did you speak about the business with your husband?"

"Not recently," she replied curtly.

"You and Mr Collins were in the process of getting divorced?"

Raylene stopped pouring wine into a glass, glanced at Kayleigh, then turned to me.

"I already covered this with the detective, for heaven's sake," she groaned. "We were separated but working on our relationship."

"So, you were in couples therapy and all that crap?"

She shoved the cork back in the bottle and returned it to the fridge, kicking the door closed with her foot.

"What the hell does that have to do with you, or anything that's happened here?" she snapped.

"We try to paint a picture of da victim's life, ma'am," Jacob said before I could answer, probably attempting to avoid another verbal conflict. "Standard tings to complete da investigation, and we appreciate your patience."

Raylene took a swig of her wine while giving Jacob a condescending look over the rim of her glass.

"You two can take your damn paintbrushes and fuck off. We're the victims here," she said, becoming animated and pointing between herself and her stepdaughter. "Perry just thought about himself, as usual. I've answered all the stupid questions I plan to, so now you can leave."

"No problem," I said, cordially. "Sorry for the intrusion. One final question and we'll be on our way."

I'm pretty sure I heard Jacob groan, but I pressed on.

"What can you tell me about his partner? Nigel Braithwaite."

"I know who his partner is, you imbecile," Raylene spat. "What are you, twenty? Twenty-five, tops, right? How the fuck do they let an embryo like you ask your ridiculous questions at a time like this?"

The woman swung around and leaned against the kitchen counter with her back to me. She'd probably be calling Whittaker and complaining after we left, but I didn't care. I was right. Raylene Bradford-Collins knew something and wasn't sharing.

Kayleigh walked over and shrugged her shoulders, mouthing the word *sorry*. I shrugged my shoulders in return and followed Jacob towards the hallway. Pausing for a moment at the corner, I turned and caught Raylene's eye. I knew I shouldn't antagonise the woman, but she deserved it. I gave her a wink, then continued to the front door.

"We're sorry for da trouble, Miss," Jacob said, opening the front door and stepping outside. "We are truly sorry for your loss, and we'll leave you in peace."

"He wasn't involved much anymore," Kayleigh said quietly, and I paused just outside the door. "Dad was the engineering brain behind the company, and Nigel was more on the management side. But when the company grew, they hired in a managerial team who really took over all the logistics, so Dad focused on development, and Nigel sort of didn't do much."

"Except take half the money, right?" I ventured.

Kayleigh nodded. "But Nigel is a spender, plus he just went through a nasty divorce, which I think is final now. From what I heard, his ex cleaned him out."

"Could that have affected your father in any way?" I asked, glad to have a moment alone with Kayleigh. "How was their relationship?"

"He didn't talk about it much, and I'm away at school most of the time," she replied. "But I think it had become strained. Dad was doing all the work. StarLife was everything to him."

"Kayleigh!" Raylene shouted from the kitchen, and I heard her footsteps approaching on the tile floor.

"Call me, I'll meet you anywhere, anytime," I whispered before briskly walking away with Jacob.

Behind us we heard the door slam closed.

Serena Reyes' apartment was in the middle of West Bay. A small loft over the detached garage of an unassuming concrete block home, all in need of fresh paint and a good clean-up. At least from the outside. Jacob walked up the steps beside the garage while I waited by the car. We'd tried her mobile again with no response, so the chances of her being home were slim.

He knocked on the door and I heard the sound of a sash window being dragged open. Jacob must have heard it too as he pointed to the back of the house. I signalled for him to stay where he was and picked my way around the side of the garage through the long weeds and stony ground. Peeking around the corner, I saw a woman hanging by her fingertips from the upstairs window, looking down to see how far the drop was.

"It's a long way," I said to help her. "But you're committed, so you might as well get it over with."

Her head whipped in my direction, and she cursed under her breath in what sounded like Spanish.

"Get me a ladder or something, quick!" she gasped, switching to English.

"I forgot to bring my ladder to work today, sorry," I replied, but I did look around for anything useful to help her down.

An old washing machine lay on its side in the undergrowth, but I doubted I could move it on my own.

"Hang on a bit longer and I'll see if I can budge this piece of shit," I told her, and she grunted and squealed in return.

I gave the rusty old machine a good shove, and to my surprise, it rocked a little. Stepping behind it, I gave it a another heave, and managed to roll it over onto its back. The side that had been against the ground was covered in clammy dirt and wriggly insects which scurried in all directions.

"Hurry!" the woman I presumed to be Serena begged, "I can't hold on."

"This is a bit disgusting, so you need to hang on longer, I'm working on it."

Jacob must have heard us as he arrived around the corner and looked at the woman hanging from the window, and then at me giving the old washing machine another roll. Rocks crunched, weeds shredded, and more bugs evacuated their homes. I carefully picked where to place my hands before pushing again, and with Jacob's help we got the rusty lump one roll away from the wall, when Serena dropped like a stone.

We both jumped back as she clattered to the ground with a scream, sat heavily on the washing machine, then tumbled backwards onto the ground.

I looked at her legs to see if there was anything obviously broken, but her feet appeared to be pointed in the right direction. I stood over her as she lay awkwardly slumped, catching her breath.

"So, Serena, when did you deliver Mr Collins' envelope to the offices of Jackson, Robins, and Smith?"

15

LOADED LIKE A CAMEL TRAIN IN A ROW OF GEESE

Thursday 1:00pm

"I don't know what you're talking about," Serena replied, trying to shuffle clear of the washing machine.

"You've been positively ID'd from the CCTV," I exaggerated. "We know he handed you the envelope in the stairwell, and you came in and out through the employees' storeroom."

She struggled to her feet and looked at the ground as she dusted off her shorts and T-shirt. I guessed the woman to be in her late twenties, with dark, curly hair which had been managed by a hairband until she'd dropped from the window. It was now a mess, and she swept her locks away from her face, finally looking up at me.

"So?" she said. "I didn't break any laws."

"Maybe not, but I wonder how the Caribbean View management feel about employees using their key cards to run personal errands?"

Serena groaned. "I need this job. They don't need to know. Come on, I haven't done anything wrong."

"Then there's no reason not to tell us all about it," I replied.

"We can't promise da condo people won't find out 'bout dis, but we can put in a good word if you help us," Jacob encouraged.

"He swore me to secrecy."

"Well, he removed himself from the picture, so you don't have to worry about that now," I rebutted.

Her brow furrowed when she looked at me again. "He was a nice man."

"I just need to know what he had you do and why, so we can wrap up this case."

Serena stood awkwardly, favouring her left leg.

"Want to sit down?" I asked. "You can sit in the patrol car while we take you to the station. Of course, that'll mean a formal interview with all the paperwork that goes with it."

"I hate all dat paperwork," Jacob added.

Serena groaned again. "I don't know why he had me do any of it, and I've no idea what was in the envelope," she began.

"How did you know Mr Collins?" I asked.

"I've worked there five years now, and he was always polite. I used to clean his condo sometimes as part of the usual rotation, then I heard he'd asked for me to always be the one whenever possible," she explained. "Happens sometimes. Owners get comfortable with one of the staff after a while, you know?"

"Was there anything going on between you, beyond that? Did he take a personal interest in you?"

Serena frowned again. "No! Nothing like that. He was just a pleasant man who liked to know who was in his home, I think."

"Okay, so what were his instructions?" I asked.

"I was supposed to meet him by his parking spot, but I remembered the security guard did walkthroughs, and Mr Collins didn't want me to be seen, so I decided to hide in the storeroom. I kept peeking to see when he arrived, but I guess I missed him as I looked, and his car was there. That's when I scrambled to the stairwell and just caught him."

"And he gave you the envelope?"

She nodded.

"And then?"

"Then I went home, and the next morning I delivered it to the lawyers' office in George Town. The one you mentioned."

"Did da man pay you to do dis?" Jacob asked.

Serena nodded again.

"Was there anything else in his instructions which stood out to you?" I asked.

She shrugged her shoulders. "Not really. He was adamant that the package be delivered when the lawyers opened yesterday morning, but otherwise it was all pretty simple. He said I'd be doing him a big favour that was very important."

The woman was right in that she hadn't done anything illegal as far as I could see, and her story raised more questions again, but about the details surrounding Collins' suicide rather than his death itself. I was itching to know what had been going on in the man's life leading up to this, as I still couldn't pinpoint a reason for his death.

I was about to ask another question, when my mobile buzzed in my pocket. I retrieved it and looked at the caller ID. It was Detective Whittaker. I took a deep breath as I walked away from the other two, and answered.

"Sir?"

"Constable Sommer, was I unclear in some way about not harassing Perry Collins' family?"

Dritt. This was bad. Whenever he led with *Constable Sommer* instead of *Nora*, it was either because others were within earshot, or he was really pissed off. Knowing he rarely disciplined anyone in front of an audience, combined with the fact Raylene wouldn't have been able to resist ratting on me, I was in deep shit.

"She's hiding something, sir," I replied, and knew as the words came out that I'd taken the wrong tack.

"Everybody's hiding something, Nora," he said firmly. "Doesn't mean we get to interrogate them without probable cause. Especially when a superior officer tells you not to."

His voice was even as usual, but his tone was impatient and, worse than that, disappointed. I'd rather he yelled at me.

"I'm sorry," I said sheepishly, because I was sorry for doing something that made him sound this way.

I wasn't sorry for grilling Raylene Bradford-Collins. The woman made me want to punch her in her bird-like beak. And, he hadn't *actually* told me to leave her alone, but this wasn't the moment to point that out.

"I create these opportunities for you to learn, but also so you can prove to the department that you're ready for official detective training," he continued. "Understanding the rules and codes of conduct are a big part of the job. You've already been labelled as a loose cannon, Nora, one that gets results, but a loose cannon none the less. All it takes is one black mark and you'll be denied your request to enter the detective program."

Fy faen. Sometimes it was clear to me that I was simply not cut out for law enforcement, and there was no way I could fake it long enough to call this a career. It felt like a house of cards. But the 'one that gets results' part stuck out more than it should have, given the rest of his speech had been less than positive. I did get shit done, despite the stupid restrictions and rules. And I had one more *drittsekk* to put away before I could quit or be kicked out.

"I can apologise to Mrs Bradford-Collins if that would help, sir?" I offered, not at all sure that I could force apologetic words from my mouth in her presence.

"No, it's best you stay as far away from her as possible at this point," Whittaker replied, to my relief. "This will be wrapped up in a few hours, and tomorrow you can report for normal duty at West Bay station."

"Yes, sir," I said, trying not to sound as deflated as I felt.

"Anything new to report on Collins?" he asked.

"I delivered the envelopes to the lawyers, and we just tracked down the woman from the CCTV who took the mystery envelope from Collins on the night of his suicide," I explained, trying to think how best to deliver what we'd found in a way that might possibly buy us more investigation time. "He paid her to specifically deliver the one envelope the next morning."

"What was in it?" Whittaker asked, and I could tell I'd piqued his curiosity.

"We don't know, and the lawyer I spoke with this morning didn't offer up any insight."

"Should I expect a call from the lawyer?"

I wondered what he meant for a moment, and then I realised. "No, sir, we had a pleasant conversation."

I left out the bit about making up signature stories to get an audience with her, but important detectives don't need to trouble themselves with such inconsequential details.

"All right. Anything else?" he asked.

"I believe the daughter, Kayleigh, has something to tell me, sir. She's indicated that she'd like to call me. I think it's probably something to do with her stepmother."

I heard a sigh over the phone. "She indicated she'd like to talk?"

"Yes, sir," I replied, stretching the truth to the limit.

Well, actually turning the story 180 degrees around, as it was me who'd asked Kayleigh to call. But I knew she had more to share.

"It sounds like Collins and his partner weren't on the best of terms, and according to what Kayleigh was able to tell me, her father did all the work."

"She might be biased in that regard," Whittaker pointed out.

"Possibly," I conceded. "But one envelope contained a new contract worth a lot of money from what I could tell, so why would Perry Collins check out when the business he loved - again, according to his daughter - was doing so well?"

"And Kayleigh brought up the prenup agreement with you, correct?" he asked.

"She did."

"Hmm…"

"Be interesting to see a copy of that, sir."

I gave the detective a few moments to think.

"Let me ask you this," he began. "In a clear-cut suicide case, is there any law which can convict another party for their involvement?"

It was a rhetorical question of course. He knew the answer but was testing me.

"Yes. But you have to be able to prove coercion or bullying, sir."

"Have you come across anything which might suggest Perry Collins was victim to either of those things?"

"No, sir. But I also haven't found as much as a hint of motive for his actions."

"This isn't a case involving more than one person, Nora. We don't have to prove motive in a suicide," Whittaker said.

"I understand, sir, but Collins was a logical man who didn't appear to do anything in his life without purpose. He may well have been simply getting all his geese in a row with the envelopes, but it feels like more than that."

"Ducks," Whittaker replied.

"Sir?"

"Ducks in a row, not geese."

"*Dritt.* Swans, ducks, geese, camels, whatever. I'm trying to say he had more going on than simply wrapping up his business affairs. There's a reason Raylene is so pissed off, and it's not because she misses her husband."

I heard a quiet chuckle over the line. "We're still a long way from coercion or bullying, Nora."

"Life insurance!" I blurted. "Suicide voids life insurance policies, right?"

"I think in almost all cases, yes, but she wasn't about to get a life insurance payout unless he died. The autopsy already confirmed he was healthy," Whittaker retorted.

I was clutching at straws, and I knew it. *Or was the saying clutching at something else?* Pretty sure it wasn't ducks. Regardless, he was right, as usual. I had nothing to suggest there was any foul play outside my own gut feeling. Which was more reliable than my use of English sayings, but not infallible.

"Can I meet with Kayleigh if she calls?" I asked, deciding to ask for permission instead of forgiveness, seeing as my forgiveness bank was overdrawn.

"Yes. But do I have to spell out the parameters associated with such a meeting?" he asked.

His question was loaded like a freight train. I had no clue what that saying meant, but I'd heard it once and it sprang to mind in the moment for some reason. I didn't think it had anything to do with bias or trains.

"No, sir," I replied, figuring I'd take my best guess at his rules if the situation presented itself.

16

GALACTIC MANAGEMENT

Thursday 2:30pm

I walked back around the corner of the garage to find Jacob half hanging out the upstairs window with Serena below him, standing on the washing machine they'd rolled closer. She stretched to reach his dangling foot, and with a final shove, he tumbled into her apartment.

"I left my key inside," she said, stepping down from the rusty metal box.

We returned to the front, where Jacob opened the door and held it until Serena climbed the steps and thanked him. Jacob looked down at me.

"We can go," I told him.

"What about my work?" Serena asked, propping the door open with her foot. "I can't lose my job."

"That's up to them," I replied. "But we'll make sure they know we don't have an issue with you."

Jacob smiled at the woman as he reached the bottom of the steps. "See, I told you it would fine."

Her expression didn't look so sure, but she thanked him again. But not me. Things always seemed to end up with Jacob being thanked and me being the bad guy, which would bother me if I gave a shit about what anyone thought.

"Dat Whittaker?" Jacob asked once we were back in the car.

"Yeah."

"We in trouble?" he asked nervously, driving slowly across the gravel driveway to the road.

"You're not."

"But you are?" he persisted.

"It'll be fine," I assured him. "As long as I avoid Raylene."

He pulled out onto the lane, heading back towards Seven Mile Beach. "What now? Back to da station?"

I'd been rolling that question around in my head and I gave him the same conclusion I'd kept coming up with. "We're stuck unless Kayleigh calls me."

"You tink Whittaker will give us any more time to work on dis?"

"Not a chance."

"Oh," he mumbled in return. "Where we going, den?"

"Did you see the CCTV of the employee going into the condo? The one they think took the bottle?" I asked.

Jacob shook his head. "Dey had da security company look through da footage for dem. Charles just told me dey know who it was."

"Tell me it wasn't Serena."

"Charles would have said if it was, 'cos we were already talkin' about her," Jacob replied.

"Let's go back to Caribbean View," I told him.

I figured the best we could do in the time remaining was to work on one of the unresolved threads. Of course, it felt like every thread was unresolved, but we seemed to be up against a brick wall on all the others. It was either go back to the solicitors' office and try to squeeze something more from Josephine, or make sure the missing bottle mystery was truly solved. I had a feeling a second visit to Josephine and her jolly mother might net me another call to the boss, so I chose plan B.

"Raylene gonna be at Caribbean View," Jacob pointed out.

"She'll be in her condo. It'll be fine," I responded, but his concern was legitimate. I would need to keep my eyes open and avoid her if at all possible.

Charles led us into a small room allocated to the security staff. I guessed it had originally been designated as storage when the condos were built because wires ran to computers in clumps through the drop ceiling as though they were an afterthought. The room was hot too, another indication the cooling needed for the servers had been overlooked. A single folding chair sat before a cheap-looking desk where a 24-inch monitor rested. If the guards were supposed to keep an eye on all the cameras around the facility from this room, I could see how someone with inside knowledge could move freely about the property without too much concern.

"Elysa's worked here for as long as I can remember," Charles said as he hunted and pecked on the keyboard. "Can't see she'd do someting like dis, myself."

"But she's clearly the one on the recording?" I asked.

"Dat true," he replied. "But dat don't mean she take nuttin'."

"Are the key cards tracked?" I asked.

"Only some of da staff entrances, not da condos," Charles replied as footage appeared on the screen.

The timestamp was early Wednesday morning and a woman in a maid's uniform walked across the courtyard by the pool and entered the hallway leading to Collins' front door.

"Is there another view?" I asked.

Charles shook his head.

"Hardly conclusive, is it?" Jacob pointed out. "We can't even see if she actually opened da door to da condo."

"Just hold dem horses," Charles said and fast-forwarded the footage a few minutes, then played it at regular speed again.

The same woman walked out of the hallway and retraced her steps across the courtyard. In her right hand hung a reusable shopping bag with something heavy enough inside to pull the handles taught in her grip.

"Where can we find Elysa?" I asked.

Charles stopped the recording and turned to me. "I believe our manager asked her to come by dis afternoon. Don't know if she did or not."

"Let's find out," I replied.

Charles kept looking at me.

"That means you need to ask your manager," I reiterated.

"Can't say I care to spend much time wit dat man," Charles said. "How about I point you his way?"

With most people I'd tell them to get their shit together and man up, but I liked Charles, and he'd had a tough week. I also figured his judgement wasn't far off the mark, so it made me curious to meet this manager guy.

"Sure. Where will we find him?"

"Office behind da reception desk," Charles replied. "Dat's where he gets paid to sit all day and play games on da computer."

The old man's expression didn't shift, but I couldn't hold back a chuckle. I thanked him and Jacob followed me to the lobby area. I happened to glance towards the restaurant and bar, which were open to the expansive entry, and spotted the last person I wanted to see. Raylene sat at the bar, alone, sipping a cocktail. I nudged Jacob.

"Oh lordy, lordy," he muttered. "Best we move on."

If Raylene was on her own, then so was Kayleigh, and I pulled my mobile from my pocket and checked, but I didn't have a missed call. I'd had a strong feeling Perry's daughter would reach out when she could, but maybe I'd been wrong.

"It'll be fine," I whispered. "Just stand between me and her. Block the view."

Moving to the reception, I smiled at Valerie. "We need to see the manager."

"He's wit someone at da moment," she replied, nervously looking over her shoulder. "Hard to say how long dis take."

"Elysa?" I asked.

Valerie looked surprised. "Yes, miss."

"Perfect," I replied and started for the gap in the counter.

"Nora!" Jacob hissed, and I briefly paused.

Valerie looked terrified. Apparently, this manager fellow had everyone on edge.

"Don't worry," I insisted. "I'm sure he'll be keen to help the police."

I continued, with Jacob scrambling to keep up and Valerie not looking appeased in any way.

I knocked and opened the office door without waiting for an invitation to enter. The man behind the desk looked to be forty-ish, plump, wearing an ill-fitting business suit and a scowl on his face. The name plate on the desk read 'Theo Branson - Manager'. Based on his appearance, I guessed he was no relation to Richard Branson, but he could be a virgin.

"Please wait outside," he snapped, and I detected an American accent. "I'll be done shortly."

I looked at Elysa. She was probably a little older than her manager, with dark, curly hair tied back in a ponytail and a round, friendly face. Which currently had tears running down her cheeks.

"I'm Constable Sommer, and this is Constable Tibbetts. We're investigating the incident with Mr Collins. We'd like a word with Elysa."

Branson stood and pointed to his door. "Then wait out there and you can do what you like with her when I'm done."

"She seems upset," I pointed out.

"She should be," Branson retorted. "Now leave my office, or I'll..."

"You'll what?" I asked with a slight grin. "Call the police?"

Jacob closed the door. "Please sit down, sir," he said firmly, which made me proud of my partner.

Branson reluctantly sat. "This is private company business," he began to protest, but with less gusto than before.

"That's been…" I turned to Jacob. "What's the word for taken over? Like something more important comes first."

"Superseded," Jacob and Elysa both answered.

I smiled at her. "That's it," I continued, turning back to the manager. "Your private company business has been superseded by our police business."

Branson fidgeted in his seat but stayed quiet.

"I assume you were discussing the missing bottle from Mr Collins' condo?"

"We were," Branson replied.

"He sacked me," Elysa added with a sniffle.

"Did you take the bottle?" I asked her.

She nodded.

"And that's why she's fired," Branson commented smugly.

I flashed a quick glance at Jacob, with a subtle nod towards the manager. For a moment my partner looked confused, but then his eyes lit up.

"Sir, would you mind stepping outside for a moment with me?" he directed at Branson.

"You want me to leave my own office?" the man responded as though we'd asked him to sacrifice his firstborn.

If he ever had the opportunity to reproduce of course. I checked his finger and saw no ring, further confirming my suspicions.

"We can talk here, or at da station," Jacob said. "Your choice, sir."

Branson stood, grumbling under his breath. I noticed he was several centimetres shorter than me, which added another notch to his lack of manly prowess. He begrudgingly followed Jacob out of his office, and once the door was closed, I sat on the corner of the desk.

"So, what's going on?" I asked Elysa.

"He sacked me. I tell him I didn't steal da bottle, but he don't wanna listen."

"You're on CCTV taking something and you've admitted you removed the Scotch from the condo, so he has a point."

Her head dropped and a few more tears ran down her face, dripping onto her blouse.

"Do you still have the bottle?" I asked, and she nodded.

"Have you drunk any of it?"

Elysa's head whipped up and she gave me a horrified look. "I would never!"

Her reaction had me baffled for a few seconds, and then an idea came to me.

"You're not telling me something," I said, and her head dropped again.

"Someone put you up to it, didn't they?"

Her body tensed, and my mind raced, double-checking the timeline of events from the past few days, especially when Raylene and Kayleigh had flown in. They would have been in the air at the time Elysa took the Scotch, but it didn't mean she couldn't have organised it beforehand. I pictured her sitting at the bar, sipping her drink. Hardly a vision of the grieving widow.

"Did Raylene Collins pay you to take the bottle?" I asked, wondering why Elysa would still have it.

Surely, if the bottle contained something Raylene didn't want discovered, she'd have hired the maid to dump the contents and destroy the evidence.

Elysa looked up at me once more, now with a puzzled expression. "I've never spoken a word to his wife," she replied.

Fy faen. I was on the wrong track. "Perry Collins hired you, didn't he?"

The woman's face switched to something between unsure and agonised.

"It's okay, you didn't do anything illegal," I assured her. "But I need that bottle right away."

17

BETTING THE GRANDCHILDREN

Thursday 4:00pm

I walked to the door and paused a moment. "Where do you live?" I asked Elysa.

"West Bay," she replied. "Off Mount Pleasant Road."

"Okay, we need to go there now and get the Scotch."

She turned in her chair. "What about Mr Branson?"

I opened the door and looked for Jacob. Valerie pointed to what appeared to be a conference room opposite the restaurant. Not wanting to walk out into the lobby for fear of being seen by Raylene, I texted Jacob. Almost immediately he appeared at the doorway, and I waved him over. He pointed at Branson, and I gave him an okay hand signal. I watched him say something to Branson, and once the two men started towards me, I ducked back inside the manager's office.

"I'm allowed back in my own office now, huh?" Branson started, and I felt like tasing him, but I let him take his seat.

"What's your grounds for sacking her?" I challenged him.

"She stole from an owner's condo," he replied as though it were completely obvious.

"I think you'll find, if you bother to let the woman explain herself, that she didn't steal anything," I countered, turning to Elysa. "Did Mr Collins give you specific instructions as to when and how you should remove the bottle?"

The maid looked terrified, but she nodded. I stared at Branson.

"She didn't tell me that," he said defensively, waving a hand at her. "How do we know she's not making it up."

I shrugged my shoulders. "The Royal Cayman Islands Police Service are satisfied Elysa is telling the truth, but you're welcome of course to conduct your own internal investigation. That is, beyond the jumping to conclusions you've already invested several minutes of your precious time into."

The manager glared at me. "If you're done here, I'd appreciate you leaving."

"No problem," I replied. "As soon as you reinstate Elysa and apologise, we'll be on our way."

I heard one of Jacob's internal groans which I'd begun to notice he made when he didn't agree with something I was doing but couldn't say anything at the time. I was becoming quite attuned to the sound as I'd heard it so many times.

Branson shook his head. "You have no control over who we hire and fire, and as for apologising…" he finished his statement with some sort of laugh-like huff.

"You're right of course," I replied, indicating Elysa should get up from the chair. "Once she's done helping us, we'll just drop her by the lawyers' office where my friend Josephine works, and you can continue the wrongful dismissal discussion with her."

Elysa stood on shaking legs, and Jacob dutifully opened the office door.

"This is bullshit!" Branson raged.

"You'll feel right at home then," I replied and ushered Elysa to the door.

"Wait, wait, wait," Branson groaned. "She can continue, but

she's on probation for three months. I need to make sure this sort of thing doesn't happen again."

"What, the following an owner's explicit and clear instructions?" I retorted. "Yeah, you shouldn't allow that sort of thing."

We'd paused, but I turned once more to leave.

"Does your boss know you strong-arm people like this?" Branson complained. "This is abuse of the uniform."

"I can take the uniform off and defend a citizen's rights just the same if it'll make you feel better. There's no strong-arming here. You're making your own decisions. Poorly, but you have every right to be an idiot."

"Fuck me," he muttered.

"I'd urge you not to use profanity, sir," I said, trying not to laugh, seeing as I was pretty handy at multilingual cursing.

My hand was on the door to close it behind us, when he called out again.

"Fine, damn it."

"Fine, what?" I asked, pushing the door open again.

"She can come back to work."

"By she, you mean Elysa, the woman you had in tears when we arrived?"

"Yes, yes, yes," he blathered. "I'm sorry for the misunderstanding."

I wanted to press him for a better apology than that, but I figured I'd pushed my luck far enough. One call to Whittaker and I'd be deeper in the shit, which wouldn't help Elysa any.

"Good call, Theo," I said instead, and we left his office.

"Thank you," Elysa said as we walked to the gap in the counter.

"He's an arse," I replied, but my mind had switched to getting away from the Caribbean View Residences without running into Raylene.

"It's clear," Jacob said, two steps ahead of me.

I breathed a sigh of relief as we headed for the stairs to the underground parking. Before I reached the steps, my mobile buzzed in my pocket. I quickly looked, dreading another reprimand from Detective Whittaker. It was a text from Kayleigh. I hurried to the landing and stopped to read the message.

'Can we meet?'

Finally, I felt like I might have a break, but we needed to get hold of that bottle. Jacob turned at the bottom of the stairs and looked up at me.

"What's up?" he asked.

"It's Kayleigh. Can you follow Elysa and collect the bottle? Pick me up on the way back."

"From here?" he asked, sounding like he didn't like the idea.

I shook my head. "No, I'll figure out somewhere close by."

Jacob nodded. "Okay. Let me know."

"Thanks again," Elysa said, and I gave her a brief smile.

I'd believed her without any proof she was telling the truth, and I hoped my instincts were correct. If Elysa were to make up a story about having permission to take the Scotch, saying Perry had been the one was perfect. He certainly couldn't deny or confirm her story anymore. But her claim fitted with all the other odd things the man had put in play. I was convinced every move had a well-thought-out purpose, but what that was I still had no idea. I hoped testing the bottle would provide another clue to the puzzle.

I brought up a map on my mobile and searched for a cafe or coffee shop nearby. There was a Paperman's Coffee House across the road in the shopping centre where a big supermarket used to be. It was a clothes shop now which I never went to. I'd never been in the coffee shop either as I couldn't see the sense in paying the same amount of money for a cup of fancy coffee as I did for a gallon of petrol. The petrol lasted a lot longer, even in the Jeep.

Texting her back with the location, I continued through the underground parking towards daylight and, beyond that, West Bay Road.

"Find him?" came Charles' voice and I saw him walking down the ramp into the parking, making his rounds.

"You're right," I replied. "I'd avoid that guy as best I could too."

He nodded. "Elysa okay?"

I waited until the old man came closer. "You sure I can trust that lady?" I asked. "People do unexpected things sometimes."

"What your gut say?" he asked in return.

"I believe her, but my gut lies sometimes."

"I'd trust her wit my grandkids," he said like it was his last word on the matter.

"Okay," I responded.

I didn't know what it was like to have a child or a grandchild, but I assumed he didn't consider them chips he'd be okay gambling with.

"Someting ain't right wit all dis business," the old man continued. "Don't add up."

It was nice to hear someone else echoing my feelings, but I was pretty sure bringing Charles along to a meeting with Whittaker wouldn't help me lobby for more time on the case.

"*Ja*," I agreed, and began to leave. "I'll let you know," I paused long enough to say.

I sensed Charles really did care, and like me, it would keep him awake at night until he had resolution.

It took a few minutes to cross over the road and walk around the outdoor shopping centre to the coffee shop I'd never been to. My friend AJ dropped by sometimes and she'd bought me coffee from them. I was sweating from the afternoon heat by the time I stepped inside to be greeted by their chilly air conditioning and Kayleigh ordering a drink.

"You got here quickly," I said, joining her.

"I was looking around the shops, so it was a short walk," she replied. "What would you like?"

What AJ usually ordered me was tasty, but I stared at the menu board and had no clue which of the many options it was.

"What are you getting?"

"A double espresso," Kayleigh replied. "Can't say I've been sleeping well, so I need a pick-me-up."

"Same, please," I said, figuring a caffeine jolt might give me a fresh perspective.

We sat at a table in the corner, away from the other patrons, and I noticed Kayleigh appeared to be nervous. I kept thinking she was about to start talking, but then she didn't, so we sat in what to her may have been awkward silence. I'm not cursed with that emotion, so for me we just sat and waited for coffee.

Once the lady brought over our cups, I leaned closer. The silence may not have affected me, but time was ticking. "What is it you need to tell me?"

I was hoping my question would break the ice, but it seemed to make her more unsure, and she fiddled with her coffee, which was nuclear hot, so fortunately she resisted trying to drink it yet.

"Whatever you can tell me about your father and his business would be helpful," I continued. "I'm having a hard time understanding why he chose to do what he did."

Kayleigh's eyes finally picked up from her cup, and she stared at me. "You're having a hard time?" she said flatly. "I don't get it at all."

Her voice cracked as she shared the last part, and I watched as she gathered herself back together and took on what appeared to be her usual stoic expression.

"I know he loved me," she said, then took a moment to keep her composure, which may have been balancing on a tightrope more than it first appeared. "And he loved his company. I don't understand why he'd leave either one."

"Do you think Raylene is involved?" I asked.

"I don't know how or why she would be," Kayleigh replied.

"You mentioned a prenuptial agreement that was about to expire. Could it be something to do with that?"

"She told you they were working on their relationship, but that was a lie. Dad filed for divorce months ago, but Raylene wouldn't sign the papers. He told me she was holding out until the ten years were up, so she'd get more money, but it wouldn't work that way. At least he didn't think so, and he would have talked to his solicitors about it, so I presume he was right."

"Surely she would've known that too?"

Kayleigh shrugged her shoulders. "I expect she did. He said something about a ninety-day resolution clause, but he filed so it would expire the day before their ten-year anniversary."

"Resolution clause?" I questioned.

"I'm not sure exactly what it entails," she explained. "But I think it was like a cooling-off period if either party filed for divorce. They had ninety days before the filing became official."

"Okay, then why else would she be buying time?" I asked.

She thought for a few moments. "I really don't know. Dad didn't speak about it much."

We both took a sip of coffee which was now only scorching hot.

"How did they meet?" I asked for no other reason than I wondered how anyone found themselves attracted to birdface and her sparkling personality.

"Some online match-making company that specialises in wealthy people and business executives. Apparently, they were a strong statistical match."

I waited to see if Kayleigh's expression or a further comment would give away her feelings on the matter, but her nervousness seemed to be gone and she was hard to read once more.

"Do you get along with Raylene?" I asked.

"Adequately," she replied.

I had a feeling I was getting a glimpse into Perry Collins' personality through similar traits in his daughter. Analytical. Logical. It was also an opportunity to see the results of a suicide from the perspective of those who cared. As stoic as Kayleigh was trying to be, I could sense how deeply she was hurting inside.

"Does your father have a will?"

"He does, but I've never seen it."

"Have you seen the prenuptial agreement?"

"I haven't."

"Do you have access to any of this paperwork?" I asked. "You're his sole heir, right?"

Kayleigh pondered for a moment. "I suppose I am."

"Do you take over his company?"

Her face tightened and she closed her eyes for a few moments. "My father's dream was for us to work together someday. I would have joined the company after university."

"What did you want?"

"I was excited about it," she replied. "My studies have always been based around that goal."

I sensed she had something more to add. "But?"

She swallowed and took a few beats before replying. "My excitement was to work with Dad. It could have been for any company or industry. He was a brilliant man, who was also my father, and we got along so well. I don't know what I'll do now."

I took a deep breath and tried to push my sympathy for Kayleigh aside. It was already after five, and this case would be shuffled through the system without me after today. I was self-aware enough to know that my stubborn curiosity was driving me to find out more, but the conclusion on the death of Perry Collins wasn't going to change. The man committed suicide. If coercion was involved, I was still a long way from having any evidence to support it, yet somehow I knew the man didn't take his own life through depression or despair.

"Did you know your father had retained solicitors here on the island?" I asked.

"He mentioned that," she replied. "Probably for his residency paperwork."

"More than that," I commented. "In fact, the people I met with don't practise immigration law from what I saw."

"Are you talking about the other envelopes he left?" she asked.

"I am." I took a sip of coffee and thought about my next move. Maybe there was a way to extend the case after all. "How would you feel about visiting their offices and seeing what we can discover about all that paperwork?"

Kayleigh's brow creased in contemplation. "If you think we'll learn something more about why my father did this, then yes," she replied.

"I'll pick you up in the morning at nine o'clock," I said. "Bring your passport and any other ID you have with you."

Her face brightened. "Should we make an appointment?"

I looked at my watch. I doubted the old lady would still be at her desk.

"You can try, but I say we wing it in the morning regardless."

"They're my father's advisors and you have a badge," Kayleigh responded, managing a grin. "I think they'll speak with us."

I smiled in return but wasn't quite so sure inside. I was doing a good job of wearing out my welcome around town. Plus, I still had to convince Whittaker that a representative of the Royal Cayman Islands Police Service had good reason to accompany Kayleigh Collins to her father's solicitors' office.

18

VIKING TONGUES

Thursday 6:00pm

Jacob picked me up and we headed back to central station in George Town. It was slow going as the commuter traffic inched along Seven Mile Beach. I looked at the boxed bottle of Scotch in a plastic evidence bag in my lap and wondered if it held the key to anything important. It must, or surely Perry Collins wouldn't have gone to the trouble of arranging to remove it. *Or was he securing evidence?* Which begged the question, why didn't he place it on the counter with the envelopes if he wanted it examined? Instead of making progress, I was becoming more confused with every new discovery.

Rasha had left for the day, but one of her group was working late and signed in the bottle. She assured us it would get priority attention, but not to expect results until next week. I asked if it could be dusted for prints before then and she wouldn't commit, but said she'd bring it up with Rasha in the morning.

On the ride to the station, I'd filled Jacob in on my conversation with Kayleigh, and he insisted on sticking around while I met with Whittaker, who was just about to leave when we caught him in his office.

"Give me a very brief briefing please, constables. I have somewhere my wife tells me I'm supposed to be, and it's always wise to stay on the good side of the boss."

He looked at me when he spoke the last part.

"We recovered the missing Scotch bottle," I said, leading with what I hoped would be the most intriguing part. "Perry Collins paid the maid to remove it the next day."

"Same maid as the envelope?" he asked.

"No sir, different maid."

"Seems like he had half the staff running errands for him," Whittaker said, slipping his suit jacket on. "Have you given the bottle to Rasha?"

"Yes, sir, but she's gone for the day."

"Okay," he said, eyeing the door as a hint for us to leave. "I'll follow up with her tomorrow. You two are expected at West Bay station in the morning."

"About that, sir," I began. "I also met with Kayleigh Collins this afternoon. She contacted me," I quickly added.

Whittaker sucked in a breath but resisted looking at his watch. "Was she able to shed any light on her father's actions?"

"Not really, sir. She's as baffled as we are. Her father told her there was a clause in the prenuptial agreement which froze the divorce filing for ninety days, but he filed in time so the clock expired before their tenth anniversary."

"There's a chance we may never know why he chose to take his life," Whittaker responded, lifting his briefcase from the desk.

"But Kayleigh wants to visit the solicitors' office in the morning to take a look at what was in the envelopes," I hurriedly continued. "She's hoping to find some answers there."

"I truly hope she does," Whittaker said, and took a step towards the door.

"And she asked me to accompany her, sir."

The detective stopped and I think his shoulders sank a little, but I couldn't be sure. "Let me guess, you said you'd be glad to."

"I told her I was certainly interested in what she might find, but I'd have to check with you, sir."

Whittaker looked at Jacob.

"I was collecting da bottle at da time of dis conversation, sir," Jacob said, and I began weighing up whether to slap him or kick him in the balls once we were outside.

"But I do tink dere's more to dis case dan we bin able to discover so far, sir. I tink it's worth spendin' anudder day on."

I almost smiled. He'd just redeemed himself.

"Tibbetts, you do understand the concept of coercion, don't you?" Whittaker asked my partner.

"I do, sir."

"In that case, can you swear to me that our Norwegian friend here didn't coerce you into saying that? I understand she's quite persuasive when she chooses to be."

Jacob laughed. "She can be, sir, but not in dis case. Dere's someting more to dis situation."

Whittaker shook his head. "You have the morning. If you don't have something new and substantial by lunchtime, I'm closing the case."

"Thank you, sir," we both said, and hurried out of his office.

Sitting in my Jeep, I looked around to make sure no one was within earshot, then dialled the number.

"Hair, nails, and dreams, sugar, which one you lookin' for?" Baby-G answered her phone.

"It's Nora."

"Who's dis?" she responded, instantly sounding suspicious.

"Nora Sommer. We talked two nights ago."

"Da blonde copper. Why didn't you say, hon?"

Because that's not how I'd ever introduce myself, I felt like saying, but I resisted and moved on.

"I have a plan."

"Dat's good, sugar. What's dis plan of yours about?"

"Woods, like we discussed," I said impatiently, wondering if she'd completely forgotten our conversation.

I also considered what could be going on to cause her to be distracted, and quickly shoved that thought out of my mind.

"Don't be sayin' shit like dat over da phone, girl!" she snapped back. "We gotta meet to talk dat kinda business."

Dritt. I was tired and ready for dinner and bed. I should probably spend a little time with Jazzy too. But I'd been the one who'd called, so I had to follow through.

"Where and when?" I asked.

"You in uniform?" she asked.

"Yeah, but I can change."

She had a point. It would be better if I wasn't spotted roaming around chatting with prostitutes in my police uniform.

"No, no," she replied. "Keep it on, sugar. Meet me at Flip-Flops Bar as soon as you can get dere."

"Okay," I agreed, and ended the call.

"*Faen,*" I grumbled, and started the Jeep.

Not only did I not have the time to meet, it was now at a lively waterfront bar which catered to the tourists and cruise shippers. It was gone seven, the sun had set, and the place would be filling up. My idea of hell in paradise.

The drive took three minutes, and I parked across the road in a spot I sort of invented. Half in the car park and half on the pavement, but there was enough room for pedestrians to get by without going on the road, so I called it good. Music thumped from the bar across the street, and I reluctantly dragged my arse that way, waving off the bouncer at the door trying to stamp my hand.

The place was big, with a covered main section housing the bar at one end, and an open-air lower patio overlooking the water. Lights flicked through a spectrum of colours, and the music was so loud everyone had to shout to hear one another. I spotted a bundle of colourful dreads wound up in a bundle above the crowd, and headed that way.

"Great place to chat," I yelled near Baby-G's ear, and she grinned in return.

"Dis works out for me, sugar, and a way for you to make tings square wit me."

"Square with you?" I asked. "I thought not arresting you covered that."

"Call dis a bonus," she shouted in return.

Now I wondered what she had in store, but figured if I could quickly handle my own business, maybe I could get out of there before I was roped into anything else.

"You need to meet Woods and tell him you're unavailable for a while."

The woman frowned at me. "Come again, sugar. I'm tellin' da man dis because..?"

"Because you'll do him a favour and set him up with an alternate way of satisfying his sick cravings."

She tipped her head to one side and thought that over. She was very animated, and we were having to stand so close, she bumped me with her breasts or her hips every time she moved. I felt like I'd fallen into a pinball machine.

"And den what happens?"

"We record the whole thing."

"Dat's entrapment or some shit, sugar," Baby-G said, shaking her head, and all her other parts.

"Not if it's on a security camera."

She started to say something else, then stopped. "Damn. That's sneaky as shit, sugar. You got some scheming in dat skinny white ass of yours." She leaned to one side and looked past me. "Don't be turnin' around, but he's here."

"Who's here?" I asked, not really wanting to know, but I could tell it was unavoidable.

"Dis shit-for-brains guy, Duran, bin stalkin' da shit outa me. He don't get da concept dat mama's love ain't just for his wallet. A lady gotta make a livin'."

"So what do you want me to do?" I reluctantly asked.

"Go put dat police scare on his ass. Tell him to leave mama alone."

"That's it? Just tell him to leave you alone?"

She shrugged her shoulders which created a ripple effect, making her chest jiggle like two bowls of jelly. It was sort of mesmerising.

"Dere's a possibility he may have a little ganja about his person if you were to check real good," Baby-G added, her face the picture of innocence. "Dat'll get him off da streets and outa my hair for a time."

"I don't give a shit if he has a little weed."

"You a copper! You supposed to care 'bout dat shit."

"Well, I don't. If he's peddling pills or coke, I'll bust his arse, but a few joints isn't worth the paperwork."

"You can't pick and choose which of da laws you okay upholdin', sugar."

"Okay, then I guess I have to run you in for prostitution."

She threw her hands up, smacking a guy on the back of his head. He didn't seem to notice or care.

"Listen here, Lara Motherfuckin' Croft, here's da way dis works. You want me to help you out in your crazy plan to take down dat shithead Woods, den you gotta throw mama a bone."

"Who's Lara Motherfucking Croft?" I asked, unsurprised by the rest of her rant.

"Tomb Raider. Don't you ever play no video games?"

"Not once."

"You shittin' me? Dey not have TVs and shit where you from?"

"Of course."

Baby-G shook her head and waved her hands and body parts

around some more. "Fuck dis shit. Get your skinny white butt up dere and bust that creep, 'fore I mace him myself."

I finally took a glance and it wasn't hard to figure out which guy she meant. He was tall, thin as a stick, and leaning on the upstairs railing, peering down at us. Later, I could ponder how I'd got myself into this mess, but right now the best thing I could think of to do was get on with it so I could go home.

"Give me a hug like we're friends," I instructed.

"We are friends, ain't we?" she replied, hands on hips.

"Sure. Now hug me and we'll say goodbye like we just had a drink and I'm leaving."

"I gotcha," she said and threw her arms around me.

I felt like I was being hugged by a bouncy castle, and up close her perfume could double as tear gas. When she let me go, I waved and forced a smile, then moved through the crowd without looking at the upper deck. Near the entrance, I slid into a crowd of people around a table and blended in. Except that everyone looked at me strangely, and I remembered I was wearing my uniform.

It didn't take long until Duran moved across the deck and down the steps to the patio. He shouldered people aside as he homed in on Baby-G. I followed, staying a good distance behind in case he turned around, but he never did. Once I was four or five people away, I paused and waited to see how he'd behave when he reached her. Both of their voices instantly rose above the crowd, but were still incoherent with the annoying music throbbing, which seemed to be the same song constantly playing over and over.

Moving closer, I could see Duran now had hold of Baby-G's arm and was trying to lead her away. She glanced past him and glared at me. I pointed to the exit, hoping she'd get the idea and let him take her out of the bar. Confronting him would be much easier and safer away from hundreds of eager mobile phones capturing the event.

Baby-G resisted enough to make it seem genuine, but allowed herself to be steered to the exit. I shrunk into the crowd and followed. Once I reached the steps to the deck, I ran up and pushed my way past the bar to the upper entrance, where I quickly ran down the front steps to the pavement.

Their voices met me before they both appeared, and hiding behind the steps I waited until they walked past. I was about to step out, when I noticed the bulge at the base of his back, hidden under his shirt. *Dritt.* A gun changed everything.

I unclipped the strap on my Taser and fell in step behind them. "Police. Stop walking. Put your hands on your head."

Baby-G froze, and Duran startled, his whole body tensing. I could almost hear the gears grinding in his head as his stoned brain slowly processed his options. I knew right away he was going to make a poor choice.

Duran's right hand wrestled with his shirt in search of his weapon.

"Don't!" I shouted, but his hand kept fumbling.

It stopped hunting for the gun in a hurry when my Taser hit him between the shoulder blades. His skinny frame jolted and spasmed on its way to the ground, where he let out a squeaky yelp.

"Damn, girl!" Baby-G yelped. "I thought you'd bailed! You zapped his sorry ass!"

I used my foot to pin Duran to the ground, and pulled his shirt up. Sure enough, a gun was wedged in the waistband of his shorts. I ejected the Taser cartridge, then reached down and removed the handgun, shoving it under my own belt. Pulling out my mobile, I called 9-1-1 and told the dispatcher to send a car to Flip-Flops Bar, then stepped on Duran's hand as he tried to reach into his shorts pocket. I now knew where the weed was stashed.

"Stay on the ground. Put your hands behind your back," I ordered, and after a moment of drug-filtered processing, he complied.

Once he was cuffed, I leaned against the building next door to the bar. According to their sign, they were overjoyed to take tourists to sandy beaches, snorkelling trips, Stingray City to pet the stingrays, or any other of the attractions the island had to offer.

I let out a long sigh and began mumbling to myself. "*Alt jeg ønsket var å komme hjem til en rimelig tid, ta en dusj, spise middag og få litt søvn, men denne idioten må ødelegge alt. Hvorfor må folk være så dumme?"*

Baby-G stood over Duran with her hands on her hips. "You really made da girl mad now, she all jabberin' in Viking tongues."

19

THE LOVE-BUNNY SHOW

Thursday 8:30pm

I finally watched the patrol car pull away with Duran in the back seat, and texted Baby-G. I'd sent her back into the bar before the constables had arrived, figuring it was simpler to leave out the stalking and harassment part. Baby-G was better off steering clear of the legal system whenever possible, and Duran wasn't going to be bothering anyone but a cellmate for a while without the additional charges.

"Dey all gone?" I heard her say after waiting for a few minutes with no reply on text.

"*Ja.*"

"Den we good, sugar, tanks for da help," Baby-G slurred as she turned to go back inside.

It appeared she'd made the most of her time at the bar while I was sorting out her *dummenikk* former client.

"Not so fast," I said and grabbed her shoulder before she could leave. "We still need to handle the business I came here for in the first place."

"What dat, sugar?"

"Woods."

"Oh shit. Dat's right. What was your crazy-ass plan?"

I took a deep breath and tried my best to remain patient, but it was a battle I'd lose if this went on much longer.

"You need to call him and tell him to meet you. It's not something to discuss over the phone."

Baby-G nodded enthusiastically. "I gotcha, sugar. Den what?"

"Then we'll get your car set up with a dash camera."

"Dash camera?" she echoed, as though I'd suggested she change careers and join a gym. "My little red car don't have no cameras."

"That'll be the setting up part," I replied, clenching my teeth. "Just call the man, tell him you need to discuss something with him, and arrange a time and a secluded place where he'll feel safe."

Although, upon reflection, he was comfortable meeting a prostitute at his own seafront condo, so it didn't need to be too cloak and dagger.

"Tell him it'll only take a few minutes," I added. "And remember, it needs to be somewhere you can have him get in your car. A dark car park is perfect."

Baby-G looked at me with her big, dark, slightly glazed-over eyes, and I wondered if any of what I'd just said had sunk in. But she pulled a glitter covered mobile from her glitter covered purse and began sending a message on WhatsApp.

I was about to tell her to just call the guy, when I realised the messaging app was even better. I really didn't want any trace of how we set this up on record, and WhatsApp was renowned for not keeping any records of messages after the user deleted them.

Almost immediately she received a reply, and quickly typed something back. This was happening a little faster than I'd planned, and I wasn't getting the chance to vet what she was sending.

"Hey. What did he say?"

"Huh?" she mumbled to me as her mobile buzzed and she instantly replied.

"Let me see what he's saying," I urged, and she looked up and smiled.

"All set, sugar."

"Okay, great. When?"

"Thirty minutes," she replied, looking rather pleased with herself.

"Thirty minutes!" I exploded. "How can we do that?"

Baby-G waved me off with a hand. "It's all good, sugar. We just meetin' over dere."

She pointed in the general direction of Hog Sty Bay, then tottered around and corrected herself to the car park across the road where I'd left my Jeep.

"You're forgetting the important part!" I growled.

"What dat now?"

"The fucking dashcam!"

"Yeah, I ain't got one of dem tings," she giggled.

If I'd had more time to play with, I'd have tased her arse, but instead I pulled out my mobile and called Jumbo, praying he'd answer.

"Hey, what's up," he said.

"We're in deep shit. Did you get the camera we talked about already?"

There was silence for a moment until he spoke again. "Ha! Gotcha," his deep voice chuckled. "Leave a message."

I heard a beep then stared at the phone in my hand wondering what just happened. *Dritt!* I realised he'd recorded his message as though he was answering the call. *Some joke.* Now I wanted to tase his big arse too.

"Call me, now," I groaned into the microphone and hung up.

This was turning into a complete disaster.

"You gotta text him back and arrange to meet tomorrow," I told Baby-G.

"No can do, sugar," she replied, blissfully unaware of the chaos raining down. "Mama gotta work."

"Then the day after tomorrow! *Fy faen*, there's no point meeting if we can't record him."

Her face slowly lost its carefree smile as she finally realised the problem. "You don't have no camera?"

"No! My…" I stammered as I struggled to find the right word to describe my association with Jumbo Flowers, "…friend, hopefully bought one today," I finished. Friend felt okay to say.

"Where's your friend at?" she asked.

"Not here."

"We just use a phone," Baby-G said excitedly. "I sit it in da cup holder and record da whole ting."

"Remember the entrapment part you brought up…"

"Oh shit," she mumbled. "It gotta be like a security camera ting, right?"

"Just text him back and tell him something came up, and you gotta meet him in a couple of days."

The words had just left my lips when my mobile buzzed in my hand.

"Jumbo?"

"Wassup?" his baritone voice growled.

"Did you get the camera?"

"Yeah. Dis ting is cool, man. It got…"

"Where are you?" I interrupted.

"What dat?"

"Where the fuck are you right now?"

"At da Jerk BBQ Hut. Why? What's all da panic?"

"No way! The jerk place in George Town?"

"Yeah."

I looked at my watch. We still had fifteen minutes.

"Please tell me you have the camera with you."

"Yeah."

Finally, something had gone my way.

"I'm outside Flip-Flops. You gotta come right away. Will the camera run off battery?"

"Yeah. Let me finish dis chicken, and I'll be dere."

"Jumbo, bring as many chickens with you as you want, but you gotta come now! We have ten minutes to set this camera up."

"Shit. You can't rush good chicken."

I heard him laugh which was joined by a few other voices and what sounded like hands slapping.

"Jumbo!"

"Alright, Miss Sommer, don't worry your skinny white ass. I'll be dere."

I'd always thought my arse was in proportion with the rest of my skinny white body, but maybe I needed to check in the mirror.

"Stay here," I ordered Baby-G, and she shrugged her shoulders, so I hoped that indicated compliance.

I ran inside Flip-Flops, dodging the bouncer who started to yell at me until he noticed the uniform. Shoving my way to the bar, I called to the bartender, who turned and glared at me. Until he too saw the uniform.

"What's up?" he asked after wandering my way slowly enough to show his contempt.

"I need coffee in a to-go cup."

"I'll have to make some," he replied. "I usually start a pot around ten."

"*Dritt.* What else do you have with caffeine?"

"We got energy drinks."

"The ones in the little cans?" I asked.

I drank the coffee-flavoured energy drinks sometimes which came in full-sized cans, but I'd seen the others. He nodded.

"Give me three of those."

The bartender went to a branded display fridge and brought back three cans and I slapped a twenty dollar bill on the bar.

"Keep the change," I told him, scooping up the cans.

"They're eight bucks each," he replied.

"Seriously?" I said, looking at the little cans I was holding in one hand.

He shrugged his shoulders. "Don't worry about it," he replied. "Just remember me if you ever pull me over."

I would rather pay the stupid price than owe a favour to a random bartender I had no chance of remembering next week, but I didn't have time to pay with my credit card.

"Thanks," I told him and pushed my way out of the bar.

Baby-G was within a few stumbles of where I'd left her, and I thrust the first of the cans into her hand.

"Drink this."

"Oooh, where da vodka?"

"No vodka."

"I like dese tings wit vodka."

"No doubt."

Jumbo's beaten-up car approached and pulled into the car park across the road. He looked like a giant inside with his head almost touching the roof and his shoulder pressed against the B-pillar as he had to have the seat so far back.

"Come on," I told Baby-G, who followed me across the road, sipping the energy drink and making faces.

"Which car?" Jumbo asked, as he unfolded himself from his own vehicle.

"The red Renault," I said, pointing to Baby-G's car in the opposite corner to my haphazardly parked Jeep.

"Hey now," Baby-G crooned, trying to hand me back the can as she strutted towards Jumbo, hitting the unlock on her car key. "Dey found all da extra-large parts when dey put you together, baby."

Jumbo grinned like a fourteen-year-old.

"I tink mama better check dey didn't miss nuttin' important on dem parts," Baby-G continued, brushing herself up against Jumbo, who towered over even her bundled dreads. "I feel a discount comin' your way."

"*Fy faen*, we don't have time for this shit," I intervened. "The red car," I directed Jumbo again, then opened the second can for Baby-G.

"I'm fine, girl," she resisted, but I held the can in front of her until she took it.

"Okay. You're going to tell him you're having some kind of lady parts surgery, and you're out of action for six weeks," I began.

"Lady parts?" she questioned.

"Yeah. Believe me, a guy who wants in your knickers has no interest in hearing the details of what might need maintenance down there. He won't ask. Then, tell him you have a friend who matches good clients like him with girls, and you'll introduce them."

Baby-G's face contorted, but I wasn't sure if it was the drink or the plan she didn't care for.

"He gonna be suspicious," she said, taking another sip.

"You gotta sell him on it."

"I don't know, sugar. Dis shit go wrong and he'll have mama's ass off da street and I'll be next door to Duran."

"Look, all you've gotta do is get him to agree to meet your buddy, Jumbo…"

"Dat's dat boy's name?" she interrupted me, laughing. "Dat's precious right dere."

"Hey, but don't use his actual name," I said. "Just say a friend and leave it at that."

We didn't need Woods asking around about Jumbo.

I traded cans with her once more and Baby-G started in on her third energy drink. She probably wouldn't sleep for a few days, but as long as she could pull this off it would be worth it. To me at least.

"If you can sucker him into a conversation about young girls, all the better. We might be able to get enough evidence tonight. But if not, and this is important, set up a meeting with 'your friend' for Sunday or later, okay? We need time to set up the second meeting."

"Let me show you how dis ting works," Jumbo called over and Baby-G immediately headed his way, swaying and swinging.

"I know how your ting works, sugar, don't you worry your oversized head 'bout dat."

"Just start it recording now, Jumbo, and make sure the LED screen is off. Maybe he won't even notice the camera."

"What if he does?" Baby-G asked, sounding a little more sober than she had twenty minutes ago.

"If he asks about the camera, you can't lie, or it's inadmissible," I replied, praying the problem wouldn't arise. "Hopefully he'll be too distracted by you to bother about it."

Baby-G shook her chest and Jumbo's eyes almost sprung out of his head.

"Save the show for Woods," I told her. "Now get in the car so we can hide."

Baby-G handed me the empty third can, then sat in the driver's seat of the Renault and started the engine, pointing the air-conditioning vents at herself.

"One last thing," I said, and called Jumbo's phone. "Answer it," I told him as he looked at me in confusion.

He hit accept.

"Now mute the speaker on yours," I told him, slipping my mobile onto the floor behind Baby-G's seat.

"Huh," Jumbo grunt. "You all kinds of sneaky, Miss Sommer."

"Ain't she just?" Baby-G agreed, and I closed her door.

"*Dritt!* The stickers," I blurted.

Jumbo reached into his pocket and pulled out a couple of small decals which I took from him. They were warnings stating that the vehicle was equipped with visual and audio security recordings. I stuck one on the rear glass then opened the passenger door and slid into the seat, closing the door behind me.

"What we doin' now, sugar?" Baby-G asked as I sat waiting for the interior light to go off.

"Gotta have these or it'll be an illegal recording," I replied.

The light went out, and I looked around the dash of the Renault, choosing a spot which would be clearly visible in daylight, but was heavily shadowed in the dimly lit car park. Hopefully Woods wouldn't see the sticker when he first got in.

I jumped out and Jumbo began following me across the car park when headlights swung in from the road. I shoved the big guy as hard as I could, redirecting him behind a pick-up truck and into the shadows. The silver BMW X5 SUV slowly pulled in and I hoped he could find a place to park. I hadn't thought of that.

We snuck around the truck and moved behind the back row of cars until we came to an open parking spot.

"*Dritt*," I muttered. "Back up a bit and get down."

Woods had seen the same opening, and his headlights soon lit up the area. I looked at Jumbo hunched down next to me behind a blue car of some sort. His back arched above the base of the windows.

"Get down lower, you big *elg*," I hissed.

He did his best to sink down, but there was only so much distance from ground to window, and Jumbo Flowers filled it plus a bit. The headlights turned off and the BMW's door opened. Over Jumbo's mobile I heard Baby-G humming and what sounded like the typewriter sound the phone made when she typed a message.

"Turn that down," I whispered, and Jumbo grunted a few times as he fumbled with his mobile while trying to stay low.

I heard the crunching of feet on the gravel, followed by another car door opening, and I risked peeking up. Woods was getting into the passenger side of the Renault.

"Come on," I urged, and we scrambled the rest of the way to Jumbo's car which was far enough away from the streetlamps that we wouldn't be seen inside. I winced when the interior light came on as we hustled into the seats, but it quickly went out once we softly clicked the doors closed. Jumbo had backed into the spot, so we were facing the rest of the cars, including the Renault, and I reminded him to turn the volume back up on his mobile and double-check it was still muted.

"It's a lady parts ting, sugar," we heard Baby-G saying. "But I be better dan new in a few months."

"What am I gonna do without my Love-Bunny?" Woods replied.

His old, wrinkly, sick-fuck voice made me want to throw up.

"We can find ways to work around your problem down there, Baby," he continued.

"Dey takin' my tonsils out too, sugar, so ain't nuttin' goin' in nowhere for a while."

Jumbo and I both stifled a laugh, his huge body shaking as he tried to hold it in.

"Papa's gonna miss his Love-Bunny, but you make sure I'm first on the list when you're back."

"You know it, sugar. But I can help you out while I'm down. I gotta friend who can take care of whatever you need. He works wit all kinda girls."

Everything went quiet for a moment, and I looked over at Jumbo, who checked his mobile and shrugged his shoulders.

"It's on," he whispered, which sounded like the rumble of distant thunder.

"What's that?" Woods said, and I held my breath.

"What's what, sugar?" Baby-G replied, and I could hear her shuffling in her seat.

But I figured even her impressive cleavage couldn't distract the old bastard if he thought he was being recorded.

"That," he repeated, sounding agitated.

"Dat's my dashcam, sugar. You don't got one of dem?"

"Is it recording?" he asked, and my heart sank.

"It's for recording da udder cars, sugar. You gotta get one. When some skinny white bitch runs into you, you just show up wit dat recording and she can't lie her ass off. Friend of mine, she had one when dis gravel truck backed up into her Honda, and dat company paid her a bunch of cash. Never even had to go to court."

It sounded like Woods grunted, and I prayed Baby-G's impressive performance had convinced him to move on.

"So what you tink, sugar?" she asked.

"About what, Love-Bunny?"

"Dis friend of mine."

"Da one wit da dashcam?"

"No, silly, da one wit da girls."

"Oh. I don't think so," he said.

"You goin' all soft on your Love-Bunny?" Baby-G teased in a

girlie voice that made me want to throw up again. "I know what you like, sugar. You ain't lastin' two months witout your special time."

"Nobody's gonna understand me like you," he replied.

"Oh he got girls for everyting, sugar. Don't you worry your sweet little heads over dat."

Baby-G chuckled at her own joke, and so did Jumbo.

"She's funny," he said next to me.

"I gotta go, Love-Bunny, give Papa a kiss for the road," Woods said and I groaned.

"So I'll call my friend tonight, sugar, when you wanna meet him?" Baby-G persisted, but I knew we were dead in the water.

I cringed at the faint sound of a slurpy kiss.

"Take care Love-Bunny and let me know when you're back on your feet," Woods said, opening the car door. "Or ready to get back off your feet."

He laughed as he closed the door and walked back to his car.

Maybe killing the *drittsekk* was going to be my only solution after all.

20

SCATTERING ASHES

Friday 8:30am

In the morning, two things were a major pain in the arse. I had to fill out a full report on the arrest of Duran, but the second issue fortunately involved someone else's arse, not mine. Jacob had the unenviable task of asking Raylene Bradford-Collins for her fingerprints.

I'd pointed out to Detective Whittaker that we'd have prints back today or Monday from the stolen bottle, and there was a good chance Raylene's prints would be on it. Whether we were ruling out foul play or bringing her in for questioning would be based on the contents of the bottle, but either way we needed her prints. I'd checked in our system and immigration's, but neither had prints on record. Whittaker had begrudgingly agreed with the proviso it was Jacob alone who went to the condo, and he called her first to smooth the waters as best he could.

It struck me as interesting that immigration didn't have her prints. The application for residency in the Cayman Islands was a lengthy process, which meant Perry Collins must have applied for himself, long before he'd filed for divorce. I wondered if Raylene even knew, and I'd have no problem asking her, but I decided not to burden Jacob with doing it. One of us still having the ability to speak with her was better than nothing. Although it wasn't worth much if we couldn't ask her the important things we needed to know.

I followed Jacob's patrol car in my Jeep and parked by the entrance gate to the Caribbean View Residences while he drove inside. I was ten minutes early, but I didn't wait long before Kayleigh appeared on the front steps. She looked surprised when I waved from the driver's seat.

"This doesn't look like a standard issue police car," she commented, climbing into the passenger seat.

"Jacob has the patrol car we requisitioned," I replied, pulling away from the kerb. "Is this a problem?"

Kayleigh's hair was long enough to tie back, which she did as the wind began whipping it around her face. "No. It's fine. Seems like the perfect island vehicle."

"If you don't mind getting wet sometimes," I pointed out. "I don't have a top for it."

Kayleigh looked up at the blue sky with a few wispy white clouds drifting over the island. "I think we're safe this morning."

I parked across the road from the solicitors' office as I had before. Kayleigh had left a message on their voicemail after I'd departed the coffee shop yesterday, but she hadn't heard back. Not surprising as they'd been closed when she left the message and didn't open until nine this morning. It was still a few minutes to when we tried the door to the offices. It opened, and the receptionist looked up from her desk.

The older woman stared at me disapprovingly, so I let Kayleigh start the conversation.

"I'm Kayleigh Collins. I left a message with you yesterday about meeting with Josephine Smith."

"We was closed."

"I understand that, but the matter is quite urgent, so we dropped by this morning on the chance we might be able to see Miss Smith."

"Mrs Smith. And she ain't here."

I gritted my teeth and stayed quiet while Kayleigh waded through treacle.

"May I ask when you expect her?"

The door opened behind us, and to my relief, Josephine walked in carrying a hefty soft-sided briefcase.

"Hello, Constable Sommer," she greeted me, then looked at Kayleigh. "Am I right in thinking you're Mr Collins' daughter?"

Kayleigh extended a hand and introduced herself.

"How can I help you this morning?" the solicitor asked.

"I'm not sure what my rights are with my father's passing," Kayleigh began, her voice holding steady, "but perhaps you can advise me? I'm trying to understand a little more about the circumstances that may have influenced my father's decision."

Josephine's face softened in sympathy. "I have a busy morning ahead of me, Miss Collins, most of which has to do with your father's affairs. But I'm sure he'd want me to guide you in any way that I can. Let's go to my office." Her attention shifted to the receptionist. "Some coffee would be nice, if you wouldn't mind."

The older woman nodded. Her expression also softened as she watched Kayleigh follow Josephine. It switched back to a frown as I passed by her view.

We sat opposite the solicitor, who took off her suit jacket and pulled a few files from her briefcase, placing them to one side on her desk.

"Shall we start with your rights as it pertains to your father's paperwork?"

"Yes please," Kayleigh replied.

Perry's daughter sat with her shoulders pulled back and her hands placed neatly in her lap. I had the feeling Kayleigh had prepared herself for the difficult conversations surrounding her father, and was determined to keep it together.

"The first thing you should know is that your father arranged for this office to represent you in matters pertaining to certain elements of his estate."

Kayleigh raised an eyebrow.

"I'm sure you're aware that Mr Collins became a Cayman Islands resident recently. With that status, he was able to produce legal documents subject to the laws of the land, although they do not differ much from the UK laws, upon which they were developed."

"What kind of documents?" Kayleigh asked.

The receptionist pushed the door open and slid a tray of coffee cups and condiments onto the desk.

"Thank you," Josephine said, handing a cup to each of us and waiting for the old lady to close the door behind her before answering. "Anything which falls under the umbrella of personal affairs. His last will and testament is one," Josephine explained. "We don't usually handle wills from this firm, but your father insisted in this case, and gave us permission to retain a specialist firm if needed. Although I don't believe that will be necessary."

"When do we see the will?" Kayleigh asked, then winced. "Not that I'm the least bit eager to do so, you understand. The money doesn't interest me."

Josephine smiled. "The will is presented to the named executor while also being submitted into probate. Once probate confirms the validity of the will, then the executor may begin taking care of whatever provisions were specified."

"Who is the executor in this case?" I asked.

"Miss Collins."

Kayleigh started and her mouth dropped open. "I am? I don't know the first thing about handling a will."

"I believe that's why your father retained our services, Miss Collins," Josephine replied. "In fact, I must apologise for not contacting you already, but we've had our hands full going through the papers Constable Sommer gave us yesterday."

"So the executor can see the will?" I asked.

"Correct," Josephine replied, and slid one of the files across her desk.

Kayleigh stared at the folder, then looked over at me.

"I'm sure Mrs Smith can give you a synopsis, if you're not ready to read the whole thing," I suggested.

Kayleigh nodded, turning back to Josephine.

The solicitor left the file where it was. "The gist is very simple, but the details become a little more complicated," she explained, taking a pause while she made a point of looking directly at Kayleigh. "Your father left everything to you."

Kayleigh stopped breathing. It was as though the weight of her father's death, along with the aftermath, had fallen from above and landed in her lap in one, unbearable bundle. I had no idea what the young woman had been expecting, but it didn't appear to be this.

"The company?" she forced from her lips.

"You take over your father's share of StarLife Semiconductor at noon Eastern Standard Time on the day of your twenty-first birthday."

"Isn't that soon?" I said, realising why Josephine had been so familiar with the date.

"November 14th," the solicitor confirmed.

I presumed that was for my benefit, as I'm sure even in her befuddled state, Kayleigh knew her own birthdate. We all sat in silence for a few moments, giving Kayleigh an opportunity to pull her thoughts together, and after a while she straightened her shoulders once more.

"What do I need to do now?" she asked.

"Very little," Josephine replied. "Your father requests to be cremated, and his ashes spread on the ocean in front of his condominium here on Seven Mile Beach. Your condominium," she added, correcting herself. "Department of Environment permission and the boat charter have already been arranged. Beyond that, we'll begin the process of transferring ownership of the condominium and the flat in London to you. The business portion will take some time, and is being handled by a firm in the UK who also have offices in America. That all falls under UK and US corporate law, but I'll put you in touch with our contact there, and part of the responsibilities your father left in our charge is representing your personal interests in those proceedings."

Kayleigh nodded politely but I could tell it was an automatic response. I imagined overwhelmed wouldn't come close to describing how she felt.

"What about Mr Collins' divorce," I asked. "Are you handling that?"

Josephine looked slightly taken aback and was probably wondering what my role had become in all of this. I didn't offer an explanation and stared at her expectantly.

"We are not. The divorce was filed in the UK."

"Is Raylene mentioned in the will?" Kayleigh asked.

Josephine nodded. "Briefly. But only to specify that unless your father's passing occurred after the day of their tenth anniversary, then an existing prenuptial agreement covers any benefits owed to Miss Bradford-Collins."

"Do you have a copy of that agreement?" I asked.

"We do not, but we've requested a copy from the solicitor in the UK. I expect them to email it to us next week once probate verifies Miss Collins' position in the will."

I watched Kayleigh's shoulders drop once more, and I guessed she was thinking the same thing as me. *Could her father really have taken his own life simply to stop Raylene getting more money?*

"But your dad filed over ninety days before their anniversary," I thought aloud.

"I know," Kayleigh continued. "It doesn't make sense. We're no closer to understanding any of this."

My mobile buzzed in my pocket and I kept it below the table and looked at the screen. It was Jacob texting me, asking if I could call him. I didn't want to abandon Kayleigh, but I figured

Jacob wouldn't be asking me to call unless it was something important.

"I have to take this," I said, standing and stepping outside the office.

Across the hall was a small conference room, so I went in there and called.

"Find out anything?" Jacob asked.

"Some, but not really," I replied. "What about you?"

"I got da fingerprints okay," he said, sounding echoey and I guessed he was in the underground parking. "But someting was weird at da condo."

"Weird?"

"Yah. I didn't actually see anyone, but I swear dere was someone else in da place."

"Did you ask her?"

The brief pause told me the answer. "But you didn't see anyone?"

"No, but I heard someone moving about."

"Wasn't the neighbour upstairs?"

"I checked wit da front desk. Ain't no one upstairs right now."

"Okay," I said, feeling an urgency to get back to Kayleigh. "We're almost done here. I'll meet you at Central."

I ended the call, returned to the office, and took my seat. "Sorry."

Kayleigh was staring at the top of the desk, slowly shaking her head. I didn't know her well at all, but she didn't seem like the sort to be bothered by a brief interruption. "Are you okay?"

She looked at me, then at Josephine. "Tell her what you just told me."

The solicitor looked unsure.

"Go ahead. You can tell her," Kayleigh reiterated.

Josephine sighed. "I was explaining to Miss Collins that one of the envelopes I received this week contained her father's notice to buy out his partner at StarLife Semiconductor."

"He made a bid to buy out his partner after he killed himself?" I questioned, the words falling out of my mouth before I could stop them.

"Actually, the other way around," Josephine corrected. "Mr Collins sent the notice to Mr Braithwaite on the morning of his passing. I received a copy of the paperwork the next day as it falls under his personal estate."

"Serena…" I muttered.

"I believe that was the young lady who brought it to me, yes."

21

———

HOT-ROD HONDAS AND LITTERING

Friday 11:30am

"Sir?" I said, standing with Jacob outside Detective Whittaker's office.

"How was the meeting at the solicitors?" he asked, beckoning us in.

"Kayleigh gets everything," I said, standing behind his guest chairs. "And her father made a bid to buy out his partner the day he killed himself."

Whittaker's brow creased. "He set in motion a buyout, then took his own life? Does the suicide void the deal?"

"Smith didn't say it did," I replied, wishing I'd specifically asked that question. "Kayleigh takes over the company on her birthday in a few weeks."

Whittaker slowly shook his head. "That's a lot for a young lady to handle on top of her father's passing."

It was, and I sympathised with her, but the information I'd just received from Rasha was more important to the case.

"Yes, sir. And Raylene's fingerprints are on the bottle we recovered."

Whittaker looked up at me thoughtfully. "Her fingerprints are probably all over everything in that condo, Nora. It was hers too."

"I checked immigration records, sir. Raylene hadn't been to the island in almost a year, until she came for two days just three weeks ago. I understand this is purely circumstantial, but I don't think we should allow her to leave until we have the test results from the contents."

The detective looked from me to Jacob, then back again. "That's a phone call I'm not excited to make. I need something more to restrict her travel, Nora."

I thought about campaigning further, but I knew it was pointless. As usual, he was annoyingly sensible and correct. I needed her motive. Killing Perry wouldn't get her more money, so the only angle I had was if she was angry enough about the timing of the divorce. But still, she didn't shoot him. He chose to shoot himself. This case was starting to really piss me off.

"Anything else?" Whittaker was saying, and I was about to reluctantly admit there wasn't, when my mobile buzzed.

I took a quick look. It was Kayleigh. I'd asked her to let us know who else was in the condo that morning. Her message read, 'No one else here. Raylene says alone except when Jacob harassed her.' I showed Jacob the message. He groaned.

"Something new?" Whittaker asked.

"Maybe, sir. We'll let you know if it comes to anything."

I hurried out of the office with Jacob in tow.

"What now?" he asked when we reached the stairs.

After a few steps I stopped, and he almost ran into me.

"What do you think?" I asked.

"About what we should do next?" he questioned.

I guess he wasn't used to me asking him stuff, as I usually just did things and he had to decide whether to join me or not. I should probably ask for his opinion more often.

"*Ja.* Maybe I'm trying to make more of this case than I should," I admitted.

He thought for a moment. "Da problem is I don't tink anyting changes in da end, right? Da man killed himself. All da udder stuff is weird and suspicious, but none of it gonna change da fact he did it himself."

"Unless he was coerced," I reminded him.

"True. But we got nuttin' suggestin' dat right now."

"Then why did he do it?"

"Not our problem," Jacob replied. "We investigatin' for any crime, and we haven't found one yet."

I groaned. Maybe I shouldn't have asked him. But I couldn't ignore his answer just because I didn't like it. I wanted to, but I shouldn't.

"Okay. So, what should we do next?" I asked again.

"Get some lunch," he said, his face slipping into a grin.

I rolled my eyes. "*Faen.* And then."

Jacob thought for a few moments. "Who do we tink coulda bin hidin' in da condo?"

That was a good question. It was someone Raylene didn't want the police seeing, so that should narrow it down.

"A boyfriend?" I suggested.

Jacob shrugged his shoulders. "Could be. But didn't arrive wit Raylene and Kayleigh, so had to come on anudder flight."

"We could search immigration entry records for any names connected to the case," I thought aloud.

"Not too many of dem," Jacob replied. "Don't really know where to start."

"That's true," I admitted. "Sod it. Let's get lunch."

We trotted down the steps and as we walked across the reception area of central station, my mobile buzzed again. It was Kayleigh. I opened the message and held it so we both could read it.

'I found flight number KX103 written on a notepad. Maybe she's leaving.'

"*Dritt,*" I muttered and switched to the browser on my mobile, searching for the flight number. "It's not an outgoing flight," I read aloud. "It's a morning arrival flight from Miami."

"Early enough for someone to be at da condo when I was dere?" Jacob asked.

"Yeah. Lands at eight-thirty."

I spun around and started towards the office with the community computers.

"What about lunch?" Jacob called after me.

"Coffee," I called over my shoulder, and shoved through the door into the hallway.

It didn't take long to connect with the immigration server we had access to. I began searching the manifest for a name I recognised, and once again I was reminded that we were wildly throwing darts at the board, blindfolded. Half the names triggered some sort of recognition, yet none I could place. And then I came across one which stopped me scrolling. Nigel Braithwaite. I grabbed my notebook and flicked back a few pages until I found where I'd written Perry Collins' partner's name down. It was him.

I texted Jacob and told him to hurry up and meet me outside the station, then brought up Braithwaite's immigration entry paperwork. I double-checked his picture captured at the agent's booth against the bio page on the StarLife Semiconductor website. His online picture was from a few years back and professionally staged, but it was the same person looking slightly dishevelled and fifteen kilos heavier. He'd listed the Kimpton Seafire as his hotel.

This could be our break. The two people who had the most reason to be upset with Perry Collins were secretly meeting here on the island. If it was indeed Braithwaite hiding in the condo that morning.

I briefly toyed with the idea of telling Whittaker, and even asking him for a warrant, but I knew he couldn't get one even if he wanted to. We were still stretching. No judge would grant a warrant based on my suspicions.

It was a fine line between following a gut instinct and blundering around chasing illogical leads, and I was beginning to second guess myself. But my desire to figure this out kept me pressing on, even though warning bells were beginning to ring on my head.

I waited another ten minutes outside before Jacob arrived, handing me a veggie wrap and coffee. As he drove us north, I caught him up in between bites of the wrap and sips of my drink. I was hungrier than I'd realised. When we arrived at the hotel, Jacob stopped just beyond the valet parking attendants, and when we got out, I told the kid we wouldn't be long. Kid. He was probably the same age as me, but I didn't feel my age inside. Too many battle scars.

"You know dey can't give us da room number witout a warrant," Jacob reminded me, and I stopped walking and looked around.

The valet guys had a small hut where they hung all the keys and kept out of the sun. I walked over and looked around inside.

"Can I help you, miss?" the teenager asked me, peering up from his mobile as he sat on a stool in the corner.

"Can I have that box under the desk?" I asked, pointing to a small cardboard box which appeared empty.

The kid shrugged his shoulders. "Sure."

I picked up the box and took out the packing slip I found inside, placing it on the table.

"Call the front desk and have them put you through to Nigel Braithwaite's room," I told the kid, and he eyed me suspiciously.

"You can use that phone, miss."

"Better if you do it," I told him, but he didn't move.

"I bet you drive that sporty little import we passed in the car park, don't you?" I asked, playing the odds.

He frowned at me. "It's legal."

I grinned at him.

"Okay, but I'm waiting on the exhaust parts. They'll be here in a week or so, I swear."

I pointed to the phone, and he slipped off the stool, picking up the receiver.

"What's the name?" he asked me.

"Nigel Braithwaite. Tell him there's a package at valet he needs to sign for."

"This all legal, miss?" he asked suspiciously.

"We're coppers, aren't we?' I said, gesticulating towards where Jacob had been a few moments ago. I think he'd backed away from the escalating incident.

The kid paused, contemplating his options, then finally dialled the front desk. I was relieved they put him straight through then surprised when someone answered in the room. The kid delivered the line without enthusiasm, which probably made it sound genuine, and after a short back and forth which appeared to revolve around Braithwaite not expecting any packages, the kid hung up and said the guy's on his way.

"What does your car look like?" I asked, leaning against the desk.

The kid frowned at me. "I thought you'd seen it?"

I grinned.

"Shit. I ain't telling you *now*," he replied, waving a hand at me.

"Okay. I won't know who not to pull over then. Makes no difference to me." I leaned outside the hut. "Hey, Jacob. Get in here so he doesn't see you."

"Are you allowed to be this devious?" the kid asked, shaking his head. "I feel like I'm aiding and abetting something here."

"Don't overtink it, my friend," Jacob said, stepping inside. "It's best to do as she say, den duck when da you-know-what hit da fan."

The kid laughed. "It's a red Honda CRX with a matte black bonnet."

I gave him a nod and another grin, then peeked outside to watch the hotel entrance. A tall, portly man in a business suit appeared and paused to light a cigarette. Looking around, he spotted the hut and strode our way, his tie fluttering in the breeze. As he neared, I stepped out and tossed the box towards him.

"Here you go, Mr Braithwaite."

He stopped in his tracks, batted the box away, then turned and hurried for the hotel lobby. On his way, he flicked his cigarette aside. Not the reaction I'd hoped for or expected.

"*Fy faen,*" I muttered and took off after him. "Stop, sir!"

I don't know where he thought he could run to, or how he was going to magically overcome his unathletic physique and sprint away, but he tried. Shortly after he entered the lobby through the sliding doors, I grabbed him by the jacket and steered him into the back of one of the overstuffed chairs in the reception area. He half fell over the cushioned back, but the chair began sliding across the lobby floor, and man and furniture skidded and stumbled until both crashed into the reception counter.

Every head turned, a security guy came running, and lots of gasps and yelps echoed around the place. Perfect. I'd run across the management at Seafire before and one thing they hated was a fuss in their expensive, pristine hotel. This would be another complaint about the crazy foreign blonde copper.

"What the bloody hell..." Braithwaite muttered in a northern English accent, gathering his breath.

"I'm Constable Sommer, and this is Constable Tibbetts from the Royal Cayman Islands Police Service, sir. We have a few questions for you, if you don't mind?"

"Well clearly I do bloody mind," he growled, "You just assaulted me for no reason at all."

"I didn't assault you, sir. You ran, and now I'm arresting you."

"For what?" he snapped, straightening his jacket and tie, his cheeks flushed.

"Littering. You tossed your lit cigarette away, sir," I explained. "We take pride in our island and won't stand for littering."

"Nora!" Jacob hissed from behind me.

"Constables, what on earth is going on here?" a man I recognised from my previous visit said, coming from behind the counter. "Could we please take this scene somewhere more private?"

"That would be the station," I said. "We'll be out of your hair in a moment."

"This is outrageous!" Braithwaite complained. "I'm not going anywhere with you."

"Constable," the manager intervened, "our driveway and fore-court are private property, so we'll handle the cigarette business as an internal matter. It will be cleaned up and I'll discuss our smoking policy with our guest. Now if you'd please leave, you've caused quite enough commotion."

A larger crowd had gathered in the lobby and everyone's eyes were on the kerfuffle.

"Provide us somewhere private where we can speak with Mr Braithwaite, or we're taking him out of here in handcuffs," I responded, looking at the manager.

"I'm not going anywhere with you," Braithwaite insisted.

I shrugged my shoulders and continued looking at the manager.

"This way," he finally conceded. "We have a small conference room."

"No, I refuse to speak with this woman," Braithwaite huffed.

"Handcuffs it is then," I said, unclipping them from my belt. I heard that odd noise from Jacob again.

Braithwaite threw up his arms. "Fine, fine. You get two minutes, that's it."

We followed the manager past the gawking crowd to a room with a long, rectangular table surrounded by a dozen chairs.

"We're in big trouble dis time," Jacob whispered to me.

"*Ja.* Probably," I admitted. "So we'd better learn something."

Once we were all inside, the manager left, closing the door behind us.

"Why would you run from the police, sir?" I began.

"I was startled, that's all. And you threw something at me."

I knew I only had a short time, so rather than debate his logic, I decided to get to the more important questions.

"Can you tell us the nature of your visit to the island, sir?"

"I think you bloody well know my partner just..." he began, then paused and gathered his thoughts for a moment, clearly trying to calm himself down before he said something he'd regret. "Mr

Collins was my partner, and I came here to see if there was anything I could do."

"But you hid from the police at the condo this morning, then ran from us just now. How is that helping anything?"

His eyebrows rose in surprise. "Mrs Bradford-Collins mentioned you were harassing her, so it seemed best not to complicate matters this morning, and like I said, you startled me."

"Mr Collins served you with his intent to buy you out of the company. That must have startled you too."

His jaw clenched. "He can't buy anyone out of anything now, can he?" he retorted, then visibly reigned himself in, fussing with his tie while he took a few deep breaths. "We're done here. Anything else you want to ask me you can do through my solicitor."

22

CONSEQUENCES

Friday 2:00pm

I didn't notice for a while, because I liked the quiet and was deep in thought, but I finally realised Jacob hadn't said a word since we'd left the hotel. Glancing over, I could see he was leaning away from me, his face tense, and his stare somewhere off in the distance.

"Are you okay?" I asked.

He shrugged his shoulders and didn't say a word.

I was about to ask again, as something was clearly bothering my partner, but I hated these games. If he had a problem, he should tell me. We weren't children. I went back to running all the elements of the case through my mind, but I couldn't concentrate anymore. Jacob was probably upset about how things went at the hotel, and while I'd have preferred them to have gone more smoothly, there was no point pouting about it. We'd learnt Braithwaite's up to something in all of this, and there was a good chance he was involved with Raylene in some way.

We'd learnt, might have been a strong way of putting it, as all we really had was a suspicion based on his defensive behaviour, but I was sure Braithwaite wasn't here to mourn the loss of his partner.

We had more notes for the file. It may have cost us *another* angry phone call which would mean *another* talking to, but we were about to be done with the case anyway. All we had were long shots to uncover anything which might support our suspicions that there was more to the case than a simple suicide. *My suspicions*, I corrected myself. Jacob didn't necessarily disagree with me, but he was taking Whittaker's view that it didn't change the end result.

"*Fy faen,*" I muttered and smacked my fist on my thigh.

I always seemed to end up down these rabbit holes with no clear end in sight. Jacob wasn't agreeing with Whittaker just to kiss his arse. He was thinking along the same lines because they were both right. I was making the case far more complicated than it needed to be over a group of characters from the UK and America. If they'd influenced Perry Collins, then it was unlikely to have happened on the island. I was wasting police time and resources when there were far more pressing local matters to address.

"I'm sorry I dragged you along on a wild…" I was already frustrated and now I'd forgotten again which bird was the chasing bird, which made me even angrier. I smacked my fist on the door handle this time. "I'm sorry, okay?"

My words ended up sounding like an outburst which wasn't how I'd intended the apology, but I shut up as I was sure more words would only make it worse.

Jacob almost imperceptibly shook his head and didn't say anything.

"I mean it," I said, determined to sound sincere, or at least calmer.

So much for no more words. I was usually an Olympian at uncomfortable silence.

"You tink you mean it," he finally responded. "But you'll do it again next chance you get."

There was that disappointed tone again. If people didn't have these misguided expectations of me, then they wouldn't be disappointed all the time. Jacob was so annoyingly optimistic. I'd given him no reason to think I'd do anything but what the hell I wanted to do, regardless of the consequences, and yet he followed along, and was now surprised somehow. All this responsibility and expectation was crushing me. I couldn't breathe.

"I probably will," I said. "And you should know that by now."

"I know dis uniform means someting to me, and it should mean someting to you," Jacob replied, his voice controlled but angry. "I get you don't care what happens to me, but you should tink about how you represent dis island and da police service, Nora. Some of us actually care about dat."

Usually, I had the ability to ignore anyone's opinion of me. It wasn't that I defended myself or made excuses that countered their accusations or insults, I simply didn't give a shit. I heard the words and the intention behind them, but they didn't affect me. It wasn't a trait I'd worked at or developed; I'd always been that way.

But Jacob's words were different. A lump formed in my throat and my stomach clenched. I would defend Jacob with my life. He was a good man with a lovely family, and his life was worth something. Far more than mine. I couldn't believe he didn't know that. He was right about the other stuff regarding the police and the island. I didn't really care that much. It wasn't to say I didn't appreciate both, because I did, but joining the police had been a means to an end. It had given me purpose at a time when I was lost and directionless. Sure, it had become more to me over time, but in the back of my mind I knew it wouldn't work out in the long term. Nothing ever did.

I loved the Cayman Islands, and yet they also held the worst memories of my life. It was here that Ridley had been murdered. My soulmate taken from me. Dead in my arms. I should have left and gone somewhere else in the world, but I couldn't tear myself away. Leaving would feel like I was deserting Ridley. I was chained to 200 square kilometres of limestone and sand. I had my shack, that one day I would give back to Archie Winters, the old man who'd given it to me to protect. Maybe then I could force myself to leave the island, but probably not.

"You're right," I said. "I don't care about a uniform or this place in the way that you do, but what happens to *you* matters to me."

Jacob let out a sigh and briefly glanced my way before returning his eyes to the road ahead.

"I need dis job, Nora," he said, his voice stern but quieter. "I want to keep dis job. You act like you don't care at all. Whittaker is trying to help you, but all you do is disobey da man and put him in a bad position. Dis affects me too, you know? We're supposed to be partners, but you never tink about dese tings from my side."

He pulled into the car park at Central Station and found an open spot. I knew I should be saying something more, assuring him and swearing I'd do better, but I didn't. We both got out of the car and walked towards the building. I'd be lying if I told him what I knew he needed to hear. Jacob's ridiculous belief in human kindness and empathy would give him just enough hope that I'd change, only for us to end up in this same place again. Although I had to admit *this place* we were in now was new territory. He'd never complained with such commitment before. Maybe he was already at the end of his rope.

I forced my mind back to the case as we crossed the reception area. I wasn't sure what to do next, and followed Jacob, who appeared to be heading for the office with the shared desks and computers. Detective Whittaker's voice stopped me before I reached the door to the hallway.

"Constable Sommer," he called out, just loud enough for me to hear.

I stopped, turned, and saw him at the bottom of the stairs.

"I'd like to speak with you and Constable Tibbetts, please."

Without another word, Whittaker went back upstairs. I called out to Jacob, who reluctantly rejoined me in the lobby. I presumed he'd heard or seen the detective too.

"He say what it's about?" Jacob asked.

I shook my head.

"Let's get dis over wit, den," he added and led the way to the steps.

In the past I would have been preparing all the ways to justify my actions, explaining how I'd moved the case forward, but my mind was elsewhere. I trudged up the steps and followed Jacob down the hall to Whittaker's office. Once inside, the detective indicated I should close the door. While I did so, I readied myself to vigorously defend my partner rather than my actions.

"This will be a short meeting," Whittaker began. "Nora, you're suspended pending an internal investigation into your actions over the past few days."

That weird groan Jacob let out once again seemed to echo my own feeling of being punched in the gut. I'd been expecting a thorough bollocking, but not this.

"Jacob, Sergeant Redburn will assign you a partner. You're back to West Bay as of now. Currently, you're not under investigation or suspended, and I hope you'll not give me cause to reconsider that decision."

We all stood in deathly silence for a few moments. I couldn't speak. Knowing that one day this would undoubtedly happen turned out to be a million miles from the feeling of it actually taking place. Apparently I did care about my job a lot more than I'd realised.

"I'd like an opportunity to defend my partner, sir," Jacob said.

I should have been surprised, but I wasn't. Constantly, I'd put him in compromising situations, without regard to the consequences for either of us, exactly as he'd described in the car. Yet here he stood, ready to fight on my behalf. I reached out and put a hand on his shoulder.

"It's okay. You were right, I had this coming."

For a moment, Whittaker looked back and forth between the two of us, and I could tell he was curious what was behind our exchange, but he didn't ask. I'm sure he thought this wasn't the time, or perhaps it simply didn't matter anymore.

"You're dismissed, Jacob," he told my partner. "Report to Redburn this afternoon."

Jacob didn't move. He turned to me, his expression desperate and heartbroken.

"I'm sorry, Nora. I didn't want nuttin' like dis."

"It's okay," I managed to utter, but it was all I could say. I couldn't find any more words and was certain if I did, they'd be hollow and meaningless.

Jacob left the office, closing the door behind him.

I stared at a coffee cup on Whittaker's desk. Anywhere but in the eyes of my mentor. The mug had the logo of the Fox and Hare pub on it. One of the few places I ever went to socialise, and a favourite of Whittaker's as well. In fact, it was Friday, so our friend Pearl Moore would be singing on their little stage this evening. The thought of being amongst a throng of people and having to explain my current situation to my friends was overwhelming. What would I do when I saw Whittaker there? These things which never normally bothered me raced through my head like a chain-wielding biker gang, smashing everything in their path.

"You realise you left me no choice?" Whittaker said, and I finally looked up.

I nodded.

"The people around you want you to succeed far more than you do yourself," he continued. "I couldn't allow your blatant disregard of procedure to go unchecked any longer, Nora. There are consequences to our actions and responsibilities which come with the badge. They apply to us all."

I nodded again.

We stood in silence for a few moments, then he sighed as though he'd given up, exhausted.

"You're dismissed. You'll not report for duty, wear the uniform, or represent yourself as an active police constable until further notice. You'll receive an email with details of your internal hearing, which will probably be as soon as Monday," he explained.

"I'll be fired, won't I?" I said, forcing the words from my lips.

"Go home, Nora. My advice is that you show up at your interview with a plan of how you intend to turn your law enforcement career around. Maybe, if you say the right things, you'll get another chance, but there's no guarantee. I can't protect you anymore."

We stared at each other for a few moments. A million emotions seemed to swirl in his eyes behind his glasses. Frustration. Resolution. And of course, disappointment.

"You shouldn't," I said.

And I meant it. Some people were beyond helping, and I realised that I might be one of them.

23

___

A NAGGING OBLIGATION

Friday 4:00pm

I drove from George Town to West Bay in a trance. My normal reaction to a situation like this would be a mix of anger and determination, but I felt neither. Operating on autopilot, I found myself turning left on North Point Drive and pulling into the car park for my friend AJ Bailey's dock. She and Reg Moore – her mentor and family friend – ran their dive boat operations from the small wooden dock extending into the Caribbean Sea from the ironshore coastline. I parked behind AJ's Ducati motorcycle as all the other spots were taken.

Switching off the engine, I sat for a moment and wondered what I was doing there. I'd subconsciously steered my way to the dock, but facing a discussion about the shitstorm my life had become held no appeal whatsoever. AJ usually had a way of putting things in perspective and helping me unravel the knots I occasionally tied myself in, but this felt more like a weld than a knot. Permanent. Undoable without destruction.

"What's cooking, good looking?" came AJ's cheery voice, and I turned to see her walking up the jetty towards the Jeep.

"You, if you sit there in this sun all afternoon," she added, chuckling at her own humour.

I swung my legs out and stepped out of the Jeep.

"Bloody hell," AJ breathed. "What's the matter?"

Apparently, my insides had projected themselves onto my outside, which wasn't usually the case.

"Shit day," I muttered in return.

"If you were a normal person, I'd give you a hug and tell you it'll be alright, but I know that won't work, so how about a dive?" she suggested. "We can take the boat out. I think I've finally fixed a pesky wiring issue I've been chasing for weeks, so we'll call it a test run."

She turned and walked towards the little hut which served as their office, bathroom, and storeroom. "I'll get you a wetsuit unless you feel like diving in your uniform," AJ said, laughing again.

I looked down the pier where her boat was the only one tied up. One of Reg's three Newton custom dive boats bobbed on its overnight mooring a hundred metres offshore, but his other two were yet to return from their afternoon trips. The dock was quiet, and we would probably slip away before Reg's customers returned.

A dive with just the two of us would be food for the soul. A perfect distraction from the thoughts swirling around my head. AJ's infectious spirit would slowly bring a smile to my face, and plunging into the underwater world always helped me gain perspective.

But not today.

I reached into my pocket and pulled out my mobile, holding it up to read the screen. AJ reappeared from the hut with a wetsuit in hand.

"I have to go," I said, holding up my phone in way of explanation.

"Bugger," AJ said, her shoulders dropping and the wetsuit

dangling from her hand. "I got all excited to go and have some fun. What case are you working on?"

"The suicide at Caribbean View Residences," I said, omitting the part about being suspended from all cases and shifts.

AJ winced. "I heard about that. Sounds nasty."

I nodded and pretended to type something back to the mystery texter who hadn't sent me anything.

"Was the bloke all kinds of depressed, or terminally ill?" she asked.

I shook my head. "We don't know why."

"Blimey. Just goes to show," she continued. "You never know what's really going on in someone's head, right?"

She looked at me as though she were searching my face for everything I was feeling inside. I knew AJ desperately wanted me to open up and talk to her, and she could also read me well enough to recognise that I knew it too. Walking away was blatantly shutting her out after driving here specifically to see my friend. But I couldn't stay. Beyond my lack of ability to share raw emotions was the overwhelming feeling that I didn't deserve a respite or escape. I'd brought all of it upon myself.

"I have to go," I said again, and walked to the Jeep.

AJ followed and once I'd climbed in, she stood with her hands draped over the roll bar above where a door would be if the Jeep had them.

"Call me later, please. Or come by the pub. Pearl's playing tonight."

I started the engine.

"I need you to promise me," she urged.

Summoning the courage, I finally looked at my friend. "I will," I lied, and she reluctantly stepped back as I reversed out of the spot.

Ten minutes later, I'd driven the rest of the way home, parked by the side of Conch Point Road, and walked through the woods to my shack. Edvard, sitting on a limestone rock warmed by the afternoon sun, stared at me with his head cocked to one side. He didn't move as I trudged by and climbed the steps to the deck. The door was locked, which meant Jazzy wasn't home from school yet, which was good. It was another explanation I dreaded. I recalled she'd talked about stopping by her friend's house to do homework, so I was off the hook for an hour or two.

It took me five more minutes to change into a swimsuit, gather up my fins, mask, snorkel, and weight belt, then head to the small, protected cut in the ironshore where the steps led into the water. Dropping a towel on the ground and kicking off my flip-flops, I jumped into the ocean, plunging into the warm water, and relishing the complete immersion in a foreign yet familiar world.

Kicking to the surface, I slipped my mask in place and took a deep inhalation before the weight belt around my waist slowly pulled me under. Reaching down, I fitted a long fin onto each foot then kicked towards the open ocean past the breakwater. Occasionally gliding to the surface for a breath, I swam a metre or so underwater across the sand flats to where the reef began. Ahead of me, fingers of coral extended into deeper water, and below me the pale-yellow sand gave way to a colourful sea floor alive with creatures of all shapes and sizes.

I swam a little farther before rolling onto my back with my nose and mouth just above the surface. My legs dangled beneath me and with minimal effort I kept myself afloat with soft, long sweeps with my fins as I filled my lungs with fresh air. After a minute of breathe-ups, I held a final inhalation and ducked below.

Usually, I'd cruise around, checking out whatever activity or landscape caught my attention, but today I finned into the entrance to a swim-through which traversed a finger of reef. Settling gently into the sand, I kneeled and closed my eyes, letting my hands fall into my lap.

You never know what's really going on in someone's head. That's what AJ had said, echoing a reality I'd often pondered. It seemed beyond our comprehension to truly realise the quantity of observations, judgements, ideas, emotions, and decisions processed by another human being. Despite the fact that our own minds constantly raced through all these things, churning information at an alarming rate, it was strange to consider the person we're speaking with was doing the same thing. All we had to go on was their spoken words, actions, and body language.

I wondered what was happening in Perry Collins' mind on Tuesday evening. From everything I'd learnt it appeared he was clear headed and logical, typical of his personality. Maybe the noise had become too much. *Had he decided the daily grind of living wasn't worth it anymore?* I truly couldn't see it, and no one close to him appeared to understand his actions either.

If I stayed where I was and never surfaced alive again, would people be surprised? Would they say they hadn't seen it coming? Surely not. I'd just been suspended from the only lawful job I'd ever had, my partner was ready to find someone new, and my boss, mentor, and de-facto father figure was the one who'd suspended me. I'd let them all down.

Pioneering my own vendetta, my plans to take down McKinley Woods had crumbled after months of effort. A paedophile would continue walking the streets and preying on underage girls whenever he could. Because I'd failed. A typical half-baked scheme which disintegrated under the slightest challenge. *How could I protect Jazzy when I couldn't even stop a monster like Woods?*

And what about Jazzy? I had no business being responsible for another person, let alone a child. The kid needed stability and balance, not the train wreck of a life I provided. She never knew if I'd be home of an evening or running around screwing up an attempt to take down an errant politician.

My lungs burned as I sat on the ocean floor considering the reasons why my life wasn't worth continuing. I was twenty-one years old and for one quarter of that time I'd been running from the authorities, breaking the law, or - unimaginably - working for them. I'd experienced abuse, violence, death of people close to me, and the sickening power of taking another's life. All these things had happened from decisions I'd made. There was no avoiding the conclusion that I was shit at this life business.

Maybe Perry had the right idea. Make the noise stop. No more obligations, expectations, responsibility, or failure. Just the nothingness beyond the pain of existing in a fucked-up world. I was fully aware that my loss would cause trauma to those close to me, but my selfish need to stop these feelings tearing me apart inside was stronger. It wasn't that my immediate situation was unliveable - far from it in some ways - it was the accumulation over time of returning to a similar place. My continuous self-destructive cycle and the knowledge that I'd never love again in the way I'd loved Ridley made it all seem pointless. I needed a reset. If we reincarnated, perhaps I could try again.

Once before in my life I'd reached a point where I simply didn't care anymore. After Ridley's murder I'd slipped into an all-consuming, heartbroken depression, and while I never tried to take my own life, I'd teetered on a knife edge of doing so. I'd been too apathetic and paralysed to take action, but I'd have welcomed anything that would have made the world stop for me.

Neither then, nor now, did I feel even a hint of self-pity. The world wasn't against me in particular - in my mind it simply didn't give a shit about anyone. We lived on a planet which spun in circles as it looped around a star, and things grew and died every day. Fate didn't kill Ridley. A *drittsekk* from a Mexican cartel with a gun killed him. Destiny had no hand in me being suspended. That was all down to my lousy decisions. Whittaker and Jacob were disappointed in me because they'd hoped I'd be a better person than I am.

I had no idea how long I'd been in the entrance to the tunnel, but my lungs were screaming for clean air, my brain's natural urge to sustain life by swimming up kept at bay by my apathy. I continued to kneel in the sand with my heart rate lower than if I was fast asleep in bed.

Thirty feet below the surface. All I had to do was stay still and do nothing.

Eventually the necessity for oxygen would overpower my mammalian diving reflex to hold my breath underwater, and I'd draw in a lungful of seawater. It would probably feel awful for a brief amount of time, but as the final reserves of oxygen depleted, the panic and inevitable moment of regret would be fleeting, and it would be over.

Thoughts were becoming heavier and harder to move through my mind. I knew I was in the midst of making the most important decision of my life, but I could no longer sense why. I felt the presence of a surreal balance, like a set of scales, tilted in one direction, demanding I not move. Yet, from the vague, swirling depths hanging on the last vestiges of consciousness, I felt a nagging obligation. I was well beyond the point of completing a thought, and as hard as I tried to clutch hold of any whole notion, all I could do was sense the balance moving. Like the scale tipping from dark to light, the urge to stay shifted, along with my finned feet.

Barely aware of which way was up, my feeble limbs wouldn't respond, and I remained on the sea floor despite my desire to find the surface. This was it. I'd made my decision and whatever drove me to change my mind at the last moment had been too late. My throat convulsed as my mouth fought to stay closed for a few moments longer. I touched something firm and metallic with my fingertips, which suddenly gave way, and I began to rise.

From somewhere deep inside I found the last ounce of strength to make a few, desperately weak fin strokes. Willpower I hadn't known I'd possessed kept my lips together. But the distance was too far. Lost in the water column with no more strength, and the certainty of death upon me, my lips parted. Water surged into my mouth, and I gasped. Then spluttered. I'd swallowed water, but not only water. The rest of my inhale had been air.

For what felt like minutes, I floundered, choked, and spat until finally I settled and caught my breath. My head pounded. I dipped my masked face in the water and saw my weight belt lying in the sand below me. I never would have made the surface if I hadn't found the strength to open the metal clasp.

Picking my head up, I turned and looked towards the shore. The first truly clear thought that ran through my tired and throbbing brain was that I'd promised to call AJ.

Obligations were part of what drove me to sit on the sea floor, and yet an obligation had brought me back to the surface.

24

BITCH-CATTY AND THE CHURCH

Friday 6:00pm

I felt like I had a terrible hangover. Exhausted, with my head throbbing, I trudged from the little marina to the shack, with the western horizon lit up in deep orange. Edvard had moved on now his heater had set for the night, and the house was still empty. I filled a drinks bottle from the cool water supply in the refrigerator door, and guzzled as much as I could stand.

Picking up my mobile from where I'd left it on the bed, I saw I had a text. It was Jazzy asking if I could pick her up at seven. She'd sent the text an hour before. I quickly typed a reply telling her yes. While I had my mobile in hand, I also texted AJ and told her I was okay and not to fuss like an old woman. Before I'd put the phone down, she'd replied with a series of insulting emojis and a smiley face. I almost grinned.

The mobile buzzed again, but this time it was a call. Baby-G.

"Hey," I answered.

"We on girl," she said, her voice a mixture of excitement and uncertainty. "What we do now?"

"Woods?" I questioned, my mind still slow and dull. "He wants to meet Jumbo?"

"He don't know no Jumbo, but yeah, the perv wanna meet my contact," she replied. "Which happens to be your fine young man, Jumbo."

"When?" I asked, trying to readjust to the fact that one of my half-baked schemes was still in play.

"I ain't replied 'cos I called you. Last time you yelled at me for gettin' tings all messed up."

"I'll call you right back," I said and heard Baby-G complaining as I hung up.

I dialled Jumbo.

"Wassup?" he answered, and I waited to see if it was his voice-mail trick again. "Miss Sommer?" It wasn't.

"Woods wants to meet. How soon can we set something up?"

"What you tinking? Someplace like a hotel, or in a car again?"

"Car would be easiest, but we'd need a nice vehicle," I pondered aloud.

"Like a pimp would drive, right?" he answered.

"*Ja.*"

"I can handle dat," Jumbo replied.

"You can't steal one for this."

He laughed in his deep guttural tone. "Nah, I know a guy."

"Okay," I agreed, deciding not to probe his resources any further. "When can you set it up?"

"When you need it?"

"Maybe tonight," I replied, liking the idea of making it happen while the revolting old *drittsekk* was keen. "Or tomorrow."

"Gimme a minute," Jumbo said. "I'll call you back."

We ended the call, and I texted Baby-G. 'Setting it up. Let you know shortly.'

My phone buzzed almost instantly with a response. I had no idea how she could type so fast, especially with her long, colourful acrylic nails.

'Hurry your skinny white ass up.'

I walked to the refrigerator and refilled the drinks bottle, downing another long swig of the cool water. My clarity of mind was returning, and I was aware of a sense of purpose building once more. Not much to rely on, but less than an hour ago I'd contemplated ending it all until AJ's subliminal message literally pulled me from the deep. If there was a chance of putting Woods away, I had to see it through. If I failed in the legal path, then maybe I'd stay on the sea floor next time, but not before I paid the filthy old man a visit. He was going in prison, or going in the ground, one or the other.

My mobile buzzed and I answered right away.

"Ja?"

"I can have it tonight after nine," Jumbo replied. "I'll set up da dashcam like before."

"Okay, we'll try for tonight. I'll get back to you," I replied. "Where do you think would be a good spot?"

"I bin tinkin' 'bout dat. Christ da Redeemer Church on Reverend Blackwell Road. Nuttin' happenin' dere late on Friday night and da car park is dark."

"Well, if there is a God, that ought to get him off his arse to strike Woods down with a lightning bolt," I said, not wanting to pursue how Jumbo knew about the secluded spot for dodgy deals. "Oh, and try to put the camera in a different place. If he sees the same one, he may freak out."

"We be sittin' in da back, rollin' like big balla wit a homey at da wheel."

"What?" I asked, trying to decipher what on earth he just said.

Jumbo laughed. "Don't worry your skinny white ass, Miss Sommer, I got you covered."

"Okay," I replied. I was ready to stop talking which was overriding my desire to micromanage the situation. "Don't forget the stickers."

"I got it," Jumbo said, and we ended the call.

I kept forgetting to tell Jumbo to drop the Miss Sommer business, especially if he insisted on referring to my arse in the same sentence.

I dialled Baby-G. "Talk to me, girl," she answered on the second ring.

"Tonight, after nine-thirty," I told her, giving Jumbo thirty minutes leeway. "Christ the Redeemer Church on Reverend Blackwell Road in West Bay."

"Damn," she muttered. "You tink dat man gonna see da light?"

"Woods couldn't see the light if a choir of angels carried his sorry carcass up to the gates," I spat in reply.

"Dat da truth. I see what he say. I gotta be dere again?"

"It would be better. He trusts you."

"Damn fool," she muttered. "Fine. But if it run past ten-thirty I gotta be somewhere else, honey. Mama gotta pay da rent."

I wasn't sure how to respond. The town heavy and a hooker with a pressing engagement were helping me set up an essentially illegal sting at a church on a street named after a reverend. We'd all be lucky to walk away unscathed.

"Okay. Let me know what the *drittsekk* says."

Baby-G laughed. "It sounds so cool when you get all bitch-catty. I bet dem men like it when you get all up in deir faces, huh?"

"Let me know," I said, and got off the call as quickly as I could.

Getting all bitch-catty up in their faces had played a major role in getting me suspended, or at least a significant contributor, so I didn't want to be reminded about it. Baby-G was just kidding with me, but it was still too raw.

What I felt like doing was crashing face down on the bed and going to sleep, but now I needed to pick up Jazzy, produce food for us both, then try and stay awake for my impromptu sting operation. I glanced at my watch. It was almost six-thirty. I started a small pot of coffee, peeled out of my swimsuit, and stood under the shower, leaving the water on cold.

Washing the salt from my skin felt wonderful and the water cascading down my body created a mental as well as a physical cleansing. The planets had aligned for me today. Unfortunately, it had been in the perfectly wrong way. I needed to be careful how I moved forward as it would be easy to slip into the same hole again where nothing felt worth the trouble anymore.

Maybe finding another job was the right thing for me to do. If I could gather the evidence needed to put Woods away, then part of the reason I'd joined the force in the first place would be complete. I wasn't completely sure how much money I had in my bank account, but I wasn't going to starve for a month or three. Archie Winters had left me with access to a bunch of money if things got really sticky, but it would be a last resort to fence the diamonds hidden in an urn on the reef. I hoped it wouldn't come to that.

I slipped into one of AJ's super comfortable Mermaid Divers sun dresses she sold from her website and poured coffee into my travel mug. Using the torch function on my mobile I picked my way across the woods and ducked through the hole I'd made in the fence. The Jeep started on the first crank, and I let it idle for a minute before pulling away.

Jazzy's school friend lived off Powell Smith Road in the middle of West Bay, so I wound my way around the small streets until I found the house I'd been to several times. As I was about to climb out of the Jeep, the front door opened, and Jazzy's mop of wild frizzy hair appeared. She waved back to her friend in the doorway, then skipped across their front garden and swung herself into the passenger seat, tossing her rucksack in the back.

"Thanks," she said, giving me a broad smile.

A wave of guilt swept over me. I found this kid living on the streets, scrounging for food wherever she could find it, stealing, and sleeping in an abandoned, run-down brick pump house. The life I was providing might not be perfect, but it was certainly better than what she'd had before.

Somewhere, back in the depths of my memories, I could remember being a carefree kid like she was slowly becoming after fending for herself for years. For a fleeting moment I allowed myself to wish that I could be fourteen again. Before my schoolteacher decided he fancied me. Before the shit hit the fan. Before the rest of my adolescence was stolen.

"Hey," I said, and reached over, holding her petite, soft chin in my hand. "How was your day?"

Jazzy looked back at me as though I'd just asked her if she'd had fun behind the bike sheds.

"You okay?" she asked.

"*Ja,*" I replied, fluffing up her unruly hair. "Now tell me how your bloody day was."

The kid didn't draw breath from her friend's house until we pulled into the car park of the Fox and Hare pub. Once she saw we were at one of her favourite places to eat, she forgot about the story she'd been telling me involving a kid she didn't like and began reciting the menu, trying to decide what to order.

By the time we pushed through the double doors and were greeted by Pearl's raspy voice from the stage, Jazzy had settled on fish tacos. She'd probably change her mind five times between then and ordering time, but I didn't care. The kid was happy, which made me happy, and I was slowly starting to allow myself a little joy into the day.

We reached Reg and AJ's usual table where the crowd all stood and made a fuss over Jazzy. AJ came around and grabbed me by both arms.

"You scared me today," she said just loud enough for only me to hear.

"Sorry. I didn't mean to," I replied, unsure what else to say.

"I've seen that look on your face before, and I hoped to never see it again."

I nodded, and for once, it was me that pulled my friend into an embrace. I usually tolerated her hugs as I knew it made her feel better, but this one was me too. Another small wave of tension seemed to melt away.

After a few moments, I drew back, as I was sure AJ would go on hugging me all night. In my hand, my mobile buzzed once more. I waited until we were all seated and stole a look.

'9:30 at the church.'

It was happening. We might actually take down a man who'd managed to slip through every net over who knew how many years. There was no way the resort had been his first venture into the dark side of his desires. I texted Jumbo with the news.

"Hey," I said, turning to AJ. "Can you watch the kid later?"

She looked at me suspiciously.

"No, this is real," I assured her.

"The case?" she asked.

I shook my head. "No. I'm not actually on that case anymore. In fact, I'm not on any cases anymore."

I knew my confession would spark a longer conversation and a million questions, but if I was sticking around, it was time to face what lay ahead. AJ leaned closer with a look of deep concern, and I told her all about it.

25

PIMPIN' BIG POPPY

Friday 9:10pm

I heard a vehicle pulling in and I stayed in the shadows of the church until I could see who it was. I'd left the Jeep in the gravel car park for Miss Pansy's, a small local food shack which was closed at this time of night, and walked to the church. A white Cadillac Escalade with big chrome wheels appeared, parked in the middle of the space behind the church, and turned its lights off. The rear door opened, and Jumbo Flowers unwrapped himself from the back seat.

"What are you wearing?" I asked, walking towards the vehicle.

Jumbo beamed at me in the dim light reaching us from the street. His huge frame was packed into a silver-grey suit, shiny black shoes, and a snazzy white shirt, with the three top buttons undone. He spread his arms out and spun around more nimbly than a man of his size should be able to do.

"Pimpin' Jumbo, Miss Sommer."

I couldn't help but smile. For a brief moment.

"You can call me Nora," I remembered to say. "Who's driving?" I asked, unable to see through the heavily tinted glass.

"A friend," Jumbo replied. "He's cool."

It was too late in the process to worry about that now. I'd leaned on Jumbo for help, and he'd run with it more than I ever could have asked for. While I didn't like another person being involved – especially one I didn't know - it fitted the charade perfectly.

"The camera good to go?"

"Yeah. Not many places to hide dat ting though if it need to seem like da real deal."

I shrugged my shoulders. "It'll have to do. Hopefully he'll have his mind elsewhere."

I took out my mobile and scrolled through my photographs until I found the one of Jazzy I had in mind to use. A cold shiver ran through me as I contemplated a paedophile leching over a photograph of my foster kid. I wasn't sure I could do it. Although Jazzy was perfectly safe with AJ, and I didn't believe Woods had the balls to go as far as kidnapping anyone if it came to that, the whole idea of using her likeness was unnerving. Jumbo stepped closer.

"It's okay, Miss Sommer. I won't let nuttin' happen to your girl."

I looked up at the big man and nodded. I'd beat Woods to death with my bare hands if he ever went near the kid, but it was comforting to know someone else would help me bury the body. I texted the picture to Jumbo, along with another photograph of a teenage girl. The second option was white with long blonde hair and blue eyes. It was one of the few pictures I had of myself as a kid. I'd cropped my father from the shot, leaving me standing on a dock on a summer's day, wearing a swimsuit.

I was betting on the politician preferring his girls to be black, but it didn't matter. As long as he committed to meet one and verbalised it for the recording, I figured we'd have him.

"Make sure you discuss age," I reminded Jumbo. "We won't be able to prove which pictures he was shown, so he has to say something acknowledging the girls are underage."

"I ain't so good at talkin' folks into sayin' tings, Miss Sommer, but I'll try best I can," Jumbo replied.

"Call me Nora," I told him again, and checked my watch. It was 9:25. "Okay. Ring my mobile and make sure you mute yours. I'll be hiding by the church."

Jumbo waved his own phone in the air as he walked back to the Escalade, and I sunk back into the shadows of the building. The church was a modern take on a classic style with interesting pitches to the roof and tall, arched windows. While I wasn't religious at all, it did feel slightly disrespectful to be conducting such an under-handed endeavour in the grounds of a church. But then again, I pondered, surely there was no better place to bring the worst of sinners to justice.

Nine-thirty came and went. Jumbo texted me and I replied, telling him to sit tight and be patient. I paced around in the dark-ness, swatting at buzzing insects, resisting the urge to call or text Baby-G. She would have contacted me if Woods no-showed or had backed out. Her lack of communication suggested she was with him and running late for some reason. Or her later client had moved his appointment up. At 9:45 I was beginning to think that was the case, and I was really tired of smacking bugs against the side of my own head.

Finally, I heard a car pulling off the road into the car park. Headlights swung across the empty asphalt, lighting up the trees at the back. Baby-G's red Renault Clio came into view, moving slowly. She turned towards the middle of the car park, and spotting the Escalade, pulled alongside. My mobile buzzed and I took the call from Jumbo, muting it on my end for now.

The Renault's driver's door opened, and Baby-G stepped out looking resplendent in a multi-coloured striped dress which perfectly matched the colours woven into her bundle of dreads. The front door of the Escalade opened and for the first time I saw Jumbo's friend as he came around and opened the back door of the Cadillac. A skinny guy in baggy jeans and a white vest who certainly looked like he might work for a pimp or a drug dealer.

The man leaned down to look through the Renault's windows and gesticulated for Baby-G's reluctant companion to join Jumbo. Slowly, the passenger door opened, and Woods stepped out. He surveyed the car park carefully before walking around and peering into the Escalade. I wanted to hear what was being said so I unmuted the phone and cupped it tightly to my ear.

"Are you police?" I heard Woods asking.

"Nah, man. We ain't police," Jumbo replied, sounding amused. "Get in man, you're lettin' out all my AC. Let's have a drink. Talk a little."

McKinley Woods took another look around in the darkness, then after a brief pause, stepped into the back of the Escalade, letting the driver close the door.

"Here, brudder," I heard Jumbo say, and presumed he'd handed Woods a drink of some description. "Our girlfriend out dere tells me you interested in entertainment."

Baby-G and Jumbo's driver got into the Renault which I hadn't thought to plan, but was glad they did. As nervous as Woods appeared, the less eyes and ears on him while he talked business, the better.

"Are you wearing a wire?" Woods asked, and I prayed he wouldn't ask about a camera.

"No man," Jumbo said, laughing, and I heard the rustling of his jacket. "You can feel me up if you want, brudder, but you gotta pay for anyting you touch." Jumbo laughed again. "But seriously, my man, whatever your taste, I got you covered."

My mobile fell silent, and I wondered if I'd lost the call until Woods finally spoke.

"What's your name?" Woods asked.

"You can call me Big Poppy," Jumbo replied, and I choked back a laugh.

I wondered if he'd used that play on words before, or come up with it tonight.

"How does this work?" Woods asked.

"Simple, man," Jumbo replied. "You tell me what you like, and

I'll tell you what options I got. Choose from a picture, den we set up da one-on-one time. Hourly, nightly, daily, you name it."

"Do you have someone like Baby-G?" Woods asked, keeping his voice low.

I groaned and swatted at another mosquito buzzing around my ear. This was turning to shit in a way I hadn't anticipated. I was so sure he'd jump at the chance of a young girl, I hadn't considered him choosing any other path. I listened carefully to see how Jumbo would handle this.

"Ain't nobody out dere like Baby-G. I can get you someone similar, brudder, but she'll be a distant second. God only made one like dat girl."

I subconsciously cringed and figured if lightning was coming, referencing the Big-G in the same context as Baby-G ought to bring it on.

"Got a picture?" Woods asked, and I wished I'd figured out a signal code to abort.

I didn't want to compromise Baby-G if this wasn't going to work out, and it certainly appeared to be going pear shaped as AJ would say. We couldn't actually set Woods up with a prostitute to earn his trust enough for him to ask for an underage girl. That would be going way too far and would never hold up in the legal system. Or, more likely, Woods would go free again and he'd finagle a way for me and Jumbo to go down for running an illegal brothel.

"Dis girl fine, but like I say, she ain't no Baby-G," Jumbo said, and I wondered where he'd found a picture at such short notice.

If Woods had an audible reaction, I couldn't hear it.

"Scroll to da next one," Jumbo said. "Udder way, brudder, dat's my momma and even I ain't rentin' out my momma."

The vehicle fell silent again. I couldn't believe Jumbo Flowers was putting on such an Oscar-worthy performance. Baby-G had been a star the other night, but this was next level. He was casual in a take it or leave it way that surely had Woods believing he was legit.

"What you tink, man?" Jumbo asked. "Scroll over one more. That girl is fine, fine, fine, brudder."

Silence again. It was driving me crazy not knowing exactly what was happening. In the distance I heard a police siren, which was growing louder. The timing couldn't have been worse.

"I can set dat up for you dis weekend," Jumbo said, laying on just enough sales pitch while still sounding relaxed.

I hoped they couldn't hear the siren inside the Escalade, but if it came closer there'd be no avoiding it.

"Hear that?" Woods muttered.

"Relax, man," Jumbo assured him. "Dey run around all over da place on a Friday night."

The police car was getting closer, now loud enough where I could hear it in stereo, with the phone's speaker quieter, and the louder raw sound in my other ear.

"I have to go," Woods blurted and I heard him fumbling with the door.

The siren screamed from the street in front of the church, passing by and steadily quietening as it kept on going.

"Told you, brudder," Jumbo said, sounding unperturbed. "Get you anudder drink?"

The door closed again, and Woods remained inside the Cadillac.

"I'm good," he said, declining the drink.

"What's it gonna be, brudder?" Jumbo asked, applying a little more pressure. "See someting you like?"

"Maybe," Woods replied. "How do I reach you?"

"You reachin' me now, my man. Best deals are done man to man, you feel me?"

"I'm unsure of my schedule. Can I contact you on WhatsApp?"

"No disrespect, my friend, but I don't know shit about you 'cept Baby-G vouches for you. Dat goes a long ways wit me, but not all da way. I took da time to meet you tonight, and dat's cool, I happy to make da connection, but we either meet in person where I control da venue, or you reach me through Baby-G. Down da road, once we done business, you get my digits. Dat cool, my man?"

"Understandable," Woods replied. "I'll be in touch."

I heard the car door open and looked up. Woods exited the Escalade and Jumbo's friend jumped out of the Renault, holding the door for the politician.

"Sorry, Miss Sommer," Jumbo said over the phone. "I tried."

"Call me Nora," I replied into my mobile, watching Baby-G pulling away. "You did great. We'll just have to hope he reaches out again."

"He gonna call, Miss. I could tell. You shoulda seen his eyes light up when I showed him your girl, Miss. All I could do not to beat dat man into next week."

I ended the call and walked out of the shadows with my palms sweating and my teeth clenched so tight my jaw ached.

26

EDVARD'S NO HELP

Saturday 7:30am

I opened one eye and saw light sneaking into the house by the edge of the curtains. After a few moments, relieved my headache had finally dissipated, I swung my legs out of bed. Behind me, a frizz of hair protruding from the covers and the soft sounds of breathing told me Jazzy was still sleeping. I flipped my mobile over on the bedside table and was surprised to see it was 7:30am. I couldn't remember the last time I'd slept in this late. Even on my days off. Which they might all be moving forward. That thought was a gut punch to start the day.

My mobile screen also showed me I'd missed two texts and a call. All from Kayleigh. After a quick visit to the loo, I splashed water on my face, started the coffee maker, and tip-toed out to the deck. Dropping into one of the wooden chairs, I took a moment to soak up the view. I'd missed the magical time during and after sunrise, but it was still a gorgeous vista with small swells gently rolling in and lapping against the ironshore less than ten metres away.

The first text apologised for messaging so early and asked me to call her. She'd sent it at 6:55am. The second text, sent twenty minutes after the first, stressed an urgency. The missed call with no voicemail had come ten minutes after that, so just before I'd woken up. The silenced but vibrating mobile may have been what woke me. I called her back.

"Nora," she answered, whispering. "I'm sorry to bother you so early, but something is going on."

"What?" I asked, annoyed she was wasting time with unimportant details instead of getting to the point.

"My father's partner, Braithwaite, is here."

"I know," I replied, and realised I hadn't spoken to Kayleigh since I'd confronted Braithwaite and caused another shitstorm. "I saw him yesterday."

"You did?" she responded, understandably surprised. "Well, I think he and Raylene are up to something."

"Up to what?" I asked again, getting more frustrated, but really at myself.

Whatever they were up to didn't matter anymore. I was impotent to do anything about it, but Kayleigh didn't know that.

"I overheard Raylene talking to him on the phone a while ago. She thought I was still asleep in my room, and she stepped out to the patio. But I got up and could hear from the living room. They're meeting someone this morning. She's getting ready now."

"Who?" I asked.

Kayleigh paused for a moment. "I don't know. I couldn't tell. I think he'd set up the meeting."

"Where?"

"I'm sorry, I didn't hear that either, but it sounded like he was picking her up."

"When?"

"At eight," Kayleigh replied. "I did hear her say she'd be out front at eight."

I glanced at the time on my mobile, then put it back to my ear.

"Okay, that gives us twenty minutes," I began, and then

stopped myself. *Fy faen*. "I can't do anything, Kayleigh. I've been suspended."

"What?" she gasped. "Why? What happened?"

"I interviewed Braithwaite, and it didn't go that well," I said, unsure exactly how to explain the situation.

"The police don't want to investigate my father's case anymore?"

"It's not that," I stammered. "Actually, it's partly that, but not in the way you're thinking." This was a real pain in the arse to discuss without getting long winded. Which for me was using more than five or six words. "Look, I'm suspended because I pushed a few rules too far. But what it means is I'm not an active constable right now, so I can't do anything to help you. I'm sorry."

I waited through a long pause.

"Then help me as a friend," she finally said.

I wasn't sure how to respond. Calling me a friend was a stretch at best, but Kayleigh didn't strike me as a manipulating person, so I took her appeal as genuine. She was desperate. The pain of losing her father was being compounded by the news of his will, and the odd behaviour of Raylene who she'd had no reason to distrust before. None of which should be my concern at this point, as I had my own problems to deal with.

I sighed. "We'll follow at a distance and see where they go, but that's all I can do. If anyone finds out I did this, I'll never get my job back."

"Thank you so much, Nora," Kayleigh whispered, palpable relief in her voice. "I promise we'll be careful. I'll hide by the entrance and meet you there."

"Fine," I muttered, and ended the call.

Of all the impetuous things I'd done lately, this simply added to the reasons why Whittaker shouldn't reinstate me. Movement at the other end of the deck caught my eye as Edvard clambered over the edge and stared at me.

"What am I supposed to do?" I asked him. "Turn my back on her?"

As usual, the stupid lizard was of no use to me, so I went back inside to get dressed and pour coffee into my travel mug. Jazzy stirred, rolled over, and ignored me as I hurriedly threw on leggings and a T-shirt. I only owned three baseball caps, two of which had RCIPS or police emblazoned across the front, so I grabbed the third. It was one AJ had given me with a Mermaid Divers logo on it. Perfect for blending in around the island which was so popular as a dive destination.

Opening the fridge, I searched for anything that would pass as breakfast and was reminded once more that groceries didn't magically appear like they did when I was a kid. I tore off a wilted-looking leaf of lettuce, snatched up my coffee and headed for the door. Edvard watched me cautiously as I trotted down the steps of the deck, and started when I threw the lettuce his way, but he was already munching by the time I'd disappeared into the woods.

I pulled into the north entrance to Caribbean Plaza, a U-shaped shopping centre opposite the Caribbean View Residences. It was two minutes before eight and most of the businesses hadn't opened yet, so the car park wasn't busy. I found a spot which mostly hid the Jeep behind a hedge but allowed me to see across the road, and I texted Kayleigh to let her know I was there.

'Raylene is waiting in the lobby,' she messaged back.

The driveway from the gates to the front entrance of the main tower rose above street level as the parking below was only half underground to avoid flooding. Being this close to the ocean on the flat island meant they couldn't dig any lower without going below the water table. From where I sat, I couldn't see the elevated entrance which was also hidden behind landscaping. I called Kayleigh.

"Can you make it across the road without being seen from the lobby?" I asked before she had time to say a word.

"I think so," she replied.

"Hurry before Braithwaite gets here," I told her and hung up.

A moment later she appeared from behind the guard hut at the entrance, and briskly walked across West Bay Road. I was pleased to see she'd chosen shorts and a plain blouse to wear. She'd blend in with the tourist crowd.

"Hey," I greeted her as she climbed into the passenger side of the Jeep.

"Thank you for doing this. I don't know what I'd do without your help."

A hire car turned into the entrance to Caribbean View Residences and stopped at the guard hut. I was glad of the distraction, so I didn't have to respond to Kayleigh's flattering words. They made me uncomfortable for too many reasons.

The guard waved Braithwaite on, so he turned right and drove up the slope to the lobby entrance, disappearing from our view. I backed out of the spot and pulled down to West Bay Road, stopping a few metres back to remain somewhat hidden. A few moments later, the hire car appeared at the condo's exit, and after waiting for a gap in traffic, turned left and drove north. I pulled across West Bay Road and blended in from the turn lane, placing me four cars behind Braithwaite.

A little over a kilometre up the road, the hire car eased to the centre lane, and waited on two oncoming cars. I slowed and was preparing to go past the turn, as I didn't want to pull up right behind them, when they turned right on Lime Tree Bay Avenue. I nipped into the turn lane and braked hard, slowing enough to make the turn as well. Now only 50 metres ahead with no cars between us, Braithwaite turned left into Governors Square, another shopping centre, although this one was a lot bigger with more shops and businesses. I passed by.

"They went in there!" Kayleigh said loudly over the wind and tyre noise.

"I know," I replied, and turned into the next available entrance. "Try and see where they went."

Following directly behind them was bound to earn a glance in the rear-view mirror so I chose to use another entrance, but now we ran the risk of crossing paths with them.

"I don't see them," Kayleigh said, unbuckling her belt and pulling herself up higher. "There," she shouted, pointing across the car park.

I turned left, heading in the general direction she'd indicated.

"I'm pretty sure that's them," Kayleigh said. "They've parked in front of the far building."

Stopping where my lane met the one they'd turned in on, we both looked right and saw Braithwaite and Raylene entering a business. I turned their way and drove slowly past.

"Stay in your seat," I told Kayleigh. "Cayman International Financial Advisors," I read aloud from the sign over the door. "That mean anything to you?"

"I can't say it does," Kayleigh replied as I pulled around to park on the next lane over.

Shutting the engine off, we sat in the Jeep and kept an eye on the building through the two rows of cars between us. The sun was getting intense and, not for the first time, I wished I had a top of some sort for the Jeep. One day I'd get my shit together and order one, but getting odd items like that to the island was always a pain in the arse.

In the corner of the shopping centre was Perk Up Coffee Shop & Cafe, and my stomach was beginning to complain about the lack of breakfast.

"Want a coffee?" Kayleigh asked, presumably seeing me staring longingly at the sign.

"I missed breakfast," I replied.

"I'll get us something," she said. "I haven't eaten either."

I was about to tell her to stay in case Braithwaite and Raylene came out, but I figured if they had a meeting scheduled, it ought to take more than a few minutes. I handed her my travel mug.

"Coffee. Black. And something to eat, please."

Kayleigh hopped out and began walking away.

"Don't order anything fancy. It'll take too long," I called after her.

She looked a little disappointed, so I guessed she'd planned on ordering one of the drinks with the long names that tasted so good. I needn't have worried about time. Kayleigh was back, breakfast consumed, and we sat sweating in the hot sun for another fifteen minutes before Braithwaite and Raylene reappeared. They did not look pleased.

I couldn't make out what they were saying, but they were both doing the whisper shouting thing at each other, fighting to keep their voices down while barking and hissing back and forth. Their doors slammed closed and by the body language, their disagreement continued inside the car.

I managed to manoeuvre myself into position five cars behind them by the time we returned to West Bay Road, and we followed them back to the condo building. I parked in the same spot across the road, and after just enough time for Raylene to have exited the hire car, Braithwaite pulled down the slope to the road and drove away.

"I don't know what I was expecting them to do, but that wasn't worth bothering you over," Kayleigh admitted.

I shrugged my shoulders. "I disagree. We learnt something."

"I suppose it is odd that they'd be talking to financial advisors in Grand Cayman," Kayleigh said, mulling it over. "Raylene never really liked it here. It was always Dad's place."

"And one thing is now clear," I added. "Whatever they're up to, they're doing it together."

My mobile buzzed and I looked at the screen. Baby-G was calling.

"Hey," I answered.

"Dis shit messin' wit my beauty sleep now, girl," she said, and I could picture her rocking her head from side to side and pointing a long-nailed finger at me.

"What happened?"

"Dat filthy old bastard wanna meet da girl, dat's what."

"*Dritt*," I mumbled in surprise.

"Okay, dat one don't sound so nice when you say it," Baby-G responded.

Despite Jumbo thinking Woods would call again, I'd doubted it. Once again it had felt like the scheme had run aground. So much so, that I hadn't given it any thought since I'd calmed myself down last night. Now I had a big problem. *What to do next?*

"Gimme an hour. I'll call you back," I said, and hung up.

27

COFFEE AND IMPLODING PLANS

Saturday 10:00am

Kayleigh ran to get back to the condo before Raylene. Taking the path alongside the edge of the property and avoiding the tower building altogether would get her there first. I hoped. But now I had something else altogether to worry about. I couldn't see a way McKinley Woods was going to hand over money to Jumbo without seeing the girl he'd be paying for. That would mean using Jazzy as bait, which was wrong on so many levels.

I'd been bound and determined to keep the kid away from the likes of Woods and his kind of depravity and perversion, so putting her right in the middle of a dangerous operation was unthinkable.

Still sitting in the car park, I gripped the steering wheel so tight it made my hands ache. Usually, I'd go straight to detective Whittaker to lean on his experience and level-headedness to come up with a solution, but how could I do that now?

I stewed that notion over in my mind for a few minutes. *What difference would it make at this point?* He'd be livid that I'd been chasing Woods in my spare time, adding another nail or two to my already hammered tight coffin. My professional and possibly my personal relation with Whittaker was down the toilet, but he was still the smartest man I knew, and he might just have a solution up his sleeve. I hoped that solution would include the police taking over the operation, but I wouldn't know unless I asked. I dialled his number.

"Hello, Nora," he answered in a stern tone. "If this is about your situation, I'm afraid I can't discuss it with you until your hearing."

"It's something else," I said.

"Okay. How can I help you?"

"It's better if we meet to discuss this," I said, wishing I'd thought through my spiel a little better.

"I need at least a clue as to what this is about, Nora."

I took a deep breath. "I've created a situation you won't like, but you'll appreciate the intent. Now I need your help."

There was silence on the end of the line. I waited.

"If you're ever offered a job selling anything, Nora, turn it down. The world's not ready for your level of honesty, and you'll never make a penny."

"Where can I meet you?" I asked, hoping his reply meant he'd agree in some way.

"I didn't say I would," he responded.

"I know. But you will," I replied, praying more than believing. "For your own curiosity if nothing else."

I heard what sounded like the briefest of laughs, but it could have been a bird squawking.

"It does sound like the RCIPS ought to be aware of whatever mess you've created now," he said. "You can buy me a coffee at Daily Grind. I'll be there in the time it takes to walk from the station."

"Okay," I said, and ended the call before he could change his mind.

Daily Grind was a small coffee shop in downtown, so he'd probably get there before me. I backed out of the spot and pulled down to the road. The tourist traffic had picked up now everyone was awake and running about enjoying their holiday. A local soon let me in the line of traffic, and I tooted my thanks with the horn. The guy in front driving a hire car waved a hand in the air and looked in his rear-view, annoyed that I was annoyed at him. Which of course I wasn't. Except for the fact he was part of the slow-moving line that would make me late. So, I guess I was becoming annoyed at him after all.

It took me twenty minutes to travel the four kilometres, find a parking spot, and jog to the shop. Whittaker was sitting at a table sipping a cup of coffee. I nodded to him and ordered a black coffee. The young woman rang it up on the till.

"Seven dollars CI," she said, and I frowned.

She pointed towards Whittaker who held up his cup. I paid the tab and left a dollar tip. The woman handed me a cup of scalding hot coffee and I carefully carried it to the table.

"Thanks for the drink," Whittaker said as I sat down.

"Thanks for meeting me," I replied.

"Well, tell me what this is all about, and I'll decide whether I made a mistake or not."

I wanted to sip my coffee to buy myself time, but it was way too hot. Usually, I preferred getting straight to the point, but too much was riding on this conversation, and I found myself unsure. Perhaps even nervous.

"McKinley Woods," I said, diving right in. "We've been after him for years now, right?"

Whittaker nodded slowly and didn't say a word. I wasn't sure if he was trying, but he couldn't hide the concern on his face.

"He was a member at The International Fellowship of Lions," I continued.

"He wasn't on the list we had," Whittaker said, his frown deepening.

"He was a member," I reiterated.

"Can you prove that?" he asked.

"We wouldn't be sitting here having this conversation if I

could," I replied, a little too smartly. "Sir," I added in a belated effort to soften the delivery.

He considered questioning me further on the validity of the claim, but either kept his doubt to himself, or decided he believed me. "Fair enough," he said. "Continue."

"I discovered he's been hiring a local prostitute. I had planned to come to you with this so we could set something up, but I met the woman in question and she's willing to help us put him away on a greater charge."

"We can't simply ignore what this woman is doing if we have knowledge of it, Nora. Prostitution is illegal, as you well know."

I held up a hand. "Would you rather bust Woods and a hooker on prostitution charges which will net her more trouble than him and nothing more than fines, or leave her alone and take him down with something substantial?"

"In theory that's an easy answer," Whittaker said cautiously, "but you haven't got to that part yet."

"Okay, I will. The prostitute - let's call her Gee," I said, and Whittaker grinned.

"You mean Baby-G."

"*Dritt.* You know her?" I asked in surprise.

"I've arrested her in the past, if that's what you mean by knowing her," he made clear.

I sighed. This was going as poorly as I thought it would, and I hadn't got to the part he really wouldn't like yet.

"She knew he likes younger girls, so we set up a situation where Woods met with a man who could arrange an underage girl for him," I said, and waited a beat for the wrath to come down on me.

Instead, Whittaker looked at me blankly. "Continue," he repeated.

"Woods has been hesitant at every step, and I was trying to record him on a traffic cam in the car where they met, but he's too careful with what he says out loud."

"That's actually quite clever," Whittaker said thoughtfully.

"He's had more than a few run-ins with the law, so I think he's very guarded," I replied.

"Not Woods. Using a traffic camera. I'm not certain it's admissible, but I assume you'd argue it was similar to security camera footage."

"We put a sticker on the outside and inside of the vehicles," I pointed out.

"Then you might have a chance," Whittaker admitted.

"Regardless, he didn't incriminate himself to a prosecutable extent, so it doesn't matter. Which brings us to the problem," I said, surprised Whittaker hadn't read me the riot act about what I'd told him so far.

"You have to put together an actual meeting involving an underaged girl," he said, pre-empting my next line.

I nodded. "Exactly. It's tonight."

Whittaker sipped on his coffee, so I drank some of mine now it was cool enough, and waited for him speak next. We sat in silence for a good while.

"Who is the other person involved?" he finally asked.

"Jumbo Flowers."

His eyebrows shot up. "You had Jumbo Flowers playing a pimp?"

I nodded again. "He was brilliant. Actually, they both were."

"I get Baby-G is doing this in trade for not being prosecuted, but why is Jumbo helping you?"

"Because I asked him, and he hates Woods," I replied.

Whittaker allowed himself a slight grin, before quickly returning to a stern frown.

"Obviously, none of this helps your situation, Nora," he began, just as I'd let myself think he was putting aside the fact I'd run an off-duty sting operation. "You should have come to me with the concept at the very beginning."

I think he'd been lost and intrigued by the story, but was now slipping back into his official role and realising how I'd wandered outside the lines once more. Well, actually I'd started and ended outside the lines.

"This is exactly the behaviour which has earned you a suspension, Nora. Why on earth am I only hearing about this now?"

"Because there was nothing to tell you at first," I said, struggling not to sound defensive. "I followed the guy to see what he was up to. He's a pervert, so I knew he'd be up to something at some point. You never would have approved me doing that."

"Correct!" he said, louder than I think he'd intended.

The young barista looked up briefly then continued cleaning behind the counter. Fortunately, we were the only patrons.

"That's because it's harassment when you follow someone without probable cause."

"My probable cause is that I know he's a fucking paedophile!" I snapped back.

Fy faen. Talk about throwing petrol on the fire. I continued to be my own worst enemy.

"I'm sorry, sir. I really do see and understand that some things I do are unacceptable for a constable. I don't deserve the badge. But we have to get McKinley Woods off the street. He's a predator."

Whittaker puffed out his cheeks in a long sigh. "I agree. I think we all know Woods is an unsavoury individual. But he has an amazing network of connections and manages to walk every time."

"Or delay and delay until it falls out of the public eye," I pointed out.

"Correct. Which means to get a conviction to stick, it has to be squeaky clean from beginning to end, and what you have going is not even close, Nora."

"But it can be," I replied. "If *you* take over from here. Everything that has happened to this point has involved me and concerned citizens. Right now, McKinley Woods is waiting to hear where and when he can be introduced to an underage girl who he's expecting to pay for. An undercover operation I put in motion as a constable, and handed to you when the perp took the bait."

Whittaker drew in a sharp breath. "I don't think a judge will see it that way."

"Why?" I countered. "Because I didn't inform you until now?

That's not illegal, sir. It might not be ideal procedure, but there's nothing illegal about it."

"And when it comes to light that this operation took place while the constable involved was under a suspension?" Whittaker asked. His voice was firm, but there was sympathy for what he had to point out to me.

"It's not ideal, I know, and I'm sorry that I've made everything difficult for you, but we can't let Woods get away. Whether I've cornered him, or completely screwed up, one thing's for sure… if we drop this now, he'll smell a rat and be even harder to pin down in the future. I doubt we'll have an opportunity like this again."

Whittaker sipped more coffee and thought it over some more.

"He'll want to meet the girl," Whittaker said. "Who is he expecting?"

A knot twisted in my stomach. The words felt so dirty, I wasn't sure I could spit them out.

"We showed him a picture of me when I was a kid," I started shakily.

"Did he ever see you at the resort?" Whittaker asked before I could continue.

"Not in person, but I can't swear he never saw a picture of me. But I'm not his type, so he wouldn't have paid much attention."

"What is his type?" Whittaker asked as though the question tasted awful in his mouth.

"Black. He likes Baby-G so his taste in adult women seems to be big and bouncy, but it appears he prefers his young women to be… very young."

"Who did you use?" Whittaker asked, and I could already tell he knew the answer.

"He saw a picture of Jazzy," I admitted.

"Damn it, Nora," he muttered.

I'd never heard the detective swear before. Not once. Ever.

"Whose kid should I have used, sir?"

For a moment his eyes bore into me like a power drill, and then they relaxed a little, and he slowly shook his head.

"I don't have a good answer for that," he replied. "We should never have to make such decisions."

"Which is why Woods needs to be put away," I reiterated.

"Is Jazzy willing to be involved?" Whittaker asked. "Are you willing to risk her being involved? You understand what this could mean with the Department of Children and Family Services?"

I hadn't broached the subject with Jazzy, but I knew what the kid would say. Of course, she didn't really understand the dangers involved, but if Whittaker ran the operation, I felt sure she'd be physically safe. It was the exposure to the shocking reality of what other humans are capable of that worried me more. Sure, she'd need to learn about these things in order to avoid them in the future, but fourteen was just too young.

"I know. If this goes even slightly sideways, they'll take her away. But putting Woods away is worth the risk."

I said the words, and just a day ago I'd been close to leaving her in the hands of the Department of Children and Family Services, but today I knew I didn't want that. Which meant we had to succeed.

Whittaker leaned forward. "I'd have to contact them and tell them what we're doing."

"I understand."

"You couldn't be involved from this point forward, Nora. You can't be there."

"I understand."

"Where is this meeting supposed to happen?" Whittaker asked.

"We haven't arranged that yet, but I'm hoping he'll prefer his condo on the beach. It's where he meets Baby-G."

"This goes against my better judgement, Nora, but I'll see if I can put a small team together at this short notice. I'm concerned Woods might have ears in the department."

"Thank you, sir," I breathed in total relief.

He shook his head. "Don't thank me, Nora. I want Woods just as badly as you do. I just hope this crazy scheme doesn't implode on all of us."

28

EVALUATE. CHOOSE. ACT. REVISITED

Saturday 12:30pm

After a series of calls and texts with Baby-G and Jumbo, I'd finally convinced them both that having Whittaker and the RCIPS involved was a good thing. I'd assured them both that their efforts would be appreciated by the police department, and they'd be involved as little as possible in the prosecution case that hopefully would follow. They were smart enough to know that my assurances didn't mean shit, as I had zero clout, but we all agreed we'd come this far, so there was no going back.

I'd only made it as far as the Jeep, which fortunately was beneath the shade of a bitter plum tree, but was still sweating from the balmy heat. My mobile dinged once more with a text from Baby-G, who confirmed Woods had agreed to meet at his condo on Seven Mile Beach at nine o'clock. I passed the news on to Whittaker and Jumbo.

Now I had one more hurdle to clear. Jazzy. I was sure she'd readily agree to help in any way, but the problem was going to be me. I needed her to understand the gravity of what we'd be doing, without going into too much detail. To my knowledge, she was yet to kiss a boy, and while she knew all about the birds and the butterflies, it was all a far cry from the disgusting behaviour of a man like Woods.

Hearing it in my mind, I think I got the sex phrase wrong, but my phone buzzing once more stopped me from worrying about it. It was Kayleigh. *Dritt*. I didn't have time right now and if Whittaker found out I was still talking to her, he'd hit the roof. With all that in mind, I still couldn't bring myself to ignore her. She'd just lost her father.

"Hey," I answered.

"I have a copy of the prenup agreement," she said.

Her voice was calmer and steady, unlike her tone that morning. Determined, perhaps.

"Any surprises?" I asked.

"Not really, but there's a lot of legalese that's hard to follow. I've an appointment with the solicitor at one o'clock. Can you come with me?"

"What for?" I asked.

I wished I could be more patient, but there was too much going on for wasted words.

"Are you asking why I'm meeting with the solicitor again, or why I'd like you with me?" she asked, sounding surprised, or maybe hurt. I couldn't tell.

"Both," I replied.

"Because I need to understand what's going on with all this company stuff, and I want to find the reason my father took his own life," Kayleigh responded. "The answer has to be amongst this paperwork somewhere."

She paused for a moment, and I wasn't sure if she was going to continue or not, but I remained quiet.

"I'd like you there as you're the only other person I can trust who sees the whole picture. And, quite honestly, I need the support. I can pay for your time if need be."

Kayleigh's comment about money threw me for a loop. *Did she think she could buy a friend? Or was she just desperate for help?* My gut told me it was the latter, but it was tough keeping everything straight in my mind.

"I would never take your money," I told her. "I'll come and get you. We can be there by one. But afterwards I have to go."

"Thank you!" she told me again as I hung up.

I started the Jeep and let the engine idle for a minute, contemplating whether to call Jazzy. I settled for a text asking where she was and what she had planned for the day. Driving north, I resisted using the turn lane to overtake the slow and heavy traffic, but I wished I was in the patrol car and could flick on the lights. Jazzy texted back shortly before I reached the Caribbean View Residences.

'Home. Have friend over. No big plans.'

Kayleigh was standing by the entranceway, and I pulled to the side so she could hop in. Rather than attempt a U-turn in the busy traffic, I drove north and turned right on Canal Point Drive. I handed Kayleigh my mobile.

"Type a reply for me."

She took the phone.

"Keep your evening free, I need help with something."

Kayleigh typed while I drove to the intersection with the bypass. It forced me north again, but only for a short distance where I circled the roundabout and continued south, hoping Esterly Tibbetts Highway would be faster than the coast road.

"That it?" Kayleigh asked.

I nodded and she sent the text.

"Who's 'The Kid' if you don't mind me asking?" she asked, obviously having seen the name I saved Jazzy's number under. "Do you have a child?"

"More like she has a 'me,'" I replied. "I foster this kid, Jazzy. Jasmine, but she'll roll her eyes if you call her that."

"Bloody hell," Kayleigh responded. "How old are you?"

"Same age as you."

"I'm kicking around in university while you've moved to a

Caribbean Island, become a copper, and fostered a kid," Kayleigh said. "I feel like a slouch."

"Trust me," I shouted to be heard over the wind as I dodged around cars on the dual carriageway. "Do it your way. I've made a mess of things."

We made it back into George Town shortly after one, and I parked on the pavement across the road from the solicitors' office. Hopefully, any traffic police coming by would recognise my Jeep, but that was unlikely in George Town. I didn't know that many of the constables there.

The old lady wasn't at the front desk as it was Saturday, but Josephine heard us come in and called us back to her office. Once we were all seated and the greetings were over with, Josephine opened the discussion.

"I've had more time to go through the papers since we last met, and I think I have a clearer picture of the situation. My associate, Horace, also helped. I think I told you, he handles the corporate contracts."

"Okay, let's start with the business side," Kayleigh responded. "And then perhaps you can help me understand this prenuptial agreement."

Josephine looked up from sorting through a stack of papers in a file. "You know marital law isn't my area of expertise either, so I'll direct you to someone who can help you properly, but I don't mind going over it with you."

"I appreciate it," Kayleigh replied. "Now, how about StarLife?"

"I'll try and make this simple, although the details are far from it, as you can imagine," Josephine began. "At the root of everything, your father wanted StarLife to be yours. He willed his part of the company to you, and he also put into play a buyout of his partner, which would make you the sole owner if Mr Braithwaite were unable to counter. The buyout clause in the partnership contract states that either side can make an offer to buy the other out, one time in every three years."

"Every three years?" Kayleigh questioned.

"I believe the intent was to avoid a buyout situation being presented relentlessly and detracting from the business itself, but that's simply my assumption based on the language," Josephine replied. "The buyout price was stipulated as one hundred and fifty percent of the prior twelve months' company gross earnings. Which is substantial in this case."

"But what about the new contract?" I asked. "That looked to be worth a lot."

Josephine nodded. "Indeed it is, and I'm sure it influenced the timing of these events, but we'll get back to that in a moment. So, the buyout has a price stipulation, and a time to respond, which is only three weeks. When they started the company, the numbers involved would probably have been workable in that timeframe, but with the size of the business today, three weeks isn't very long at all."

"So Braithwaite has three weeks from this past Wednesday to make some kind of counter?" Kayleigh asked.

"Correct. And the counter doesn't have to be the full amount. The other partner must show proof he has one hundred percent of the prior year's gross available, which would then void the buyout."

"Is this a normal clause in a partnership contract?" I asked.

"I've never seen anything quite like this before, and neither has Horace," Josephine replied. "Again, we're guessing as to the intent, but it would force both partners to remain on somewhat even financial ground. If one of them wasn't prudent with their personal finances, then they'd run the risk of being bought out of the company."

"You mentioned Braithwaite was frivolous with his money," I directed to Kayleigh.

"He certainly spent more than Dad did on fancy trips and parties," she confirmed.

"Your father may have put this clause in knowing Mr Braithwaite had those tendencies," Josephine suggested. "Businesses have to be financially robust to ride the peaks and valleys of the economy, competition, and a myriad of other challenges. The clause was probably intended to make sure both parties could equally float the business if needed."

"And Braithwaite's divorce just became final recently," Kayleigh said, deep in thought. "Dad timed this so his partner wouldn't be able to react."

"It would appear so," Josephine agreed. "Which brings us to the new contract with Global Clean Power Technologies. It is worth a large amount of money over an extended period of time with options to continue the relationship long into the future. Horace and I both think it will triple the annual gross within three years."

"Okay, but none of this explains why my dad felt the need to end his life. He could have seen all this through and been an even wealthier man. Our plan had always been for me to start working with the firm after university. There was no reason to..."

Kayleigh trailed off, but we all got the point.

Josephine shook her head. "I'm not sure I can help you there, I'm afraid. Except, there is one oddity in the timing which I doubt is a coincidence. The three-week time to counter runs out at nine o'clock on the morning of your birthday."

"Don't contracts usually have something in there about crazy circumstances?" I asked. "I don't remember what that's called."

"Force majeure covers circumstances outside the party's control, such as weather, war, and such. We checked on death and the only relevant clause in the partnership agreement states that the agreement continues in its entirety if one or both partners pass away. The deceased's beneficiary becomes the new partner."

"Then why my birthday?" Kayleigh asked.

"Possibly to simplify the process," Josephine suggested. "Having you take over before the buyout clause ran out would have made for a lot more paperwork, solicitor fees, and complexity."

"This might explain why Raylene and Braithwaite were meeting with financial advisors today," I suggested. "Maybe they're trying to combine forces to meet the criteria for Braithwaite to keep his part of the partnership."

Kayleigh nodded. "It still doesn't make any sense, though. Dad had no reason to kill himself."

We all sat in silence for a few moments. I agreed we were no closer to finding an answer and it didn't seem to make any logical sense. Everything could have taken place exactly as Perry Collins had planned without him blowing his brains out. All except the part where Kayleigh took over. But if he wanted out for some crazy reason, all he had to do was sign his side of the partnership over to her.

"Maybe the prenuptial agreement will tell us something," I said, as much to move things along as anything else.

I was still invested in Kayleigh's situation as well as her father's suicide, but the need to see Jazzy and finish organising this evening was making me antsy.

"I have taken a look through the prenup, per your request, Kayleigh, and it's another slightly out of the ordinary document," Josephine said. "I've never personally heard of this cooling-off period they included."

She handed Kayleigh a copy, who in turn passed it to me.

"I have a copy on my phone," she said, and began opening the file on the small screen.

Josephine handed over her copy. "Here. I'll look at it on my monitor."

We all sat in silence reading, or more like scanning the document, which was ten pages long. Most of it handled legal rubbish about which court would handle a divorce, arbitration clauses, and other stuff I couldn't follow. The real details were covered in a few pages, outlining the monthly amount payable to Raylene if they divorced inside ten years. It was a large sum of money in my world, but not nearly enough to get involved in buying out half the company.

"Maybe Raylene was trying to borrow against future

payments," I suggested. "That's why they were meeting with an advisor."

"I don't think it went well by the look on their faces," Kayleigh replied without looking up.

I continued reading. It appeared Raylene would get a house they'd purchased after they were married. It was a small holiday cottage in Cornwall. Again, probably worth a lot of money, but half a million wouldn't put much of a dent in the buyout number. And then, the next section made me pause.

"Didn't you say the cool-off bullshit thing was ninety days?" I asked.

Kayleigh and Josephine both looked up at me.

"Yes," they replied together.

"That's what Dad told me," Kayleigh added.

"And he filed so it expired the day before their tenth anniversary?" I asked.

"Yes. Which is the sixth of next month," Kayleigh confirmed.

"Well, I might have found your father's reason to… do what he did," I said, pointing to a line in the agreement. "The contract reads three months, not ninety days."

"Oh my," Josephine gasped, bringing up a calendar on her computer. "That would be 92 days over those three months. The divorce wouldn't be officially filed until after their tenth anniversary. Mrs Collins would get whatever a court would award her. The prenuptial agreement expired."

"What happens to the prenup in the event of his death?" I asked, skimming through the pages.

"It becomes effective on that day," Josephine replied. "It locks in."

"He screwed up the dates," Kayleigh stammered. "My dad killed himself because he made a mistake on the bloody dates? I don't believe it!"

"Their anniversary is before the buyout three weeks expires, correct?" I asked.

Josephine nodded.

"He must have intended to go through with the buyout once he had the new contract signed with that Global whatever company, but then he realised his mistake on the dates," I thought aloud. "His only way to stop Raylene getting half his money was to…"

I managed to stop myself before I spoke the words out loud once more. Kayleigh was in complete shock, and she didn't need to hear them said again.

"Evaluate, choose, then act," I said under my breath, recalling the words he'd sent his daughter.

Kayleigh dropped her head into her hands and sobbed. I put a hand on her shoulder and felt her body convulsing in desperate sorrow as tears fell into her lap. Comforting and consoling was not a talent I possessed, but I squeezed her gently, and didn't say a word for fear of putting my foot in my mouth.

I wasn't sure that finding her answer was worth the pain it was causing Kayleigh, but I couldn't help feeling a small sense of relief. The man had lived by logic and process, and he'd died by the same sword. I respected him for his commitment to his convictions, but there was one loose end still bugging me.

Why have the bottle of Scotch stolen?

29

UNDERCOVER MISFITS

Saturday 4:30pm

"Of course I'll do it," Jazzy said immediately.

Our conversation had gone exactly as I'd predicted so far. She was all in, with no clue what she was letting herself in for, despite my efforts to explain.

"What do you think of this man from what I've told you?" I asked, as we sat on either end of the sofa.

"He's a piece of shit that should be in jail," she replied.

I held up one finger. "Correct." I popped up a second. "Don't swear." And then a third. "How are you going to react when you're in a room with him?"

Jazzy thought for a moment. "I'll have to act like I don't hate him, I suppose."

I nodded. "More than that, you have to put aside all your feelings and play the part, so he believes it."

"I have to be all flirty with him?" she asked, wrinkling her nose.

"No, not that far. Indifferent would be okay. But he can't see that you're scared, or that the situation feels weird to you."

She took a bite of the apple she'd been holding and chewed for a few moments.

"Did they teach you this stuff? At the resort place?"

I nodded again. "The biggest part of their training was convincing us that what was happening was normal and okay. We all knew it wasn't, but after a while of them assuring and encouraging us, it slowly became our lives. Creatures adapt to their environment. We were never allowed to leave the resort unless we were with a staff member, and that was only for special circumstances, so our world became the resort or the company boat. Life was as they presented it to be."

"I guess I understand how that could happen," Jazzy said, not sounding convinced.

"Remember how your life was before you fostered me?" I asked.

She grinned. "*I* fostered *you?*"

"You and that stupid lizard," I said, grinning back at her.

"Sure. It's hard to forget."

"Well, that life was your normal for a long time, right? And now your life is very different, but you've adapted to it."

"That's because I like a comfy bed, a refrigerator, and a shower," she replied, laughing.

"Of course, but before that you would steal things and sleep in the little shack you'd put together. You knew it wasn't how it was supposed to be, but it was how it was. It became your normal."

Jazzy nodded. "That's true, I suppose. So, I have to pretend that being in a room with this arsehole is normal for me."

"Language. And yes," I replied. "He won't get to lay a finger on you, I promise. Jumbo will be there, and Jumbo could carry you under one arm while beating the shit out of Woods with his other hand."

"Language," Jazzy said, and laughed.

"I'm explaining all this, because even though it sounds like it'll be okay, when you're in this strange living room, confronted by a man you know has sick desires for you, and your only friend is Jumbo who you only just met, it'll get real in a hurry."

Jazzy took a moment, and I could tell she was trying her best to mentally put herself in the situation. Even as I explained it all to her, butterflies ran rampant in my stomach, so I could only imagine how nervous she was getting. Or should be if my words were getting through.

I was struggling not to pull the plug on the whole thing. Woods hadn't shown any signs of being a physically violent man, and I figured all 42 kilos of Jazzy could probably put the bastard down with her streetwise scrapping skills, but the mental toll was still my concern.

"What do I have to wear?" was the question that came out at the other end of her contemplation, and it was a good one.

In the picture Woods had been shown, Jazzy was wearing jean shorts and a brown tank top. Normal clothes for a kid running around on a tropical island in the heat. But he wasn't looking at her through that lens.

"Your denim shorts and a tank top, but not the brown one. Something bright. That yellow top with the smiley face on it."

"My 'be happy' shirt?" she questioned. "I don't feel very grown-up wearing that shirt."

"Then it's perfect," I replied, with a butterfly maelstrom in my stomach.

***

I sat in Jumbo's borrowed Escalade's third row of seats. He was next to me, his huge form pressing in all directions, including mine. He was lucky I had a skinny white arse. Baby-G and Jazzy sat in the middle row, and Whittaker and Detective Weatherford were turned around, briefing the group from the front. It had to be the oddest collection of people ever assembled for an undercover police operation.

Whittaker had allowed me to listen in, but after the briefing I'd have to stay here in the West Bay Fire Department's car park while they moved to the Discovery Beach Club condominiums for the operation. At least I trusted everyone in the group, but it would still be torture watching them drive away with the kid.

Weatherford was a good policeman and a solid guy, both in his large-framed build and his reputation. I'd hoped Whittaker would bring a few more bodies, but he'd settled on one trusted man and a warrant for a wire. With Jumbo inside the condo alongside Jazzy, Woods would have a hard time getting away if he decided to bolt at any time.

"Because he's already asked you about being an informant, Jumbo, my concern is he may ask again, so I think it's better to put the wire on Jasmine."

"Jazzy," the fourteen-year-old reminded the detective. "Where does it go?"

"Under your shirt," he replied, and held up the unit, which was nothing more than a tiny microphone wired to a slim and compact battery and Bluetooth broadcast unit, no bigger than a coin. "The receiver unit will be this mobile phone," he added holding up what looked like a regular smartphone. "Jumbo can keep this in his back pocket as it's not a wire so he wouldn't be lying if asked."

"What if I'm asked?" Jazzy asked.

"Then I'm afraid the operation will be over, as we can't lie about it if asked directly," Whittaker explained. "It would make any recorded evidence inadmissible in court."

"Where am I gonna be in all dis?" Baby-G asked. "Don't seem like I need be nowhere, so how about I get on down da road?"

"I think it's important for credibility that you arrive with Jumbo, Miss Brookstone," Whittaker replied, using her legal name. "It will also appear less suspicious to onlookers if you arrive like a family of three. We don't want to raise any curious inquiries from neighbours, and Woods is more likely to be relaxed if he thinks the situation would be observed the same way."

"I ain't never bin..." Baby-G began and then abruptly stopped.

I was pretty sure the rest of her sentence was about to be "*both-*

ered by anyone when I came by the condo", but she'd decided it best not to incriminate herself for no reason. I shared a quick smirk with Whittaker.

"Detective Weatherford will be with me in my car," Whittaker continued. "We'll be listening live through the wire. Any sign of a problem, or when we feel Woods has given us the evidence we need, I'll text Jumbo as we reach the front door." He looked at the big man. "Do not physically engage Woods unless it's absolutely necessary for the safety of Jasmine… Jazzy. Understood?"

Jazzy turned in her seat and Jumbo reached a big hand over the seat back. They bumped fists. Her little hand against his was almost comical. He gave her a wink.

"I got you, little lady," he said in his deep, rumbling tone.

She smiled and nodded.

"Okay," Whittaker said, glancing at his watch. "Let's get Jazzy wired, and we'll all take up positions ready to go at eight. Any questions?" He looked at Jazzy. "Remember, you can call this at any time. No shame, no questions, no trouble. Understand?"

Jazzy nodded again. "I'm fine," she replied, her voice sounding firm, but it was still the small, innocent voice of a young teenager.

"Time for you to leave us, Nora," Whittaker said, and I caught his eye.

He knew it was killing me to watch them go without me. On every level.

"Someone has to fit her wire," I said, pointing to the kid, hoping to buy myself more time.

"We'll step outside while you and Miss Brookstone handle that," Whittaker replied. "Then we need to go. You know this is non-negotiable, Nora. You can't be anywhere near this operation."

"I understand, sir," I replied, which was true.

I didn't like it, but I did understand, and there was no way I was about to risk Woods getting off on a technicality based on me. I couldn't be at the Discovery Beach Condos.

The men stepped out of the Escalade while we attached the wire to the inside of Jazzy's shirt. The kid already had her game face on.

She sat patiently without uttering a word while I fitted the wire and Baby-G fussed and told her what a tiny little thing she was. Which didn't help my state of mind. Once we were done, I took a moment and looked at Jazzy.

"I'm okay, Nora," she said. "Jumbo has my back."

I forced a smile. "Call it if anything turns to shit, okay?"

"I will."

"I'll be screamin' holy hell and beatin' on dat old pervert if anyting go wrong," Baby-G assured me. "Don't worry 'bout dat."

I got out of the vehicle and started towards the Jeep before I freaked out and took the kid home.

"Nora," Whittaker called after me.

I turned. He was reading something on his mobile. I walked over to him.

"An initial report has been sent to Rasha from the lab," he said, without looking up. "She texted me a few minutes ago."

"The Scotch?" I asked, trying to switch gears in my head.

He nodded. "They found a trace of dimethylmercury."

"I don't know what that is, but if it has mercury involved, it shouldn't be in a Scotch bottle, right?"

He finally looked up. "It's incredibly toxic."

"*Fy faen.* She was trying to poison him, but he killed himself instead? Still doesn't make any sense."

"We're probably a long way from proving Raylene put the dimethylmercury in the bottle, but someone was trying to kill whoever would drink from that bottle," Whittaker replied.

"Maybe he did it himself, then changed his mind and used the gun," I suggested.

"Unlikely," Whittaker replied. "Dimethylmercury takes months to kill. He would have become sick, but by the time a doctor could diagnose the cause, there'd be no way to save him. There was a case in the 90s where a researcher was poisoned when a few drops of dimethylmercury spilled onto her latex glove. It immediately ate through the latex onto her skin. She was dead a year later. It took that long."

"After the divorce," I muttered, thinking through what we'd discovered at the solicitors' office.

"I don't see how Raylene had anything to gain from killing Collins," Whittaker said. "We already know the divorce would be final before the ten-year anniversary. But I suppose that in itself is motive for revenge."

"Perry screwed up the dates," I said, knowing I had to reveal what I knew at some point. He'd end up finding out I'd been with Kayleigh at the solicitors, but what would it matter at this stage? "The prenup said three months, and he thought it was ninety days. He filed for divorce too late. Raylene needed him alive, which is why he killed himself."

"But she'd be happy to see him die after that..." Whittaker thought aloud. He put his mobile in his pocket. "We need to go," he said, looking at me. "Later, you can explain to me how you know these things and I don't."

"Yes, sir," I replied. "But that's not the important part," I added, taking out my mobile and calling Kayleigh.

Whittaker frowned at me.

"Who does the company go to if something happens to Kayleigh?" I asked rhetorically, staring back. "If Raylene is capable of murdering her husband, I doubt she'd be opposed to killing her stepdaughter."

The phone rang in my ear, until it went to Kayleigh's voicemail.

"*Dritt*," I muttered, and left her a message to call me as soon as she could.

30

HELL IS A COUNTRY CLUB

Saturday 8:00pm

I parked the Jeep in the back corner of The Palms' dimly lit car park. Between the Discovery Beach Club Condos and where I sat was a huge private residence, so I was hidden from the detectives. I had no intention of interfering, but I also couldn't sit a kilometre away twiddling my thumbs while the kid was in the firing line. I needed to be closer.

If the sting operation went sideways, McKinley Woods wouldn't put himself at risk again, I was sure of it. I told myself I'd make a decision if that situation arose, but I knew deep inside the die was already cast. I couldn't let him get away with his debauchery anymore.

I'd tried Kayleigh again and reached voicemail, so I sent a text asking for her to call me as soon as she could. I thought about telling her why, but that could backfire if the wrong person happened to see the message, and as she wasn't answering the calls, I couldn't be sure she was near her mobile.

As I was about to put my phone down, it buzzed and I accepted the call. Jumbo had offered to let me listen in on the understanding I wouldn't go all Viking if the situation became compromised. I'd promised I wouldn't, but he'd just grinned at me and shook his head. I really did intend on trying not to get involved, but we both knew my promise was hollow.

"You good?" I heard his deep voice ask.

I couldn't hear a reply if either Jazzy or Baby-G had made one, but a knock on a door came next, so I assumed everyone was all set.

"Step inside," a voice I didn't recognise said. "I'm gonna pat you down."

"Who the fuck are you?" Jumbo asked.

"I'm the security guy who's gonna pat you down, else you can turn around and leave," the man said firmly. He spoke with a London accent.

"You a copper?" Jumbo asked.

"No," the man replied.

It was a good question and one a pimp would certainly ask, but our plan had never once addressed the issue of hired muscle. This wasn't Woods' MO at all. He slinked around in the evenings on his own and steered clear of associating himself with known criminals. He rubbed shoulders with other politicians, although in recent times many had shunned him and his bad publicity. I waited anxiously, expecting Whittaker to pull the operation with the unexpected wrinkle.

"Step inside," the man repeated. "We ain't doing this on the doorstep."

There was more shuffling of feet and a door closed. No one said anything for a few moments, and I presumed the guard was searching them. Jazzy had only developed the need to wear a bra in the prior few months and I'd tucked the listening device where that bastard better not touch, or I was in danger of going Viking.

"You best be careful where you put dem hands, sugar," Baby-G snapped. "These goods don't come free."

After a bit, the man must have been satisfied as I heard feet on a tiled floor.

"Welcome to my beach house," Woods said, and my skin crawled. "Everyone have a seat."

"Dis necessary?" Jumbo asked.

"Prudent, I believe," Woods replied, so I figured Jumbo had referred to the security man.

"I assume you're not wearing a wire, are you?" Woods asked, proving Whittaker right.

"I ain't," Jumbo replied. "How 'bout you?"

Woods laughed. "No, I assure you my home is free of any listening devices. What about you two?" he asked, and I stepped from the Jeep, holding the mobile to my ear, prepared to run.

"Someone owe me a hundred for da good time your man have makin' sure I don't, sugar," Baby-G said.

I started jogging across the car park. Even if Jazzy lied, the operation was over. It was pointless to continue. But then I abruptly stopped.

"Of course I am, but you'll have to come and get it," Jazzy said, and giggled.

Baby-G let out a laugh. "I like you," she said, and I was pretty sure I heard hands slap together.

"We got business to discuss, my man," Jumbo said, and I wondered how close Whittaker and Weatherford were to the front door.

They had to have thought this was over too. I certainly had. The kid never ceased to amaze me.

"Graham, would you mind getting drinks for our guests?" Woods asked, although it sounded like an order rather than a request.

So much for anonymity. He'd set up the meet at his own condo and given up the name of his hired help. If Graham had a gun on him, he was going away for a long time.

"Let's talk over here," Woods continued, and I realised we had another problem.

The negotiation was going to take place away from Jazzy and the wire she was wearing. I knew the microphone was powerful, but it could only pick up so much, especially if drinks were being poured and other noises made close by.

"It's a grand an hour, brudder. Two hour minimum," Jumbo said, which I heard clearly as the mobile was in his back pocket.

All I could do was hope Whittaker was also picking it up. Jumbo's second mobile was in his other pocket, but that didn't help unless Jazzy's mic caught the conversation.

"That's pretty steep," Woods replied. "I pay half that for Baby-G."

"Baby-G ain't fourteen years old, my man. You any idea how hard it is to get a girl like dat? You seen, man. She da real deal."

I held my breath. Woods' next words would be the ones that put him away for the rest of his life. *If* they were being heard on the wire. But it didn't matter.

"I'd feel better if we didn't have mobile phones around," Woods said.

Fy faen! Something had spooked him. Maybe he'd seen two phones in Jumbo's pocket, but surely that's expected from a pimp? Every drug dealer on TV has at least two mobiles on the go. Not that I owned a TV or watched any shows, but I remember someone saying that once. I stood at the south end of The Palms' car park unsure what to do next.

"Dese phones are how I do business, man," Jumbo complained. "I gotta answer when dey ring."

"Then you're welcome to step outside, but if you stay in here, the phones are being turned off and held until you leave. Graham, collect all the mobile phones," I heard Woods order.

We'd been so close. But now, even if Woods incriminated himself, we wouldn't hear it.

"How about we close our deal, den you can have da phones, man," Jumbo argued. "If we ain't doing business here, brudder, we gone anyway."

"Hand it over," Graham's voice demanded.

"What's it gonna be, brudder?" Jumbo persisted.

"We'll make a deal. After the phones are out of play," Woods replied.

The line went dead.

I stood there with my mouth open. I felt completely lost. Disconnected. Presumably, Jumbo had handed the mobile over willingly, but I couldn't be sure. If I went down the road and through the car park, I'd risk the detectives seeing me. Unless they were busy knocking down the front door in which case, I wouldn't be able to stop myself barging in too. I looked over at the side of The Palms block of condominiums to where palm trees and the dark of night hid the beach from view. I ran towards the path winding alongside the building.

Short landscape lights marked the walkway then ended where soft floodlights illuminated the powdery sand. A tall privacy hedge of beach naupaka screened the private home, reaching almost to the high tide waves lapping the beach. I ran past the front of the house, the big home's landscape lighting enabling me to see just enough to not fall on my arse.

Reaching the end of the hedge, I squinted towards Discovery Beach Club, where a row of palapas sat in front of the building, and a low concrete wall surrounded a swimming pool. Why anyone would build a pool ten metres from the warm Caribbean Sea was beyond me, but there it was. I kept running in the deep sand until I reached the pool, lit with those fancy underwater lights which changed colours every few seconds. A couple sipped drinks and chatted quietly, sitting on the steps with water up to their waists.

Woods' condo was at the far end of the second building. I was about to move around the pool when I saw movement on the beach in the distance. Someone was heading towards the water. I couldn't make them out clearly in the dark as they'd moved north of the illuminated area, but they'd come from somewhere near the last condominium. There was no way to hold myself back any longer. I stayed low, moving around the low wall, and called Whittaker on my mobile.

"It's all going along fine, Nora. Let me call you when it's over, okay?"

Moving closer, I could tell the figure was struggling to walk in the sand, and he wasn't alone. *A couple going out for a romantic dip in the ocean?*

"I don't think it's fine," I hissed into the phone. "Can you still hear them?"

"I'm listening to Woods ramble on right now," Whittaker replied. "In fact, he won't shut up."

The two figures reached the water's edge and paused. One was tall, and the other much smaller, but they were clear of the condo's lights and becoming even harder to see. The tall one reached down and wrestled with something in the sand, then kept going, splashing into the ocean. I broke into a run, moving to the firm sand where the Caribbean Sea lapped against the beach, beyond the reach of the lights. Sounds of more splashing and a knocking noise reached me from the water as I came closer. I squinted into the night and recognised the sound. Someone was climbing a ladder into a boat.

"Something's wrong, sir," I hissed into my mobile.

"Where are you, Nora?" Whittaker asked sternly.

"What's Woods talking about, sir? Does it make any sense?" I replied, ignoring his question.

"He's tooting his own horn about politics and what he's done for the island," he replied. "Are you on the beach? Why do you think something's wrong?"

"Because two people just left the condo building and are getting into a small boat anchored out front. You need to go into the building now, sir!"

"He hasn't actually incriminated himself yet, Nora. He's still talking, so there's no way he's left."

Whittaker was right. It couldn't be McKinley Woods who was getting on the boat. The detectives would have heard over the mic if he'd moved outside, but I knew in my gut this wasn't going as planned.

"I'm going out to the boat," I said. "I'll see what's going on."

"Nora! You're not supposed to be here. You're on suspension, remember!"

"*Fy faen!* Then un-suspend me, sir! I'm telling you this thing's gone to shit!"

"We need to move," I heard Whittaker tell Weatherford. "Nora. You're temporarily off suspension. Don't make me regret this."

I seemed to hear him say that last part a lot. I ended the call and tossed the mobile onto the sand as I ran into the water. From the boat, I heard a muffled young voice call out. I knew that voice.

The outboard engine started.

I reached the boat, which appeared to be a runabout no more than six metres long. Waist deep in the ocean, I threw a hand over the bow, groping for a hand hold to pull myself up, but instead smacked something metallic. It was wet and sandy. The small anchor, which must have been what the taller figure had retrieved from the beach. From the stern I could hear grunts and guessed he was hauling the second anchor aboard.

"Jazzy," I whispered, and received another muffled groan in return.

Dragging the bow anchor over the gunwale, I planned to dive down and wedge it into the sand, but the man called out.

"That you?"

I recognised Graham's voice by his London accent.

"Get some help," I growled in the deepest voice I could manage.

I hoped the sound of the ocean against the boat disguised my pathetic effort enough to fool him. I heard movement in the boat, and the figure blocked out the stars above me. With all the strength I could muster, I swung the anchor, smashing against some part of his body. The anchor clanked loudly into the open bow, bashing against fibreglass as Woods' security man splashed into the water.

Swinging a leg up, I grabbed the railing and pulled myself into the boat, dropping down next to Jazzy, who was curled up on the deck. Fumbling around her face, I found the duct tape and pulled it from her mouth.

"Woods gotta gun," she blurted, her Caymanian accent kicking back in. "He got Jumbo and Baby-G. He took da microphone from me."

"The detectives are going in now," I told her, feeling for her bindings.

Her wrists were held by duct tape as well, which I was quickly able to unwrap.

Just as I finished, the boat rocked, and I heard Graham attempting to clamber over the side. I yelped as he grabbed my ponytail and yanked me backwards. Fortunately, I hit cushions with my back and while he awkwardly struggled to get over the railing, I reached up and pulled him headfirst into the boat.

I hoped Jazzy had scrambled clear as the man's firm frame hit the deck with a thud.

Not giving him a moment to recover, I leapt on top and punched his face, aiming repeatedly at his nose. His arms came up defensively as he groaned and gasped, my fists, wet with blood, now smashing against his forearms.

He bucked his body, trying to throw me off, and his legs thrashed. From behind, I heard a body slam against something solid. Jazzy screamed, then must have recovered enough to pin his legs as the bucking lessened. I heard a dull thump and Graham gasped, his hands attempting to reach past me. I stole a glance behind, and realised Jazzy was punching the man in his groin for all she was worth. I went back to work on his nose.

All strength drained from the man and just as I paused from hitting him, exhausted, he vomited. I could hear the thumps continue from behind me and Jazzy grunting with each punch she threw.

"Okay, kid," I gasped. "We got him."

I lifted myself up and heard splashing coming from the water.

"Graham?" hissed Woods' voice, then a light shone in my eyes.

I dropped just in time. The bullet flew through the glass windshield of the boat.

"Jazzy!" I yelled, and felt for her.

"I'm okay," she hissed.

I turned back to the bow, staying low out of the light from Woods' torch. I grabbed the anchor once more. He splashed alongside the runabout, heading for the stern and the ladder. The light beam was flying around all over the place as he fought through the waist-deep water.

Jazzy and I could both jump overboard and probably swim clear in the dark, but then Woods would get away.

"Jazzy," I whispered. "Get over the side. Swim to shore."

"I'm not leavin' you!" she hissed back.

"Yes you are," I snapped. "Get in the water, now!"

Jazzy grumbled under her breath, but slipped under the railing and dropped with a splash into the ocean. With her on her way to safety, I crouched in front of the helm as I heard Woods struggling into the boat at the stern.

From the condominiums I could hear shouting, but I knew they couldn't make it out here in time. Woods' torch beam swung all around the little boat and from its angle, I could tell he was standing at the stern.

The light moved down to search the water and I took the brief opening to swing the anchor through the walkthrough gap. Woods fired a wild shot before howling in pain as the anchor connected with some part of him.

Spinning around, I launched, taking two strides before barrelling into the paedophile as he tried to regain his balance. We crashed over the outboard motor and hit the water. Wheeling my arms, I found him and grabbed hold, rolling until my foot felt the seabed. Pushing off, I broke the surface and gasped in a breath while I moved my hands to his throat.

The man's arms thrashed at me, clawing and scraping my shoulders, but I kept his face underwater. Immediately I knew I had the upper hand. He was a soft, old man who'd probably never worked a day of manual labour his whole life. I doubted he could hold his breath for more than thirty seconds, especially having been winded by my charge. The mammalian diving reflex might buy him a little longer, but by fifty to sixty seconds, he'd be breathing water and drowning.

Thirty seconds could feel like an eternity sometimes.

A long time to think.

Don't make me regret this.

Whittaker's words hung in my mind like a wind chime suspended in a desert. Clinking and clanging repeatedly in a vast space with nothing else to be seen or heard.

In a matter of seconds, I would remove the last member of The International Fellowship of Lions resort from this world. The last member living in the Cayman Islands at least. *And what then?*

There'd be no hiding the fact that I'd executed McKinley Woods. I would go to jail for the crime. Jazzy would be back in the foster care system. My friends and family would be devastated. Edvard would miss his free snacks.

Woods' thrashing was becoming more desperate, but much weaker.

I could hold him under until he stopped, then swim off into the ocean and finish what I'd started the other day. Take myself down to the reef and stay there. *And what would that change?*

Nothing, except I'd be dead instead of spending the next twenty years in prison.

"Nora!"

Jazzy's voice reached me, and I heard her splashing my way.

Don't make me regret this, the wind chime continued.

Regrets? I already had too many to count.

Would this be another regret?

I pulled the man's barely conscious body to the surface, where he spluttered and choked and coughed.

I don't know that I could have let him live if Jazzy hadn't come back. But I couldn't murder the man in cold blood, however despicable he might be, in front of the only person who looked up to me. She deserved better.

"McKinley Woods, you're under arrest," I said instead.

"You're going to Hell," the man wheezed, wiping the seawater and spittle from his face.

"I was already there," I replied as Jazzy wrapped her little arms around me from behind. "It looked like a country club for you and your *drittsekk* friends."

Recognition sparked in his eyes, and I knew he'd just placed me. A vague memory of a picture on a screen. An option he once upon a time could have chosen.

But his options had just run out.

31

TWO TRUTHS AND A LIE

Saturday 9:00pm

Jazzy wouldn't let go of my hand. Truth be told, I didn't want to let go of hers either.

Graham was taken away in an ambulance. His nose and possibly his cheek were broken, and he had a large contusion on the side of his head from the anchor, as well as swelling and bruising in the crotch area. With a bit of luck, the *drittsekk* wouldn't be able to reproduce.

Woods had ranted for a while about everything from entrapment to police brutality, up until I pulled the gun from the sea floor and let him know it hadn't been down there long enough to lose the fingerprints. Only thing we could get out of him after that was the word 'lawyer'.

Jumbo couldn't stop apologising. Woods must have seen the two detectives out the window as they returned to Whittaker's Range Rover after what they considered a false alarm. That's when Woods demanded the mobiles. Jumbo had covertly ended the call to me, and continued fussing about handing them over, but

Graham pulled the gun and held it on Jazzy. He quickly covered her mouth and with simple hand signals, the captors had made it clear any talking would result in a bullet to the kid's brain.

Woods soon found the microphone and clutched it in his hand while running water in the sink so he could give his orders without the detectives hearing, then went on his diatribe to throw them off. Whittaker had thought it was some kind of negotiation tactic and hoped he'd get back to the price discussion. Until I'd called.

We didn't have a recording of Woods incriminating himself, but we had three witnesses to his intent, and the gun possession alone would put him away. He'd have a hotshot solicitor try to throw it all out, and they'd come at me for excessive force, no doubt bringing up my suspension, but once he fired the gun, he'd pretty much cooked his turkey. *Was that the right bird?* English phrases seem to pick on birds a lot.

Regardless of the birds, if Woods had simply told everyone to leave, we would have had a much tougher case to make stick. His decision to bring in hired muscle and escalate the events to a level he'd never dabbled in before turned out to be his undoing.

"I'm in your debt," Whittaker said to Jumbo and Baby-G once Woods had been taken away. "I hope our paths don't cross in my line of duty, and I certainly can't promise anything, but your cooperation will be taken into consideration as much as possible."

"Don't owe me nuttin', Mr Whittaker," Jumbo replied. "I did dis for Miss Sommer, and 'cos dat piece of shit had it comin'."

Whittaker shook the big man's hand.

"You can owe *me* all you want, sugar," Baby-G said, with her hands on her hips. "I'll take it."

The detective wasn't sure how to respond.

"I should get the kid home," I told him.

He rested a hand on my shoulder. "You both did well tonight. I'm sorry I didn't read the situation more accurately."

"We got him, sir," I replied. "That's all that matters."

His eyes told me he had more to say, but I was glad he decided it could wait. We were all damp, salty, and ready for a shower. I had a glass of wine planned in my future, and the kid deserved one tonight as well.

"I'll see you on Monday morning," he said.

We'd almost reached the Jeep when I suddenly remembered Kayleigh. A knot instantly twisted in my stomach. I guess it was understandable, but I'd forgotten about her in the chaos.

I took my mobile from my pocket and dusted more of the sand away. I'd been lucky to find it again in the dark on the beach. I looked at the screen and was disappointed I hadn't missed any calls or texts. We climbed in the Jeep and as I let it warm up, I tried calling Kayleigh's number again. It rang until it went to voicemail.

I crossed the car park and paused at West Bay Road.

"I need to make one stop on the way home," I told Jazzy.

She didn't look impressed. "It better be to buy food."

"We should do that too. But I have to check on a friend first."

"AJ?" she asked.

"Another friend."

"I didn't know you had another friend."

"Thanks," I muttered, and drove south.

The opposite way from home where a shower and wine awaited.

Turning into the Caribbean View Residences, I stopped at the guard gate.

"Is Charles here tonight?" I asked the uniformed security man who stepped out.

"He is, miss. How can we help you?"

I showed him my police badge, which may or may not have been active depending on Whittaker's opinion on the timing of my temporary reprieve.

"I'm following up on the suicide case," I said. "Ask Charles to meet me by the south building. I'll park there."

The man looked at me, then Jazzy, and then my old, faded blue Jeep.

"Wait right here, miss. Let me call Charles," he said, stepping back into the hut.

I thought about driving in anyway, but decided I shouldn't generate more fuss than necessary. We could hear the guard calling Charles on the radio. After a few moments he stepped back outside.

"Go ahead, miss. He said he'll meet you there."

I drove into the complex and parked by a no parking sign behind the oceanfront villas building. Less than a minute later, Charles walked towards us.

"Evenin' Constable Sommer. Everyting okay?"

"Probably. Have you seen Kayleigh Collins this evening?"

Charles leaned on the roll hoop of the Jeep. "Can't say I recall seein' da girl, no Miss."

"How about Raylene?"

"Don't believe I seen her neither," he replied, peering past me at Jazzy. "Who da lovely young lady wit you tonight?"

"This is Jazzy. Can you stay with her a few minutes while I check on Kayleigh?"

"I'll just come with you," Jazzy volunteered.

I stepped out of the Jeep. "You've had enough excitement for one evening. Hang out with Charles. I'll be right back."

"I'll keep an eye on her for you," Charles said, smiling at Jazzy.

"Keep a hand on your wallet, and don't let her talk you into betting on her game two truths and a lie," I warned the old man. "She cheats."

I left with the sound of Jazzy professing her innocence to Charles, fading as I turned the corner of the building.

Banging on the door to the condo didn't seem like a great idea, knowing Raylene could well be the one answering, but I had no choice. Whittaker would be at Central Station by now, tied up with McKinley Woods for the next few hours. If Kayleigh was truly missing, I'd call him, but right now all I had was an uneasy feeling as she wasn't answering her mobile.

I was sure Whittaker planned on interviewing Raylene tomorrow, but the poison in the Scotch bottle couldn't be tied to her without some other damning evidence. He'd start with why she was here a few weeks back, but I was sure she'd shrug that off as a quick holiday.

Having tumbled all that over in my mind ten times, I knocked on the condo door.

Listening carefully, I was sure I could hear muted voices from inside. I knocked again. Footsteps approached and after a brief pause, when I assumed the person looked through the peep hole, the door opened. Only far enough for Raylene to fill the gap.

"What the hell do you want at this time of night?"

"Hello Mrs Bradford-Collins. May I speak with Kayleigh, please."

Being polite with the woman took all the strength and self-control I could muster.

"She's not here."

"Where is she?"

"I don't know. Not here."

"Who else is here?" I asked.

"No one, but that's also none of your damn business. Now leave me in peace."

She started to close the door.

"May I step inside for a minute?" I said and stuck my soggy trainer in the door.

"Get your foot out of my door right now, or I'll call your boss. Again," she snapped, barely opening the door enough to glare at me.

"This isn't actually your door. It's Kayleigh's. Now, how about I come inside, and we talk about your stepdaughter?"

I had no clue what I could bluff my way into discussing, but I wanted inside the condo. She wasn't alone and Kayleigh was missing.

"I told you she's not here and you need to leave. I'm calling security," she retorted, bashing the door against my foot again.

It hurt like hell, but I didn't move.

"Braithwaite's with you, isn't he?" I persisted. "You won't let me in because he's here."

"I'm done with this," she ranted. "I'm calling security,".

"Okay. Go ahead," I replied, guessing she hadn't brought her mobile with her to the door.

Raylene pushed the door harder against my foot, swearing under her breath, which proved I was right about the phone.

Now I'd had enough. I doubted my antics earlier in the evening had helped my case on Monday, seeing as they'd begun with me ignoring Whittaker's directives. Again. So, one more strike against me wouldn't make any difference.

I swung my fist through the gap and caught Raylene on the chin.

My forearm snagging on the end of the door stopped the blow connecting with the full force I'd intended, but it was enough to make her stagger back. My fist stung from the scrapes and grazes I'd picked up from Graham's face, but I quickly shoved my way inside.

Grabbing Raylene by the arm, I moved down the hall and stopped at the first bedroom door, kicking it open with my foot.

There, laid on the bed, was Kayleigh. Bound, gagged, and staring at me with terror in her eyes.

I started to move into the room, but before I could take a step, something hit me across the side of my head, sending me flying.

32

THE NIGHT OF POOR DECISIONS

Saturday 9:45pm

My legs turned to jelly and as much as I willed myself to stay on my feet, I'd lost all control and tumbled to the floor. The hallway spun and I fought back the urge to vomit. Two voices echoed around me. I wanted to get up and fight, but I couldn't tell which way was up. The cool tile floor felt good against my cheek, and I drew in long breaths to fend off the nausea.

"You should never have let her in," Braithwaite's voice hissed as my mind slowly began to clear.

That explained who hit me.

"I didn't have a bloody choice, Nigel. She punched me in the face. Look, you idiot, I'm bleeding."

Now I really cursed the door for taking the sting out of my blow. If I hadn't been dragging Raylene along, maybe I would have seen or heard Braithwaite. He must have come from the opposite bedroom. This night wouldn't end. I'd been a five-minute drive from a glass of wine, and now I was on the floor with a concussion and two people who I was sure would like to see me disappear.

"Now we have to deal with her too," Braithwaite continued arguing, confirming my suspicions. "What are we going to do? She's a policewoman for Christ's sake."

I stayed on the floor, banking on the fact they weren't ready to face killing me just yet. The more strength I could regain, the better shape I'd be in to make a move. My head was ringing, and I still felt dizzy, but at least the building had stopped spinning.

"Tie her up before she comes to her senses," Raylene ordered, and I heard them both moving around.

Now would be the ideal time to fight back, but I was still feeling sick, and I wasn't sure my legs would work properly. A hand took hold of my arm and rolled me over. I kept my eyes closed and moaned a little, pretending to be dazed, which wasn't hard as certainly didn't feel very alert.

"Hold her hands together," Braithwaite said, and Raylene roughly did as instructed.

I half expected a retaliatory punch in the face, but it never came, and I allowed them to secure my wrists together with what felt like a large zip tie. That didn't worry me too much.

One of them pulled my mobile from my pocket, then Braithwaite picked me up by my armpits, and dragged me across the tile into the living room. I moaned some more, remained limp in his hands, and barely opened my eyes as though I was coming in and out of consciousness.

I had a hell of a headache building, but the nausea had passed, and I was feeling like I might be able to stand. Fighting would be a lot to ask, but adrenaline does wonders. He left me on the floor behind the sofa so if anyone happened to be on the beach this late, they wouldn't see me.

"Let's get on with it," Raylene said, and I peeked through one cracked eyelid to see what they had in store for me, but they had both left the living room.

"Wait a second," Braithwaite said, and I heard his footsteps getting louder.

He pulled my legs together and tried fastening another zip tie around my ankles. I kicked weakly, just enough to make it difficult. He put his leg on mine, and his considerable weight pinned me to the floor.

"Bugger," he cursed, got up, and left again.

From the bedroom, I heard Kayleigh's voice, hoarse and scared. "What are you doing to me?"

Raylene must have removed the tape from her mouth. They were finishing whatever they had planned for Kayleigh. It wasn't hard to guess what that would be, but I had no idea what method they'd choose. Raylene would call the police in the morning, devastated and inconsolable, having found Kayleigh dead in her room. The daughter who couldn't bear to go on without her father. The fight for the company would be back on.

Except I'd added a layer of complication to their scheme.

"Lay still, you little bitch," Raylene fumed.

I heard gagging and spitting noises, so I figured pills were the weapon of choice.

"Nigel! What the hell are you doing?" Raylene barked. "I need help holding her still."

"Calm down, I'll be right there," Braithwaite replied impatiently, and his footsteps approached once more.

He must have gone to get a second zip tie. Two together would easily reach around my ankles. I couldn't let him bind my legs. Ready or not, it was time to act, although I certainly didn't feel ready, and a knot was growing on the side of my head.

I lay still until he knelt down by my legs, his concentration focused on attaching the two zip ties together. Kicking with as much strength as I could gather, I caught him square in the face with my trainer.

Braithwaite reeled backwards, clutching his nose, but quickly recovered. I tried kicking again, but I'd used up most of my strength, and he easily deflected the blow, following with a punch to my stomach.

All the air left my lungs and the nauseous feeling returned in an instant. I curled myself up, but he dragged my legs across the floor, then pinned me once more. He wiped blood from his nose and glared at me.

"You're a real pain in the arse."

As he slipped the zip ties under my ankles, I kept trying to wriggle free, but he was far too heavy. I swung my bound hands down and clouted him on the shoulder, but it was ineffective. My energy was gone and once he had my legs tied, I'd be screwed.

I fought to move my feet, and for a few moments I was making it difficult for him to poke the end of the zip tie through the head of the other, but he finally managed.

"Got it," he grunted, just as a loud tap came from the sliding glass doors.

Braithwaite looked up, startled. I reached over my head, then brought my zip-tied hands flying forward while flipping my elbows out. He whipped around to look at me, but too late to do anything. The zip tie bit into my wrists with a searing pain, but the force broke the lock apart and my hands came free, just as we'd practiced in police training.

Braithwaite didn't know what to do, and hesitated. He'd dragged me out from behind the sofa, so whoever was outside could see me on the floor. My captor stood there, paralysed.

Adrenaline surged. If I had any chance of saving Kayleigh, I had to move.

With my legs still pinned, I pulled myself up using my stomach muscles and whaled on Braithwaite with both fists. He threw his hands up in defence, but not before I got a few good licks in. My knuckles screamed in pain, but I switched to his ribs, then back to his head when he moved his arm down.

He rolled away from me, and I made it to my feet, swinging a foot at his midriff. Braithwaite yelped and I looked up in time to see Raylene running from the bedroom. Her lip was swollen and cut from where I'd hit her earlier. She looked at the glass slider and her eyes went wide.

It was her mistake too. In one long step I reached her and slammed her into the corner of the wall between the living room and the hallway. Her head bashed against the drywall, and she didn't even make a sound as she dropped limply to the floor.

Braithwaite was struggling to his feet and reaching for a glass soap dispenser, which I assumed was what he'd used earlier to smack me in the head.

"Give it up," I warned him. "I'm in no mood for any more shit."

He stood, panting and gasping, his face red with anger and the beating I'd already given him. Blood trickled from his nose and a cut over one eye. I stole a glance at the slider, where Charles continued to bang on the glass, his mobile held to his ear. Jazzy stood next to him banging on the glass with her little fists.

"You know they have the police on their way. You're done," I spluttered, giving myself a few moments to recover some strength. "But I'm happy to keep kicking your arse."

Braithwaite snorted. He was a businessman who'd spent his time around conference tables and expensive lunches. He had to know he wasn't fighting his way out of here. But the look in his eyes said different. This night seemed to be filled with poor decisions. For once it wasn't me making them.

Lunging forward, he launched the glass container at me. I dodged left and heard it hit something other than a wall behind me. Raylene's slumped body if I had to guess. Braithwaite tried altering his trajectory to follow my move, but he was too slow and heavy. Best he could do was slide to a stop on the tile floor.

My bloody and beaten fist caught him just below the ribs, and he doubled over. With my last ounce of strength, I brought my knee up into his face and gave the George Town Hospital surgeon another nose to straighten.

The big man fell like a stone and smacked his head on the tile for good measure.

I staggered to the slider and let Jazzy in.

"You were supposed to stay in the Jeep," I muttered.

As I turned to get to the bedroom, Charles opened the front door with a small truncheon in his hand.

"It's clear," I told him, throwing a thumb over my shoulder. "Two down back there."

"You took him out as well, huh?" the old man said, coming into the hallway.

"She kicked his arse," Jazzy added, and I hoped I'd remember to explain the whys and necessities to her later.

I ducked into the bedroom. Kayleigh was curled up on the bed, a bottle of pills spilled on the cover next to her. She was moaning and fighting to stay conscious. I picked up the bottle. Temazepam. A sleeping pill if I remembered correctly from our drug training.

"Get me a knife from the kitchen," I told Jazzy, and she ran out of the room.

I dragged Kayleigh to the edge of the bed and shoved my finger down her throat. She gagged, bit me, but then vomited all over the lush carpet.

Jazzy ran back in with a knife.

"Ewww," she gasped, holding her nose. "That stinks."

I cut the zip ties and stopped Kayleigh from rolling over, keeping her face over the side of the bed. I heard sirens wailing in the background.

"The woman is waking up," Jazzy said, having taken a few steps back.

"You can go knock her out again," I said.

"Okay," Jazzy responded a little too enthusiastically, and started to leave.

"I'm kidding!" *Dritt.* That would be another point to discuss later. "Here, don't let Kayleigh on her back. She might choke."

"Is she drunk?" Jazzy asked.

"No. They made her take pills. We need to get her to the hospital."

"Is she going to be okay?"

I paused at the door. "Yeah. I think we got here in time."

"Guess it was good we didn't stop for dinner," Jazzy replied, sitting on the bed and holding Kayleigh.

The adrenaline was wearing off, and every part of my body

either ached or felt like the skin had been shredded away. My head was killing me. I leaned on the door jamb and looked down the hallway. Charles had found Braithwaite's stash of zip ties and was securing both him and Raylene. She was groggy, but coming to, swearing under her breath.

I turned back to the bedroom. Jazzy was stroking Kayleigh's hair and telling her she'd be alright.

Maybe it was good we hadn't stopped for dinner.

And maybe it was good I'd stuck around a little longer too. The ocean floor would still be there if I ever really needed it. But that time wasn't now.

33

TOO MUCH TRUTH

Sunday 1:30am

I couldn't stop touching the knot on the side of my head. It felt like a watermelon growing out of my skull, but in the mirror, it was more like a swollen red bump hidden underneath my hair. Apparently, I had a light to moderate concussion, and I needed to be observed for the next twenty-four hours. I told the doctor I had plenty of people at home who'd keep an eye on me, so he reluctantly discharged me.

My knuckles looked like I was preparing for a fight. The nurse had covered the cuts and scrapes with ointment, then wrapped them in a bandage so I couldn't wipe the gooey mess over everything. She'd been really nice and recommended all kinds of treatments and lotions to help soften my skin and reduce the scarring. I finally had to tell her I didn't give a shit and it was better if my hands were tougher in my line of work. She didn't say so much after that.

I walked out of the room where I'd been treated in the emergency wing and went next door. Kayleigh was fast asleep. An IV led from her arm to a bag hanging on a stand and wires ran from inside her gown to a monitoring machine. I'd been assured she would be fine, but it was still unsettling to see her looking so pale.

A constable I recognised from Central Station stood between the doors to the next two rooms where Raylene Bradford-Collins and Nigel Braithwaite occupied beds. I nodded to the policeman as I left. Apparently, Graham was somewhere else in the hospital recovering from facial surgery. With a bit of luck all three of them were in more pain than me, although I bet they hadn't refused pain meds like I had, so they were probably sleeping in blissful oblivion.

I'd heard Woods had insisted on being treated for the bruising on his shoulder where the anchor had hit him, so all told, I'd brought the hospital some pretty good business. If they paid commission, I might have a new line of work after the RCIPS fired me on Monday.

Down the hall in the waiting area, I found Jazzy curled up on the floor behind a row of chairs, nestled against the wall. One good thing about living on the streets was her ability to sleep just about anywhere. I'd wanted to call AJ to come pick the kid up, but Jazzy had insisted on staying. Last I'd seen her, the nurses had been making a pretty big fuss over her, and the word ice cream had been mentioned. I'd figured she was in good hands.

I was about to wake her so we could finally go home, when I heard a familiar voice.

"I thought they were keeping you in overnight," Whittaker asked.

I turned and spotted the detective across the waiting room, a fresh cup of lousy hospital coffee in his hand.

"Doctor said I'm good to go," I replied, stretching the truth more than a little. "You should have gone home, sir. I don't think anything will change before morning."

I'd seen the detective briefly after we'd first arrived, but hadn't expected him to still be here. It was one-thirty in the morning. He walked towards me and sat down on one of the uncomfortable chairs.

"I'll be leaving soon," he replied. "I wanted to make sure you were okay first."

"I'm fine," I quickly replied, keeping my bandaged hands self-consciously behind my back.

I was longing for sleep, and thanking Charles was also on my mind, but none of that needed discussing at this hour.

"Sit with me a minute, Nora," he said, nodding to the chair next to him. "I know you need to get home, but I doubt we'll have an opportunity to talk before Monday morning."

I stifled the groan I wanted to emit. But he was right, I doubt we'd meet even if we tried to plan something for tomorrow… Well, technically today. His Sundays were usually filled with family obligations, and I planned to turn my mobile off for the day. I took the seat and wondered why we needed to talk in the first place. He'd made it clear he was done protecting me, and I didn't blame him at all. Maybe he felt the need to make that clear one more time.

"Have you thought about what you plan to say at your hearing?" he asked.

"Not really," I admitted. "I don't think there's much I *can* say. You're right. I keep screwing up."

The detective nodded thoughtfully. "Nora, let me ask you this. Do you really want to be a policewoman?" he asked with concern in his voice.

I let out a long sigh and thought for a few moments. He was looking for the truth, and he deserved the truth. So did I. I'd bull-shitted my way along with ulterior motives since he'd suggested I try joining the police force several years ago. One of my goals had been taking out anyone I could reach who'd been involved in The International Fellowship of Lions, and Woods was the last of those *drittsekker*. That I knew of.

But there were plenty of other shitheads who belonged in jail for all kinds of reasons. The question was whether wearing a uniform and chasing bad people was what I really wanted to be doing. The idea of becoming a detective held more appeal as it seemed to elevate the level of criminals I'd be dealing with, but I figured any talk of detective training was off the table at this point.

"No," I answered honestly, and his expression fell into that look of disappointment I'd seen too many times.

"I *need* this job," I added. "It's what gives me purpose."

I turned and looked at Jazzy's curled-up form on the floor, her mop of frizzy hair somewhat contained in a ponytail.

"We need each other, too," I said, nodding her way. "But it's the job that keeps my mind busy. It keeps me focused."

"Or what?" he asked softly.

I hesitated. The job had only been part of the inner motivation which had pushed me off the sea floor in search of another breath, but it *had* made a difference. A stupidly simple obligation to call AJ had moved me. Literally. Her final words had been the ones which had hung in my mind, but of course I knew there was a bigger picture in play. Her words symbolised how she felt. And Jazzy. And my parents. And Roy Whittaker, I suspected.

"That doesn't matter," I replied. "My ability to do the job is all that's in question on Monday morning."

"True, but as a friend, I'd like to know," he persisted.

It was certainly time to be brutally honest with Whittaker, and with myself, but some things were still too private. Everyone marched to the beat of a different drum, and I doubted he'd understand my personal view on life and death. It wasn't that I took either lightly in any way, and perhaps it came down to an issue of self-worth, but I had no idea how to explain myself, even if I'd wanted to.

I truly believed sharing your deepest emotions with someone is a commitment, not just in honesty, but in the burden you place on you both. If Whittaker heard me say I'd considered taking my own life, he'd feel responsible for making sure that didn't happen. That's a heavy weight to carry. For us both. It added pressure to me too.

That's one of the reasons helplines are so effective. You're telling a faceless stranger who listens, encourages, and often never knows the outcome. A personal connection without the other burdens.

Besides, how could he even consider allowing me to continue as a constable if he knew the shit that went through my mind?

It truly is a gift that we can't read each other's real thoughts.

"I'd work for Reg or AJ on the dive boats, but I'm not sure they'd appreciate my customer service skills," I said, and allowed my lips to curl into the slightest of grins.

Whittaker forced a brief smile in return. I could tell he was dying to dig for a more truthful answer - the detective in him smelled bullshit from a mile away - but fortunately he let it be.

"Then what can we do to get you to follow protocols and rules?" he asked. "Something has to change if you're to remain on the force."

"Do you want me to stay?" I asked him.

I wasn't hunting for compliments or trying to sound like a victim. I wanted to know how he really felt, and I hoped he understood that.

The detective took a moment, which gave me confidence his answer would be truthful.

"Two years ago, I had a gut feeling you'd make a good policewoman, Nora, but I knew it would be a big adjustment for you," he said, then paused again, looking at the floor for a few moments before lifting his eyes and continuing. "I think there have been elements to the job that have been more challenging for you than I anticipated. But, your natural instincts and uncanny knack of reading both people and situations are nothing short of exceptional."

I felt my forehead crease into a frown. I was uncomfortable with compliments, but he was also taking a circuitous journey getting to his point, and I was surprised by how much the content of his next few words meant to me. I cared, and I didn't think I ever gave a shit what anyone thought of me.

"But I can't condone behaviour which endangers the public, other officers, or the integrity of our investigations. Do I want you to be a policewoman? Yes. I do, Nora. But not at any price. It has to be within the system of the law, and if that's not possible for you, then no, I don't think you should continue."

Fy faen. Maybe I didn't want that much truth. But of course he was right.

Inside, I knew this conversation was either the turning point in my law enforcement career, or the end. The hearing Monday would be a formality based on how this talk ended. And what I said next would probably be the deciding factor. I took my time before responding, mulling over my true feelings more than worrying about the words I used.

"I know I need to change the way I go about certain things," I admitted. "And truthfully, I don't know that I can."

His eyes searched mine, longing for me to say something more.

"But I would really like to try, if I'm given the chance, sir. I know I haven't followed through in the past, but I promise to give it one hundred percent of my effort."

I watched the relief flood through his face, and I felt a surge of excitement in my battered and beaten body. I'd told him what he wanted to hear, but this time I'd really meant it. I would try my hardest.

Evaluate. Choose. Act. Perry Collins had lived and ultimately died by these words, and while I wished for Kayleigh's sake that he hadn't followed through so completely, I respected the man for his commitment. Without realising it, I'd also been following the same code in many ways, except for my responsibility to the police department. Whittaker was offering me one last chance, and I'd evaluated and chosen. Now it was time to act.

At least now I'd pushed the system to the breaking point, I hopefully wouldn't have to step too far back over the line to keep everyone happy.

Where would be the fun in that?

AFTERWORD

In this series, Nora has often battled the demons which lurk in the depths of many our minds through difficult times. This novel ventures farther down that complex path, and rather than sensationalise suicide, my hope is to illuminate the profound emotional struggles that can lead individuals to such a harrowing crossroads.

While the circumstances and motivations in this story are not typical - I don't think anything Nora thinks or does could be described that way! - ultimately, there's an underlying message of hope, consequence, and a path to the glimmer of light waiting to pierce through the shadows.

If you or someone you know is struggling with their personal demons, reach out to a friend, and/or call 988 to contact the Suicide and Crisis Lifeline in the US or 116 123 to reach the Samaritans in the UK. You're not alone.

Be Cool To Each Other,
    Nick.

ACKNOWLEDGMENTS

My sincere thanks to:

My incredible wife Cheryl, for her unwavering support, love, and encouragement.

My family and friends for always being there.

My marvellous editor Andrew Chapman at Prepare to Publish for his diligent work and wise suggestions.

Lily at Orkidedatter for her Norwegian advice.

Casey Keller, Craig Robinson, and Alain Belanger for their help with all things Cayman Islands related.

Shearwater Research and Dive Rite for their friendship and support.

The Tropical Authors group for their advice, support, and humour. Visit and subscribe at www.TropicalAuthors.com for deals and info on a plethora of books by talented authors in the Sea Adventure genre.

My beta reader group has grown to include an amazing cross section of folks from different walks of life. Their suggestions, feedback and keen eyes are invaluable, for which I am eternally grateful.

Above all, I thank you, the readers: none of this happens without the choice you make to spend your precious time with my stories. I am truly in your debt.

LET'S STAY IN TOUCH!

To buy merchandise, find more info or join my newsletter, visit my
website at
www.HarveyBooks.com

If you enjoyed this novel I'd be incredibly grateful if you'd consider
leaving a review on Amazon.com
Find eBook deals and follow me on BookBub.com

Catch my podcast, The Two Authors' Chat Show with co-host
Douglas Pratt

Find more great authors in the genre at TropicalAuthors.com

Visit Amazon.com for more books in the
Nora Sommer Caribbean Suspense Series,
AJ Bailey Adventure Series,
and collaborative works;
The Greene Wolfe Thriller Series
Tropical Authors Adventure Series

ABOUT THE AUTHOR

A *USA Today* Bestselling author, Nicholas Harvey's life has been anything but ordinary. Race car driver, adventurer, divemaster, and since 2020, a full-time novelist. Raised in England, Nick has dual US and British citizenship and now lives wherever he and his amazing wife, Cheryl, park their motorhome, or an aeroplane takes them. Warm oceans and tall mountains are their favourite places.

For more information, visit his website at HarveyBooks.com.